Praise for *New York Times* bestselling author
Christine Warren

Born to be Wild

"Warren packs in lots of action and sexy sizzle."
—*Romantic Times BOOKreviews*

"Incredible." —*All About Romance*

"Another good addition to The Others series."
—*Romance Junkies*

"[A] sexy, engaging world...will leave you begging for
more!" —*New York Times* bestselling author
Cheyenne McCray

Big Bad Wolf

"In this world...there's no shortage of sexy sizzle."
—*Romantic Times BOOKreviews*

"Another hot and spicy novel from a master of paranor-
mal romance." —*Night Owl Romance*

"Ms. Warren gives readers action and danger around
each turn, sizzling rom_____
each scene. *Big Bad Wo*____

You're So Vein

"Filled with supernatural danger, excitement, and sarcastic humor."　　—*Darque Reviews*

"Five stars. This is an exciting, sexy book."
　　—*Affaire de Coeur*

"The sparks do fly!"　　—*Romantic Times BOOKreviews*

One Bite with a Stranger

"Christine Warren has masterfully pulled together vampires, shape shifters, demons, and many 'Others' to create a tantalizing world of dark fantasies come to life. Way to go, Warren!"　　—*Night Owl Romance*

"A sinful treat."　　　　—*Romance Junkies*

"Hot fun and great sizzle."
　　—*Romantic Times BOOKreviews*

"A hot, hot novel."　　　　—*A Romance Review*

Walk on the Wild Side

"A seductive tale with strong chemistry, roiling emotions, steamy romance, and supernatural action. The fast-moving plot...will keep the readers' attention riveted through every page, and have them eagerly watching for the next installment."
—*Darque Reviews*

Howl at the Moon

"*Howl at the Moon* will tug at a wide range of emotions from beginning to end...Engaging banter, a strong emotional connection, and steamy love scenes. This talented author delivers real emotion which results in delightful interactions...and the realistic dialogue is stimulating. Christine Warren knows how to write a winner!"
—*Romance Junkies*

The Demon You Know

"Explodes with sexy, devilish fun, exploring the further adventures of The Others. With a number of the gang from previous books back, there's an immediate familiarity about this world that makes it easy to dive right into. Warren's storytelling style makes these books remarkably entertaining."
—*Romantic Times BOOKreviews* (4½ stars)

St. Martin's Paperbacks Titles by

Christine Warren

Born to be Wild

Big Bad Wolf

You're So Vein

One Bite with a Stranger

Walk on the Wild Side

Howl at the Moon

The Demon You Know

She's No Faerie Princess

Wolf at the Door

Prince Charming Doesn't Live Here

CHRISTINE WARREN

St. Martin's Paperbacks

PRINCE CHARMING DOESN'T LIVE HERE

Copyright © 2010 by Christine Warren.
Excerpt from *Wolf at the Door* copyright © 2006 by Christine Warren.
Excerpt from *She's No Faerie Princess* copyright © 2006 by Christine Warren.
Excerpt from *The Demon You Know* copyright © 2007 by Christine Warren.
Excerpt from *Howl at the Moon* copyright © 2007 by Christine Warren.
Excerpt from *Walk on the Wild Side* copyright © 2008 by Christine Warren.
Excerpt from *One Bite with a Stranger* copyright © 2008 by Christine Warren.
Excerpt from *You're So Vein* copyright © 2009 by Christine Warren.
Excerpt from *Big Bad Wolf* copyright © 2009 by Christine Warren.
Excerpt from *Born to be Wild* copyright © 2010 by Christine Warren.

For information address St. Martin's Press, 175 Fifth Avenue, New York, NY 10010.

ISBN: 978-0-312-94794-1

Printed in the United States of America

St. Martin's Paperbacks edition / November 2010

St. Martin's Paperbacks are published by St. Martin's Press, 175 Fifth Avenue, New York, NY 10010.

10 9 8 7 6 5 4 3 2 1

Prince Charming Doesn't Live Here

One

"Danice Carter, Esquire. Just the woman I wanted to see."

"Well, take a good, long look then, because you've got about twenty-seven seconds before I pull open a window and fling myself out."

Stocking feet slapped across the chilly marble in front of the sixteenth-floor elevators, then onto plush tweed carpet as Danice stalked toward her office. She hadn't had a particularly pleasant afternoon.

Ignoring the danger signs, Celia turned to follow.

"How did things go with Wilkinson's team?"

Danice shoved open her office door and launched her soft-sided briefcase toward the back wall with the approximate force of an anti-aircraft missile. "Peachy. Their client has decided that in addition to causing the collapse of his business, Henry Hollister and Grissom Holdings are also responsible for the boom in the Chinese economy, the global recession, the greenhouse effect, and unrest in the Middle East."

"Ah."

"They've adjusted their demands for the settlement accordingly. I believe the offer they presented me contained language about me giving lap dances in the hall of Satan while they drink the blood of all of Grissom's senior corporate officers from a golden chalice." She used one of the shoes in her hand to gesture toward her briefcase. "The papers are in there. Feel free to go over them and tell me if I'm wrong."

"I'll get right on that." Celia pursed her lips and took a seat in front of Danice's desk while the other woman flung herself inelegantly into the leather executive's chair behind it. "Do you want me to call around and see if I can find you pasties and a G-string?"

Danice glared at her. "You giving up your career as a paralegal for a future in stand-up comedy?"

"Maybe. I like to keep my options open." Celia tilted her head and widened her eyes ingenuously. "Did you offer up your sense of humor as a sacrifice to pacify the Wilkinson camp?"

"No, I dropped it on the corner of Lexington and Fifty-first, along with my afternoon latte and the heel of my three-hundred-dollar Kate Spade pump." Scowling, Danice wound up like a starting pitcher and threw her shoe toward the front wall, savoring the satisfying *thunk* of leather on drywall. If only she'd stuck with softball as a teenager, maybe she could have had the satisfaction of leaving a dent. "If only that had been Wilkinson's fat head."

"Mm, I hear clients don't appreciate being assaulted by legal representation. They might even file suit."

"Ha. Ha."

"Damn, girl, you need to lighten up."

Danice sighed and dropped her head to the back of her chair. "I'll put that on my list. Right after world peace and saving the whales." She shifted her gaze to Celia. "What was the straw you had for me?"

"Straw?"

"When I came off the elevator, you said you'd been looking for me. I assume you have a straw for my back?"

Celia grinned and took in her boss's sleek, camel-colored sheath dress. "The color's right, but there's something about the face that doesn't fit the picture."

"Thank God for that, at least. I don't have time for a nose job." Bracing her hands on the arms of her chair, Danice pushed herself upright and leaned her elbows on her desk. "You've got something for me?"

Celia offered up a slim brown folder. "This."

Danice flipped open the cover and frowned down at a short stack of papers that, at first glance, didn't ring any bells with her. "Any clue what it's about?"

"No, but it came down from on high. Ms. Eberhart brought it to me herself just after lunch."

"Really?" That actually made Danice take notice. Her brows lifted, and she looked down at the papers with renewed interest. "If it came via Patrice Eberhart, I'm assuming the responsible heavenly throne belongs to Mr. Yorke?"

"You opened the folder." Celia shrugged. "At this point, you now officially know more than I do. I was told to see that you got the folder as soon as you got back to the office. My work here is done."

"You wish, Tonto. What did Ms. Eberhart tell you when she gave this to you?"

"Exactly what I just told you. To make sure you got

that as soon as you got in. And to buzz her so she'd know you were back."

Danice rolled her eyes and reached for her telephone. "See, that last part was what I really wanted to know. I'll buzz her myself."

"I was getting to it. You're always rushing me," Celia teased as she rose. "You have notes for me from this Wilkinson meeting?"

Danice nodded toward the window. "In my briefcase."

"Okay. Thanks, boss."

Slim, creamed-coffee fingers punched in an internal dialing code then tapped restlessly on the desk while Danice waited for an answer.

"Mr. Yorke's office. How may I help you?"

"Ms. Eberhart, this is Danice Carter. I've just returned from an outside meeting, and my paralegal gave me a message that you might need something from me."

The crisp, schoolmistress voice responded promptly. "Ms. Carter. I assume that you have received the file I left with Ms. Alta."

"Yes, Celia did give me a file, though I haven't reviewed it yet. As I said, I'm just back to the office."

"Yes. I shouldn't worry. Mr. Yorke has asked me to invite you up so that he can provide you with the background for this particular assignment. I'm certain your review of the provided materials will be more productive after you've talked with Mr. Yorke."

Danice felt her eyebrows shoot up and decided it was a good thing that her Big Boss's assistant couldn't see her face at the moment. It might not instill the right kind of confidence if it were known she'd nearly passed out at the news that one of the firm's senior partners had requested a meeting with her.

Matthew Yorke IV wasn't a senior partner; he was *the* senior partner, and the namesake of one of the prestigious old firm's founders. The closest she'd ever come to speaking with him during her five years working for him had been when she'd excused herself as she walked in front of him at last year's company holiday party.

"Of course," she said, carefully keeping the shock out of her voice. "I'd be happy to make time for Mr. Yorke. When would he like to set up a meeting?"

"Actually, Mr. Yorke would like for you to come up now." There was a short, significant pause. "If you're available."

Danice stifled the urge to laugh. Not because the comment was funny, but because it was ridiculous. What did the woman expect her to say? That she'd check her calendar and get back to her? "Of course. I'll be right up."

Hanging up, Danice flipped the folder in front of her closed and pushed to her feet. Then she swore.

"Celia!"

A minute later, the paralegal's head appeared in the door. "You rang?"

Danice nodded and dropped back in her chair. She opened her bottom desk drawer to pull out the makeup bag and mirror she kept there for emergencies. "I need shoes."

"Shoes?"

"Yes, shoes. I told you, I broke mine on the way back here from the Wilkinson meeting, and I can't go up to Mr. York's office in my bare-assed feet. I need shoes."

Celia blinked and drew back in shock. "Mr. Yorke? You're going to Mr. Yorke's office? Now?"

Danice swiped a powder pad over her cheekbones and nodded. "That's what I just said, isn't it? He wants to see me about that file Ms. Eberhart brought down."

"In person? Mr. Yorke wants to meet with you in person?"

"Yes," she insisted impatiently, reaching for a mascara wand. "And I can't go up there in bare feet. So where can I get me a pair of shoes in the next five minutes?"

Celia kicked off her heeled loafers and stepped onto the carpet beside them. "You can take mine. But seriously, Mr. Yorke asked to meet with you in person to go over that file? What on earth could be so important that Matthew Yorke the Fourth, lord of all he surveys and potential secret ruler of the universe, would want to meet with an assistant associate whose name he probably can't remember unless his personal secretary is whispering it in his ear?"

"Wow, thanks for the vote of confidence." Danice grimaced and twisted the bottom of a tube of lipstick. "What size shoe do you wear?"

"Seven. I'm totally confident in you. I just didn't think Mr. Yorke was."

"I have no idea if he is or not, but I intend to make sure he becomes just as confident as I can make him." She rubbed her lips together and tossed the lipstick back into the makeup bag. "Shit, I wear a seven and a half. On my good days. Your shoes will be too small."

"Grin and bear it. Because it's either wear my shoes, or wear the sneakers you have me keep for you for the days you decide to walk home, and I don't think they'll go with that dress."

"Then I guess they'll have to do, won't they?"

She sighed as she gave herself a final check in the mirror. She appeared exactly the way she strived to appear—a reasonably attractive, twenty-eight-year-old professional woman of indeterminate heritage. Her skin glowed the rich golden color of café au lait, her brown eyes tilted up at the outer corners from within a round and slightly shallow profile, and her thick black hair fell straight and heavy to just above her shoulders.

As a child, some people had thought she was black, others Asian, or Latina, or Native American, or Polynesian. Danice had defensively referred to herself as 100 percent American. She hadn't wanted to be judged by the color of her skin or the shape of her face or the texture of her hair or even by the ethnicities of her parents. She had wanted to be judged for herself.

Until she started applying to colleges and discovered that in order to get the education she wanted at a price she could afford, she would have to make a few compromises with her dignity.

Those compromises had led her to Fordham University and then Columbia Law School without bankrupting her grandchildren. They had also gotten her foot in the door at Parish, Hampton, Uxbridge, and Yorke, one of Manhattan's most prestigious law firms. That was as far as Danice was willing to compromise her principles. She'd let her skin tone open gates for her, but she'd seize control of the castle based on skill, talent, and sheer force of will.

"All right. I guess I'm ready to go." Snagging the file

from her desk and slipping it into a slim leather note-book, Danice stepped out from behind the wooden barrier and into Celia's shoes, wincing only a little at the pinching fit. "How do I look?"

"Like a junior partner in the making, my friend." The paralegal gave her an enthusiastic thumbs-up. "Knock 'em dead."

"Don't say things like that. The man's eighty-four years old. With my luck, that's just what would happen."

Celia's laughter followed Danice out into the corridor as she strode toward the elevators. Honestly, Danice wasn't quite certain what her co-worker was laughing about. She hadn't been joking. At eighty-four, the man could go at any moment, and wouldn't it just cap off her day if he did it in her presence?

Twenty seconds on the elevator deposited her on the Parish Building's sacrosanct twentieth floor, the exclusive domain of the Senior Partners. There were four of them, one for each of the four original founders of the firm. Each had an office larger than Danice's entire apartment, guarded by one of the four fiercest personal assistants in Midtown Manhattan. And just opposite the elevator, a shared receptionist staffed a U-shaped desk the approximate size of Paraguay.

"Can I help you?" asked the woman, her pale silver hair a slightly warmer shade than her voice. She looked to be about sixty, but based on the warmth of her manner, freezing could account for having preserved her well past her hundredth birthday.

"I'm Ms. Carter," Danice returned smoothly, her posture unconsciously straightening and her own normally warm, husky voice icing over. "Mr. Yorke is expecting me."

"Is he." The receptionist's skepticism would have been insulting if it hadn't been so obviously . . . insulting. As things stood, it made Danice want to snort. "I'll just ring Ms. Eberhart and alert her to your presence."

No one got that good at insulting people obliquely without years of practice, Danice decided as she waited for the older woman to make her phone call. Maybe the gatekeeper had been here even longer than a hundred years. Maybe she was left over from the founding of the firm in 1859. Somehow, Danice wouldn't have been surprised.

A moment later, Patrice Eberhart emerged from a corridor behind the reception desk and nodded to Danice. "Ms. Carter. If you'll follow me, please."

Resisting the urge to check herself for goose bumps, Danice turned and did as instructed. She hadn't noticed the temperature on this floor being cooler than the rest of the building, but the greetings definitely were. Either everyone here needed to be kept in a meat locker to keep from decomposing, or being or associating with a senior partner required the surgical removal of one's personality.

Pausing before a paneled door of dark wood, Ms. Eberhart rapped softly, then performed an impressive move involving opening the door no more than three inches and somehow squeezing through the crack and closing it firmly behind her. For a second, Danice thought she might have turned into a mist to manage it.

Like a vampire.

The stray thought wiped the burgeoning smile from Danice's face. According to her dear friend Reggie, vampires didn't turn into mist. That, apparently, was all Hollywood mythology. And Reggie ought to know, since she'd recently married a vampire and become one herself.

Damn, Danice thought, shaking her head. Somehow she didn't think she'd ever get used to thinking things like that, especially not here within the safe and utterly normal confines of an unrelentingly respectable law firm. And definitely not without someone jumping out from behind a door and telling her she'd been punked.

The door opened again, this time wide enough for an actual human being—or an actual vampire, she supposed—to pass through, and Ms. Eberhart stepped aside to wave her in.

"Mr. Yorke will see you now."

The older woman managed to make it sound as if an audience with Matthew Yorke IV was slightly harder to get than one with Elizabeth II, and significantly more important. Danice had to stifle the urge to curtsy.

Instead, she nodded with a touch of arrogance of her own and strode forward toward the thin, stooped figure behind the huge, antique desk. As she extended her hand, she heard the *click* of the door closing behind her.

"Mr. Yorke." She smiled, shaking the old man's hand firmly but carefully. It would hardly help her career if she were to unintentionally break something. "It's certainly a pleasure to see you again, sir."

"Ms. Carter, please have a seat," he replied in a surprisingly robust voice. He gestured toward the elegant and uncomfortable Queen Anne armchairs facing his desk, and Danice sat.

She had seen Matthew Yorke up close and in person precisely three times before this afternoon, so she recognized him, but this was the first time she'd had the opportunity to observe the sharp intelligence in his faded blue eyes. Some people, she thought, might be too distracted by the wrinkled skin and thinning hair to notice that the old man watched the world around him with the canny patience of a wolf. She wasn't one of them. Instinctively, she straightened her spine and met his gaze with her own.

"I hope you won't mind if I call you Danice."

"Of course not. Please do."

Matthew Yorke settled himself carefully into the huge, worn leather chair behind his desk and laced his fingers together over his stomach. "I had Patrice bring me a few tidbits of information about you the other day, Danice. I have to say, you're certainly justifying the firm's confidence in you so far."

A long, slow blink was all the outward reaction Danice allowed herself. Inside, she couldn't decide if she should laugh or slap his face. The declaration had more than a touch of feudalism to it, carefully couched in a backhanded compliment. The man was either stuck in the Dark Ages or a master of psychological warfare.

Maybe both.

"Thank you, sir," she said, her voice bland. "I always do my best for the firm, of course."

His nod dripped with royal condescension. "You graduated at the top of your class from Columbia. We have high expectations for your future."

"As do I."

She detected a glint of what she thought might be approval in his eyes before he continued.

"I was especially impressed with your handling of the Howard-McKinley matter," he said, naming the case of a small software firm that had sued a former employee for breach of contract after he failed to prove as innovatively brilliant as he'd claimed when he'd been trying to get the job.

"Thank you, sir, but I can hardly take all the credit. Alan Thorpe was the lead attorney there. My contribution was mostly in persuading the two parties to stop and listen to each other's arguments. Once they managed that, it wasn't so hard for them to come to terms over a settlement."

"Exactly." Faded eyes gleamed as Yorke nodded. "I have a lot of lawyers working for me, Danice, and all of them know the law. Not all of them are able to talk sense into two offended parties who aren't being remotely sensible. I think that's a particularly valuable skill."

Danice shifted uneasily. On the one hand, she couldn't bring herself to downplay her achievements to her own boss, but on the other, she was beginning to get an uncomfortable feeling about just what her achievements might have earned her. Somehow, she didn't think it was an all-expenses-paid vacation to the Caribbean.

"Thank you," she repeated and carefully left it there.

Yorke rolled his chair forward a few inches and leaned his arms on his desk. "And now I suppose you're wondering why I asked you to come up here."

"I am curious, sir, but I presumed it had something to do with the file Ms. Eberhart brought me."

He nodded. "It does. Have you read through it?"

"No. I only received it a few minutes before I came upstairs."

"Good. Then let me say first, and most important, that the matter in the file is one that must be handled with the absolute highest level of discretion. It's not something I would like to hear being bandied about the building or over the watercooler."

"Of course not." Danice struggled not to allow any of her indignation to seep into her tone. It wasn't as if she didn't know when to keep her mouth shut. Hell, even as they spoke she was keeping the secret of The Others from the entire damned world, wasn't she?

"Now, don't be offended." The elderly man smiled knowingly. "When I explain matters to you, you'll understand how I take the details of this case quite personally. You see, it involves my granddaughter."

Two

"Your granddaughter?" Surprise leaked out before Danice could stifle it. She'd assumed any case that came down from On High would be an important one, but she'd never expected to be trusted with a case of personal significance to an owner of the firm. She hadn't even made junior partner yet.

"That's right. She's my daughter Ruth's child, and it might make me sound like some kind of unfeeling old bastard, but I have to tell you, the girl has always been my favorite." He nodded at the notebook folder in her lap. "You might as well open that up now. You'll likely want to take notes."

Still unsure of exactly what was going on, Danice did as she was told and opened the folder. She flipped to a blank sheet on the legal pad inside and took out a slim silver pen. Whatever this was about, she felt pretty confident it would at least be interesting.

"My granddaughter's name is Rosemary Addison," Yorke began. "Her mother, Ruth, is my youngest, and if her stubborn streak is any indication, she's also the one who takes after me the most. And she seems to have passed that trait on down to Rosemary.

"Ruth married against my wishes. I never liked Tom

Addison, and I can't say that I don't blame him, at least in part, for this whole mess. He was never good enough for Ruth, and the only time he ever paid any attention to his daughter was when he was scolding her. It's a wonder she never ran away or ended up a teenage drug addict."

So far, Danice couldn't quite decide what she was supposed to be making notes about, so she just wrote down the names he mentioned and other random words to make her appear to be listening. Which she was; she just wasn't quite understanding at the moment. She had no idea what he might be leading up to, and frankly, she couldn't even tell if she was supposed to.

But somehow she wasn't getting a very good feeling about it.

"It's all to Ruth's credit that Rosemary turned out to be a good girl, if a bit high-strung and impulsive. And stubborn. But it's Tom Addison's fault that she was always looking for a man to love her, because that son of a bitch never did."

Danice blinked at the harsh words, but continued her pretend-note-taking. *Is that so, Mr. Yorke? But tell me how you really feel?* she thought.

"So it's Addison's fault that Rosemary is in this mess. And that's where you come in."

Danice's head snapped up. "Um, excuse me, sir. Where, exactly, is it that I'm coming in?"

Her question seemed to shake Yorke out of some sort of spell of memories and irritation. He gave a tiny start and blinked at her once before his face settled into a wrinkled scowl.

"Rosemary got herself mixed up with some lowlife,"

he growled. "Some opportunistic bastard made Rosie fall in love with him, got her pregnant, and then disappeared. That son of a bitch broke her heart. He hurt her so badly, she never even told her family about it. I had to find out from some gossip columnist calling me up to ask if it was true that my granddaughter, Rosemary Addison, was unmarried and pregnant. This reporter told me that Rosie had been seen leaving an obstetrician's office and going directly to a luncheon where she had to ask people if anyone had heard from this asshole because she had some very important news for him. As if my little girl would have to go chasing after some man in order to get him to do the right thing! If you ask me, the son of a bitch ought to be shot."

For a second, Danice found herself wondering if the file in her lap contained legal documents, or a gun and a silencer. It almost sounded as if Matthew Yorke wasn't looking for an attorney so much as a hit man. Or hit woman.

Hit person?

"Back in my day, that folder on your lap would have contained a breach of promise suit," he continued, still scowling. "Too bad that went out in the 1940s. But that doesn't mean I'm letting that bastard get away with deserting my Rosie. I'm going to find the bastard for her, and then I'm going to make him pay. We can't get him for breach, but we can sure as hell get him for paternity in New York, and since Rosie tells me they spent time at the family house in Connecticut because he claimed to be from around there, we're going to slap him with their Marvin law as well. New York might not grant palimony rights, but Connecticut does."

Finally, the light began to dawn. "And you'd like me to handle the suits?"

Yorke nodded. "I would."

Danice squirmed and searched her brain frantically for a way to get out of the assignment. Not only were paternity and palimony lawsuits stigmatic and messy, they were also painfully difficult to negotiate and seldom easy to win. And the last thing she needed in her quest for a partnership was to lose a case on behalf of the granddaughter of the firm's senior-most senior partner. It would be career suicide. A warped form of hara-kiri, only messier and less dignified.

"But first," the old man continued, "I need you to talk some sense into my granddaughter. Not only is she currently refusing to let me file, she's also withholding the name of the bastard from me, so I can't even track him down and threaten to break his puny little neck."

Oh, yeah. This was just looking better and better.

"Mr. Yorke," she began cautiously, "I'm flattered by your confidence in me, but the firm has several attorneys with much more experience in family law than I have. I'm sure you've noticed that during my time here, I've spent more time in contracts and civil litigation."

"Of course I noticed that, Ms. Carter," Yorke snapped, "but I also noticed that you're female, bright, and close to my granddaughter's age. It wasn't the easiest chore convincing her to talk to an attorney in the first place, but I promised her I'd find someone she could feel comfortable with. That someone, my dear, is you."

So that was what it looked like when your life flashed before your eyes, Danice reflected morosely. It really was almost anticlimactic. In retrospect, the high points so far looked more like speed bumps than mountainous achievements.

She forced a smile and worked to unclench her jaw. "Well, I suppose if you're certain I'm the best choice . . ."

"You're the only choice." His glare did little to comfort her. "Inside that folder, you'll find the address of her parents' summer house in Connecticut where she's staying, and summaries of the New York paternity and Connecticut palimony statutes. It's up to you to fill in the rest of what you'll need to go to court. But most important is finding out this bastard's name. I want it, and I damned sure as hell don't want my Rosie to have to go begging someone else to put her in touch with him before I know it. I want that information as soon as you have it. If not sooner."

Oh, yes. An assignment like this would undoubtedly make her future with Parish Hampton.

Make it into *what,* was the question.

"Forgive me for asking, Mr. Yorke," she began, trying frantically to find a way to voice her thoughts that wouldn't have her clearing out her desk before the end of business. Which was in about six minutes from now. "But have you considered that your granddaughter might prefer to simply put this relationship behind her and move on with her life? I realize that few people dream of being a single parent, but it doesn't sound as if the baby's father is a terribly reliable sort to begin with, so maybe it would—"

"Ms. Carter," Yorke bit out, his pale eyes narrowing until she could barely make out the slits of blue in the mass of wrinkles, "I don't care what year it is, or what the celebrities or the young kids are doing these days. My granddaughter is not going to be an unwed mother. No punk is going to knock up my little girl and just walk away without being punished. It wouldn't have happened in my day, and it won't happen today. Do I make myself clear?"

Danice swallowed hard and wondered how difficult it would be to pass the bar exam in California. Or Alaska.

Maybe Argentina?

"Very clear, sir." She bent over the pad in her lap and feigned making another diligent note about the case as she watched the deep black chasm at her feet opening wider and wider. Falling in, she thought, might be inevitable, but at the moment a painful and messy death didn't sound all that bad. It might even beat the alternative of trying these cases. She'd have to give it some thought. "I'll arrange to meet with Ms. Addison immediately. Was there anything else?"

Yorke shook his head, rheumy eyes gleaming with a combination of malice and satisfaction. Unfortunately, Danice wasn't altogether sure which emotion he had directed at her. "That's all, Danice. Just make sure you handle this case as well as you've handled all your others, and everything will be just fine."

The edge of the chasm inched closer.

"Of course. I'll give it my best."

"I'm sure you will." He leaned back in his chair, his expression softening back into the dignified mien he normally showed the world. Only by looking very closely could she detect the spark of Machiavellian intent behind his mask. "And I'm sure a successful resolution of this case will be the kind of thing the partners look on very favorably when they meet to discuss promotions in three months."

And right there, he held the carrot and the stick in the same gnarled hand.

The problem, Danice reflected glumly a few minutes later as she stepped back into the elevator, was that while she would give her best to the situation, she had a feeling that the situation would be giving her little more than a headache in return. Well, a headache and some heartburn, she thought, already wishing for the pack of antacids she kept in her bottom drawer.

Both sources of discomfort would be worth it, though, if they led to her junior partnership at the end of the year. Until just a few minutes ago, she had assumed she was another year away from the brass ring, but now Yorke was dangling it right in front of her nose.

Danice glanced down at her notes as the elevator doors slid open. Hopefully, Rosemary Addison wouldn't be screening away calls from the firm's number. If this was going to be Danice's fate, she'd prefer to go up in flame right now and get it over with. Better to go out with a bang than a whimper.

Especially since she had a feeling she would still be whimpering while she burned.

Three

Danice didn't believe in allowing herself to be handicapped, so she knew perfectly well how to drive. But she also didn't believe in being an idiot, so she didn't own a car. Keeping one in the city would have cost her nearly as much as leasing her apartment, and driving one through Midtown would have cost her sanity, so on a daily basis she did what all intelligent New Yorkers did: used her own two feet and one of the few reliable public transit systems in America.

Today, however, she was working, so she very cheerfully allowed Parish Hampton to order her a car service to drive her the thirty-odd miles from Manhattan to New Canaan, Connecticut. Not having to drive herself gave her the freedom to work during the trip, and working during the trip gave her the chance to plot the strategy she would take when she met Rosemary Addison in way too short a time.

She had dialed the young woman's number the minute she got back to her desk after speaking to Yorke. For several agonizing minutes, she'd feared she'd been right about the call screening, but after nearly seven rings Rosemary had finally picked up the phone. She had not, however, sounded all that happy to talk to an employee of her grandfather's firm.

Matthew Yorke IV, his granddaughter had informed Danice, had no right to stick his nose into her private affairs. She was twenty-six years old, and way past the age when she needed to answer to anyone else for her behavior or her decisions. If she wanted to go out to the docks during Fleet Week and sleep with every sailor who stepped off a ship, that was exactly what she would do, and nothing her parents or her grandparents could say was going to stop her. If she wanted to have a dozen illegitimate children and parade them in front of the tabloid paparazzi every day of their young lives, she'd do that, too. And if her grandfather didn't stop trying to stick his nose in her affairs, she'd make sure she didn't even know the damned father's name herself the next time, so that he'd have no reason to think he deserved to know it, either.

But if Danice wanted to come by the house, Rosemary supposed she could squeeze a meeting in at around ten the next morning.

Oh, how Danice was looking forward to it.

Glancing out the window of the moving town car, she could see that the landscape of concrete and asphalt that made up New York had faded away, leaving her surrounded by the leafy, tree-lined expanse of Connecticut's Merritt Parkway. They wouldn't be far from their destination now.

Danice sighed as she shuffled a stack of papers back into her polished chestnut leather briefcase. She harbored very few illusions about how this morning's interview was likely to go. Her boss was counting on her not to return to New York without the name of the man who'd insulted his family's nineteenth-century sense of honor. Her client had about as much interest in speaking with her as with Torquemada and the rest of the Spanish Inquisitors. The paternity and palimony cases were weak and probably all but unwinnable without Rosemary's cooperation. And to make up for the time this trip to and from New Canaan would eat out of Danice's schedule, she was going to have to work through this weekend's Girls' Night event with her four closest friends.

Why was it that only international spies and war criminals got to carry cyanide capsules around with them for emergencies?

The car slowed to exit the highway and turned onto the secondary road that would take them to their destination in the expensive and exclusive enclave of the rich and snobbish. In reality, Danice could think of few places she wouldn't rather be, and few things she wouldn't rather be doing. Mostly because she could see no way that this would work out well for her.

Pulling off the road, through a set of wrought-iron gates, and down a long, winding private drive did very little to reassure her. Neither did the enormous brick structure at the end of the drive, which bore a closer resemblance to a seat of British aristocracy than to her idea of a casual "summer house."

Of course, for the daughter of an electrician and a manicurist, born and raised in Brooklyn, a summer house was a pretty radical idea to begin with. These days, Danice might dress in designer clothes and charge more by the hour than her parents had earned some weeks, but very occasionally the wealth of some people still astounded her. The Addisons now counted among those people.

She thanked the driver for opening her door and nodded at his murmur about waiting for her in the car. It might be hot today—since it was August, there wasn't much chance of it being anything else—but the humidity had broken last night, and for once the heat felt pleasant rather than oppressive. Danice didn't even regret wearing trousers instead of a dress. Of course, it was only quarter to ten in the morning; her opinion could still change.

Squaring her shoulders, Danice gripped the handle of her briefcase tight and strode briskly across the wide, columned front porch and up to the carved double doors of the quiet mansion. Despite the pleasant weather, the windows were closed, but she could see no lamps burning inside. With so many windows, though, she doubted anyone could complain about insufficient lighting.

Raising a hand, she pressed the button for the doorbell and listened to the melodious chime sound within the silent house. She waited for several minutes and rang again, but everything remained silent. And still.

And really, pretty deserted looking, now that she thought about it.

Frowning, she leaned to the left to peer in the long, narrow sidelight that flanked the door, but she couldn't see anything beyond a polished marble entry hall with a long, graceful staircase sweeping up to a second-floor balcony. She certainly didn't see anyone who looked like Mr. Yorke's twenty-six-year-old granddaughter.

She didn't even see a maid, a housekeeper, or a pet cat. The place appeared completely empty.

Danice groaned. She knew she had arrived fifteen minutes early for her appointment with Rosemary, but after their conversation on the phone last night, it really would not surprise her at all if the girl had decided to punish her by making her wait for their meeting. Rosemary had probably gone out to get her hair done, or something, and would come roaring down the drive in a tiny convertible sports car just before noon, acting as if she were doing Danice a favor by deigning to show up at all.

Not that Danice was cynical, or anything.

Still, there had to be someone in the house, she decided. She couldn't believe that in this town and with this family, there wouldn't be a single maid or gardener or something around at all times. Especially not with the driveway gates left wide open and a meddling old martinet like Matthew Yorke IV as the head of the family. Someone had to be around to answer the damned door.

Ringing the bell again, Danice followed up by lifting a fist to knock—okay, more like pound—a few times on the heavy wooden panels. To her surprise, her second thump elicited a soft clicking sound, and the left-hand door swung soundlessly open. Danice braced herself for the sound of a shrilling alarm.

Nothing happened.

Ooooooookay.

Puzzled, she used the side of her briefcase to nudge the door a little farther open and leaned forward to peer into the foyer.

"Hello?" she called uncertainly. "Is anyone here? I have an appointment with Ms. Addison. Hello?"

No one answered.

Something about this seemed a little bit weird.

Glancing over her shoulder at the black town car, Danice could see the driver had the windows open, the seat pushed back, and his black cap positioned over his face while he relaxed and waited. She was only surprised she couldn't hear him snoring. Clearly, he wouldn't notice if she let herself inside.

Her peep-toe slingbacks made a hollow clacking sound on the marble floor as she stepped through the door and eased it shut behind her.

"Hello?" she called again. "Ms. Addison?"

The house sounded almost eerily quiet. She could hear the shushing of her own clothing shifting when she moved and the muted sounds of the outdoors beyond the creamy, wainscoted walls, but she couldn't hear anything that sounded like another person. Was the house really deserted and unlocked while the owners' daughter was in residence? That wouldn't make any sense.

Taking a few steps to the right or left allowed her to peer into the rooms that opened up on either side of the entry hall. To her right, she could see what looked like a sitting room followed by a formal dining room that she guessed stretched back a fair distance. On the left, a more formal living area opened into a large, sunny room with a concert grand piano and several other instruments either hung on the walls or positioned in stands along the room's perimeter.

Still no people.

She could see a hallway opening up straight ahead

beyond the curve of the staircase, but without windows, the dim space offered no clues as to what might lie in that direction. It appeared, however, just as silent and deserted as the parts of the house she could see.

Damn it, what the hell was she supposed to do now?

Impatiently, Danice checked her watch again. Five till ten. The girl really should be here. She might be young and rich and spoiled, but she'd agreed to this meeting, and she'd designated the time herself. Could she honestly be rude enough not to be home to keep it? Maybe she was just in another part of the house and hadn't heard Danice's entrance?

Danice recalled her first impression of the massive, window-covered edifice and stifled a groan. Did it really matter what part of the house the girl was in? The place was so big that if Danice tried to conduct a quick room-by-room search, not only would it take her the rest of her damned life, but there were so many places a person could go to hide that if Rosemary didn't want to be found, odds were that Danice wouldn't find her.

So what should she do now? Sit down and wait? She certainly had enough work in her briefcase that killing a couple of hours while she waited for Yorke's granddaughter to show up at noon wouldn't pose a huge problem, but did she really want to start off this meeting in such a subordinate position? It wouldn't do her any favors when it came to exerting influence over Rosemary if the girl knew from the outset that Danice was literally at her beck and call. And if the girl had decided to blow off the appointment entirely, Danice would feel pretty stupid camping out in the hall for however long it took for someone to wander by and inform her of that fact.

On the other hand, she did not want to picture the look on Yorke's face when he found out that Danice had driven all the way out to Connecticut and not only hadn't gotten the name of Rosemary's erstwhile lover, but hadn't managed to get the girl to talk to her. Or even stand in the same room with her. That would not bode well for her continued employment, let alone her promotion.

Shit, shit, shit, she thought.

"Shit."

The curse echoed in the sterile environment, and Danice could have sworn the flowers that had been carefully arranged in a vase atop the round table in the center of the foyer gasped at the effrontery.

Then her head snapped around, because she also could have sworn that she'd heard a soft thumping sound come from upstairs.

Standing completely motionless, she strained to hear it again.

Nothing.

But she felt certain that a second ago, she'd heard a *thump* from somewhere over her head. Someone else had to be in the house. Who knew? Maybe the maid wore an iPod while she cleaned and hadn't heard Danice. Either way, did Danice really want to face the consequences of heading back to Manhattan without even checking to see if anyone could tell her where Rosemary had gone?

That thought decided her. Setting her briefcase down next to the flowers, she squared her shoulders and headed for the stairs. If there was a maid up there, Danice hoped to hell she spoke English. Because if she had to ask where Rosemary had gone and when she'd be back in Spanish or French or Russian or Martian, she might as well just give up now.

Too bad Danice Carter had never been the type to give up. On anything.

Four

McIntyre Callahan had known from the beginning that taking this case was a Very Bad Idea. He'd seen the capital letters and everything. Unfortunately, he'd also seen that the size of the payment being offered was enough to run his small private investigation agency for the next six months, even if he didn't touch another case during that period. And call him kooky, but Mac had a disconcerting fondness for paying his bills. So he'd taken the case, but he'd regretted it almost right away.

Which was nothing compared with how much he was regretting it right now.

Right now he stood concealed in the shadows across from the top of a stairway in the house of someone he'd never met, while trying to decide whether to tackle the woman climbing inexorably toward him and pump her for information, or blend in with the wallpaper and wait to see what she was doing here.

That was the way it was supposed to go, anyway, but then the woman's head and shoulders crested the stairs and Mac forgot all about what was supposed to happen. He became much too preoccupied with drooling.

The woman took his breath away. Hell, she stopped

his heartbeat, or at least made it stutter and skip in a way with which he was entirely unfamiliar.

He couldn't pinpoint the reason. For a man with Fae blood in his veins, for a man who'd experienced the awesome beauty of Fae women, he couldn't call her the most gorgeous female he'd ever seen. Her features weren't perfect enough for that. But they fascinated him, from her slightly almond-shaped eyes to her high, defined cheekbones, and the piquant shape of her chin.

He didn't think it could be the rich, dusky, honeyed tone of her skin, either, even if that skin looked so soft and fine that his fingers literally itched to reach out and stroke it. After all, Fae women might have skin that glowed with the pale luminosity of a pearl, but he lived in New York, surrounded by women with skin in every hue and shade and texture imaginable . . . and since he lived among The Others of New York, he could imagine an awful lot more than the average human.

Even the shape of her as she moved toward the top of the stairs wasn't anything he hadn't seen before, or seen perfected on someone else. She appeared to be neither short nor particularly tall, but her figure curved beneath her slate-colored trousers and silky, sleeveless top in a way that made him want to measure her softness with his hands.

From her dark, thick hair, neatly confined at the nape of her neck, to the red-polished toes peeping out of dainty designer shoes, nothing about this woman should merit more than a few appreciative glances and maybe the desire to ask politely for her phone number.

Nonetheless, something about her called to him.

Loudly enough that he found himself leaning heavily toward his tackling option, if only so that he could feel those curves and that skin pressed against him as he pinned her to the closest horizontal surface.

Practicality, however, made him hesitate. He had heard her calling out as she came through the front door a few minutes ago, had heard her asking for Ms. Addison and announcing that her name was Danice Carter, so he knew she wasn't his quarry. She hadn't, however, announced what she was doing here, other than keeping an appointment. Judging by her expensively elegant wardrobe, she wasn't applying for a job as a maid or gardener, but beyond that he couldn't hazard a guess. Still, she was looking for the same woman he was, so he did need to know what she was after, and if she knew any more than he did.

He could have, he supposed, taken her at face value, and assumed that because she had called out in the house, her actions provided evidence that she had expected someone to answer. By that reasoning, she could not be expected to have any more idea of the whereabouts of Rosemary Addison than he himself did. Mac, however, made it a rule to take very little of what he heard and saw at face value. Not only had it made him a better investigator, but it had kept him alive on more than one occasion.

Maybe Ms. Danice Carter (if that was, indeed, her real name) had an appointment with Ms. Addison that she had expected the other woman to keep, and was simply confused about why no one had greeted her at the door. But if that was the case, why was she prowling around another person's house uninvited? Especially if she was far enough removed from intimacy with that person to address her as *Ms. Addison* instead of by her given name? And if the woman merely wanted to ascertain whether there was anyone in the house, why had she headed directly upstairs instead of checking the rooms on the main floor of the house first?

None of those actions guaranteed a nefarious purpose, of course, but none of them screamed out on the side of ignorant innocence, either.

Mac had always found that even when it didn't pay to be cautious, being cautious allowed him to stay alive long enough to get paid.

With a little push of his will, he called up a tiny glamour to conceal himself from human eyes, ensuring that even if she glanced in his direction, her gaze would pass right over him without registering his presence. He might not have full command of Fae magic, but he often found it convenient to make use of what he had.

The woman's heels clicked softly on the wooden floor at the top of the stairs, then padded silently onto the thick runner that decorated the length of the upstairs balcony. Three doors led off the open area above the entry hall, and corridors stretched away in three directions toward the rear and sides of the house. Mac watched her hesitate for a moment, almost as if she were listening for something, before she muttered to herself under her breath and headed cautiously for the door closest to her.

Mac had already checked this part of the house—and enough of the rest of it to be certain they were the only two people in it at the moment—so he knew the door led to a bedroom, and he knew that bedroom to be empty. He also suspected that it had recently been occupied by Rosemary Addison.

But was it a coincidence that Danice Carter went directly into that room? Or did she know more than she was letting on?

Falling soundlessly into step behind her, Mac decided to find out.

He suffered a brief jolt when she glanced over her shoulder after stepping inside the room. It almost looked as if she knew he was watching her, but her gaze slipped easily past him, and he knew the glamour still concealed him. Which at least reassured him that she must be as human as she looked. Another Fae-blooded creature would have seen through the simple magic, or at least seen that it was there, and most other varieties of Others would have been able to sense the presence of something magical nearby if they had paid the slightest bit of attention. This woman, however, appeared nervous, but oblivious.

She stopped a few feet inside the room, looking tense and irritated and poised to flee at any moment. She also seemed to be searching for something or someone, craning her head from this side to that, almost as if she expected a crowd of partygoers to jump out from behind the furniture and yell, *Surprise!*

He'd be the one surprised if that happened.

But what was she looking for?

He watched her open her mouth as if to call out one more time, then shut it without making a sound. He didn't know if she'd realized she didn't know what to say, or if she'd thought better of announcing her presence again.

He did know, however, that her mouth had just made it onto his list of Top Ten Sexual Fantasies. Why hadn't he noticed it when he cataloged her features earlier? It definitely deserved notice, with its plump shape and inviting curve and arousing mobility. Hell, it probably deserved to be immortalized in Italian marble. When he let himself imagine what she could do with it—

He cut off that train of thought before it could leave the station and willed his body to relax. This really wasn't the time for indulging in prurient daydreams. He could do that later.

And had a feeling he would.

At the moment, though, he really did need to find out what exactly she was doing here.

Dissolving the glamour, he stepped forward, blocking the room's exit with his body, and decided there was a very simple way to find out the answer to his question.

So he asked it.

And that was when she screamed.

Ever since she'd reached the top of the stairs, Danice had experienced the deeply creepy feeling that she was being watched.

It didn't seem to matter how often she peered into corners or how many times she looked back over her shoulders. The house continued to appear completely empty, but the goose bumps on her arms and the tingling on the back of her neck insisted that someone had their eyes on her. The presence didn't feel particularly malevolent, but that didn't make it any less disturbing.

In fact, *disturbed* offered a very good description of how she felt just at that moment.

Something wasn't right here.

Danice grimaced and congratulated herself on her keen powers of perception. There was definitely something strange going on. The longer she spent in this house, the more she decided that Rosemary Addison's absence was not the result of a spoiled girl throwing a temper tantrum, or even an empty-headed socialite paying so little attention to her obligations that an appointment made only fourteen hours before had completely slipped her mind.

No, Danice decided grimly, there was more to this than that. She just had no idea what it could be.

Crossing her arms, she chafed her hands up and down the bare skin, hoping to chase away a bit of the chill. It didn't have much effect, but the defensive posture at least expressed her internal conflict a little bit better. What exactly was she supposed to do now?

She had already decided that Rosemary Addison was nowhere inside this house, and after following her ridiculous impulse up the stairs and into this bedroom, she had begun to conclude that neither were any maids. And furthermore, she had also decided that if there had been anything up here to cause the thumping sound she'd thought she heard back in the entry hall, she probably did not want to know what it was.

So, what next?

Did she leave a note and drive back to Manhattan to face the wrath of Matthew Yorke IV? Did she use her cell phone to call Rosemary and ask to reschedule their appointment? Did she tear her hair out, give up her ambitions to practice law at the elite level, and move to an ashram in Tibet?

Was that something moving behind her?

Sucking in a panicked breath, Danice whirled to face the doorway, only to find it filled by a tall, lean man with long golden hair, bright gray-blue eyes, and a menacing expression.

She had an instant to process the reality of his presence and another to realize that by blocking the door, he effectively had her trapped in a room with no exit, no obvious weapons, and a big soft bed that appeared to be the perfect canvas for a little bit of rape, murder, and mayhem.

She also had half an instant to wonder what Matthew Yorke IV's reaction would be when he learned the news that one of his employees had been found dead in the bed of the granddaughter he'd sent her to talk to, before she threw her head back and screamed at the absolute top of her lungs.

Then she had no more instants left, because the man in the door flashed forward faster than humanly possible and tackled her, clamping one hand tightly over her mouth and using the other to pin her wrists to the mattress above her head.

Oh, dear.

Five

She felt just as amazing beneath him as he'd imagined she would.

Mac allowed himself about seven nanoseconds to savor the sensation before he forced his attention back to business and glared down at her.

"Looking for something?" he growled.

She muttered a few words against his palm, but judging by the expression in her dark eyes, he decided it probably wasn't something he wanted to hear anyway. Somehow, he doubted it was complimentary.

Still, it wouldn't do him much good to ask her questions if he wouldn't be able to hear the answers.

"If I take my hand away, are you going to scream?"

She glared at him as if he were an ax murderer.

A very unintelligent ax murderer.

He sighed. "Right. While I understand your feelings, given the situation, I'm not sure that's really the wisest answer. It doesn't offer me all that much incentive to turn you loose."

Especially not since he'd heard two voices outside after the car had pulled up. Someone else might still be around to hear her scream, and while one quickly stifled cry might be explained away, two would be pushing it.

She offered another muffled reply, but he had a feeling it didn't differ significantly in content from the first. They appeared to have reached some sort of impasse.

"Look, I have absolutely no intention of hurting you," he assured her, though the expression of distrust and anger in her eyes didn't much change. "I'm not a rapist, and I'm not a killer. I'm a private investigator, and at the moment what I really need to investigate is who you are and what you're doing here. So will you promise not to scream so that I can lift up my hand and ask you a few questions?"

She did a great deal of rather disgruntled muttering, but after a minute or two he felt her wind down and spit out one last word that sounded (felt? gave him the vague feeling?) like it might have been, "License?"

"My license?" he tested and got a crisp jerk of a nod in response. "In my wallet. But I have my hands just a little too full at the moment to show it to you. As soon as you promise not to scream, I'll let you take a good hard look. Deal?"

"Nadkmgnnsnhsalg, llbmssnddskmmm."

He paused, frowning in concentration. "As soon as you see my license, you'll promise not to scream?"

Another reluctant nod.

Mac thought that one through and came up with only one feasible solution. He swore on his father's grave he had absolutely no ulterior motive in deciding on the single logical course of action. Not a single prurient thought in his head.

No, siree.

"Are you right- or left-handed?" he asked, assuring

himself he was not at all looking forward inappropriately to what he was about to suggest.

She managed to glare and frown up at him at the same time. She also managed to flex her right shoulder forward. He nodded.

"My wallet is in my back pocket, on the right. My right. I'm going to let go of your left wrist, and you're going to use that hand to reach into my pocket and take out the wallet. If you flip it open, you'll see the license. But if you use the opportunity to take a swing at me instead, I'm not going to be very happy about it. Understood?"

He watched her think that through for a second before she nodded one more time.

"All right. Don't move too fast, though. It might make me nervous."

Carefully, he loosened his grip on her slender wrists just long enough to let the left one slip free. His fingers tightened immediately on the right, pinning it in place. She didn't attempt to break free, though, and he wondered if it was because she already believed he was who he said he was, or because she was too wary of him to test his patience.

Or maybe she was just smart enough to realize that he was half again as big as her and any attempt to overpower him would be ultimately futile.

Any way he looked at it, she behaved herself with admirable restraint, moving her arm down slowly and fumbling for a minute at his hip before she oriented herself and reached warily into his back pocket to pull out his billfold.

He noticed the care she took not to touch him any

more than necessary, and felt a twinge of regret for that. He would happily give her permission to grope him from now until doomsday if she needed to, but apparently she didn't yet share his sense of strong physical attraction.

Too bad.

Her hand moved faster as she raised the leather wallet into her view and let the sides fall open to reveal two plastic-covered ID compartments, one containing his New York driver's license, the other his state-issued pocket card, identifying him as a duly licensed and authorized private investigator, pursuant to the laws of the State of New York.

He watched her eyes scan the card, saw her file away his name, the name of his firm, and the fact that the photo matched the face she had been glaring at for the past five minutes, before her gaze slid back to his. The expression in her eyes remained angry, but the tint of fear had faded.

She muttered something grumpy.

"I know we're in Connecticut. Fortunately, right behind the New York card you'll find one from the Nutmeg State. Trust me, I'm covered. Now since we've established who I am, can I take my hand away so you can tell me who the hell you are?"

She nodded, reluctantly but definitely, so Mac began to lift his hand, ready to slap it right back into place if she so much as drew too deep a breath.

All she did was curse at him.

"I am not telling you a goddamned thing until you get the hell off me, you jackass."

Mac sighed. "You know I can't do that. Look at it

from my perspective. Would you trust you not to make a break for it the minute I let you go?"

"Absolutely, because I'd need at least *two* minutes to take really good aim and kick you in the balls the hundred times that you frickin' deserve!"

"Well, that doesn't particularly set me at ease."

"And setting you at ease is so my primary concern right now."

"Considering that I'm the one in control at the moment, you might want to make it your primary concern."

"And you might want to start wearing a cup, just in case I ever have to see you again."

Instead of being angry, Mac found himself laughing, and at that point, it seemed rude to keep her pinned to the bed.

Entertaining, but rude.

He released her and stepped to the side, out of immediate groin-injury range. Folding his arms across his chest—mostly to keep his hands from going anywhere they shouldn't—he gazed down at her and lifted an eyebrow. "Well?"

"Well, what?" Pushing herself into a sitting position, she continued to eye him warily.

"Aren't you going to introduce yourself?"

She rubbed her hands around her wrists, as if erasing the feel of him holding her down. The idea made him frown, but he kept his thoughts to himself.

"This has got to be the weirdest meet-and-greet I've ever done," she grumbled, "but I'm Danice Carter, and I'm looking for Rosemary Addison. I have an appointment with her at ten. Now, how about you tell me what *you're* doing here, McIntyre Callahan, PI."

Now, that was interesting. If Rosemary had made an appointment with someone for ten o'clock this morning, that meant she must have intended to be here at that time. So where was she?

"The same thing you are, apparently," he answered. "Except I didn't have an appointment. What was yours supposed to be about?"

She looked way too satisfied when she informed him, "I'm afraid that I can't disclose that sort of information. It's privileged."

"I didn't know that shrinks made house calls."

"I'm not a psychiatrist. I'm an attorney."

"An attorney? What does Rosemary Addison need an attorney for?" She opened her mouth, but he held up his hand and stopped her. "I know, I know. It's privileged."

"Quite. But I'm aware of no laws stating that there's any such protection afforded to a private investigator." Her eyes narrowed. "So what, exactly, is your business with Ms. Addison?"

He flashed her a grin. He admired her drive.

"Just because there's no expectation of privilege regarding my business doesn't mean I have to reveal it to you, Counselor. As it turns out, you're not a police officer, are you?"

Danice pursed her lips and tilted her head to the side, looking more cunning than innocent. "No, but I am the person who can file a complaint against you for breaking and entering, harassment, and assault, at the very least, if you keep pissing me off. Aren't I?"

"That suit wouldn't make it past the file clerk. Since I came in the same way you did, you would have noticed that there was no breaking involved in my entering. And I'd hate to have to tell the court that you committed exactly the same act of trespass I did. It probably wouldn't look very good for you."

"I might decide to take my chances."

"So might I."

They stood there for several minutes, blue eyes clashing with brown, until Mac realized that the only way to get this woman to give in would be to knock her unconscious with a swift blow to the head. Somehow he couldn't quite bring himself to do that, so instead he sighed and reached out a hand for his wallet.

She handed it back immediately, which oddly reassured him. She could have tried to use it as a bargaining chip and refused to hand it over until he answered her questions. It would have taken him all of two seconds to overpower her and regain it by force, but he wouldn't have enjoyed having to do that.

"I may not enjoy attorney–client privilege," he said, tucking the billfold back into his pocket, "but I do have an obligation to my clients to maintain a certain level of discretion, which means that I can't tell you everything you want to know." He raised a hand before she could voice the objections he saw forming on her lips. "But I will tell you that my client hired me to locate a woman named Rosemary Addison. Obviously, I located her address, but the woman herself seems to have eluded us both."

He watched her weigh his answer and wasn't really surprised when she decided it felt a bit light.

"And why did your client need a PI to find Ms. Addison? She's a prominent member of a prominent family. She's not exactly living a life of anonymity."

And here, Mac thought, was where things got tricky.

"As wonderful a job as our national media might do in reporting the whereabouts of bored American socialites," he drawled, trying for a note of dismissive cynicism, "not everyone in the world watches *E!*"

She narrowed her eyes. "Your client is foreign?"

The word hit close enough to the mark to qualify as the truth—albeit loosely—so Mac nodded.

"And what does this international client of mystery want with Ms. Addison?"

"You know very well I'm not going to tell you that. That would absolutely violate my client's expectations of discretion and privacy."

Not to mention the fact that Mac had begun to realize he didn't quite know the answer to that himself. It made him frown.

Danice reacted to the change of expression with a shrug. "You know I had to ask. Can't blame a girl for trying."

Mac dragged himself back to the matter at hand and caught the tail end of her comment. He smiled. "Frankly, Ms. Carter, the last thing I'm inclined to call you is a 'girl.' "

He let his gaze trail over her, from the top of her glossy dark head to the bottoms of her petite, polished toes. And if a spark—or raging inferno—of appreciation happened to reach his eyes as he did so? Well, he was only a man, after all.

He watched her shift slightly then straighten her

spine into regal alignment. "Don't try to get around me with charm, Mr. Callahan. I'm immune."

Mac saw the instant she realized her mistake, but by then, it was too late. Much, much too late.

He stepped forward, backing her up the single, monumental step between her knees and the bed. He saw it in her eyes the moment the rear of her legs touched the mattress, saw the flare of unease.

The tiny, buried kernel of excitement.

"Are you?" he murmured, leaning close, letting his breath brush the silken skin of her cheek. Letting her scent of amber and honey fill his senses. "Are you really, pretty, pretty Danice?"

Six

Danice thought she had learned this lesson years ago. After all, a good attorney never spoke without thinking. It would be suicidal. There were far too many pitfalls, too many traps to be sprung in a negotiation or a deposition or a sworn testimony for anyone to say the first thing that popped into her head, and Danice knew it. Hadn't she spent enough time learning to pounce on that kind of mistake the minute her opponent made it?

Yet just then, Danice experienced the shift of the ground beneath her feet as she suddenly ceased to be the hunter and instead became the prey.

And judging by the glint of intent in McIntyre Callahan's eyes, this predator was feeling more than a little peckish.

She really should have known better than to call into question the charm of a man who looked like this. He stood at least six feet tall, with the kind of whipcord-lean frame that left no one in doubt of his strength. Certainly not Danice, against whom he'd already used it once.

Used it impressively, a voice inside her taunted. Used it until she'd had to fight not to appreciate the erotic feeling of his body pressed against hers, even in circumstances that she had not considered the least bit sexy. But that was beside the point.

The point was that the man was gorgeous. He wore his golden-blond hair long, which normally Danice would have found a complete turnoff, but on him it somehow managed to call attention to the sharply masculine edges of his features. He had a long, narrow face with high, slashing cheekbones and a jawline sharper than a Ginsu carving knife. He also had deep blue-gray eyes the color of the sky before a storm, with such long, thick, lush eyelashes he could have starred in a mascara commercial.

Except that no one on earth could ever mistake him for anything but a man. Certainly not Danice. And certainly not when he stared at her with that hot, hungry look in his eyes.

The one currently making her stomach roll over and beg.

She cleared her throat with a touch of desperation. "What I meant is that I'm trying to maintain a professional outlook here," she qualified hastily. "And I'd think you would be, too, since you're also here for . . . professional reasons. I meant that we should both try to be. Professional, that is."

"I've a confession for you, Danice," he murmured, stepping closer and somehow drawing out the long *E* sound so that the sound of his voice made her shiver.

"What kind of confession?"

He pressed closer and raised a lean, long-fingered hand to brush aside a strand of hair that had escaped the clip at the nape of her neck. "I confess that at the moment"—his finger trailed up the side of her neck to trace the shell of her ear, making her shiver—"I'm not feeling very professional at all."

Her eyes widened and his glinted as his head began a slow, deliberate descent toward hers. He blocked out the light—or maybe that was just her vision going dark—and she stopped breathing. Which could explain the whole vision thing. And for one numb moment, Danice could swear she tasted him on her lips.

The dark, sweet flavor jolted her back to her senses. Twisting her body away, she ducked out of the space between him and the bed—or, as she liked to call it, The Danger Zone—and put herself in a much more sensible position between him and the door. Also known as The Escape Route.

He turned to face her, and she thought she saw a hint of genuine disappointment in his expression before it shifted back into what she suspected were its normal lines of vague amusement. "I take it that you *are* feeling professional."

"I'm feeling something," she muttered under her breath. She needed another minute to let her heart settle back into what resembled a normal rhythm.

"I'm sorry, I missed that. What?"

"Nothing." She straightened her shoulders and met, if not his gaze, then certainly the space between his eyes, which she thought should really count as the same thing. "I'm assuming that if you traced Ms. Addison to her parents' house here in Connecticut, that you had information leading you to believe you'd find her in residence."

He quirked an eyebrow, his expression clearly telling her that her abrupt change of subject amused him, but he let her get away with it. "And since you had an appointment to meet her here this morning, I'm assuming you believed the same thing. Too bad both of us were disappointed."

One of us maybe more than the other, she thought.

Only she said, "I didn't exactly wander through the whole house to check. I suppose she could still be somewhere around here. The place is huge. Or maybe she's outside by the pool. I'm assuming a house like this has to have a pool. Or three."

"Lucky for you, I did wander through the house, and she's not in it. Nor was she anywhere in sight of it." He grinned unrepentantly. "I looked out the windows, too."

Danice frowned. Not at his snooping, but because Rosemary should have been here, and it annoyed her that the young woman would take her irritation with her grandfather out on a third party. Danice's mother would call that just plain bad manners.

"Well, since I wouldn't feel right prowling around someone else's home without an invitation," she said pointedly, because her heartbeat still hadn't slowed down and his smile continued to affect her stomach—and other bits—in inappropriate ways, "I guess I'll have to take your word for it. I'll call Ms. Addison on the way back to the city and ask her to reschedule our meeting for another day."

Once again, her subtle admonishment seemed to amuse the man more than anything. That made her jaw clench. Suddenly it seemed like the most sensible thing in the world to get the hell out of his presence while the getting was good. Without another word, she spun on her heels and left the bedroom to tromp back down the stairs to the foyer and the car waiting for her outside. While she couldn't hear any footsteps indicating that he'd followed her, the way the hair on the back of her neck refused to relax and lie back down, where it was supposed to, let her know he wasn't far behind.

He laid a hand over hers when she reached out to lift her briefcase off the entry table. It took more effort than it should have before she was able to turn and face him with an expression of sufficient coolness.

"Yes, Mr. Callahan?"

That grin of his flashed again, and cool became the last thing she felt inside.

"First of all, you should call me Mac. I have a feeling the two of us are going to meet up again pretty soon." Before she could argue—because she had to argue—he pulled a card out of his left pocket and handed it to her. "My number is on there. Along with my e-mail and my office address. I'd appreciate it if you'd have Ms. Addison give me a call if she gets in touch with you to reschedule."

Danice took the card, carefully ensuring that their fingers did not touch during the exchange. He noticed, too, damn him. "If?" she repeated. "You think she wouldn't return my call for some reason?"

He shrugged, and his expression shifted from amused and interested to blank and a bit hard. "I think that she was supposed to be here this morning, but she wasn't. She might have had a very good reason for missing your appointment, but who's to say that same reason won't apply to returning your phone call?" He nodded at the card she still held. "In any event, I'd appreciate you passing that along if you speak to her."

Danice nodded and slipped the card into a small outer pocket of her bag, retrieving one of her own in the process. "In that case, I'll say the same thing. If for some odd reason you find that Ms. Addison has decided to relocate to another one of her family's residences, I'd appreciate you letting me know. Just in case she is trying to avoid me."

Mac took the card and held it, but his eyes remained on hers. Damn it, he had to know those things were like weapons. It violated all the rules of fair play for him to use them against her like that. The man should go around blindfolded, for the safety of the female population.

"I'll do that, Danice," he murmured, his voice going all low and intimate again. The jerk. "In fact, I'll look forward to it."

Forget the blindfold. He should just be locked up in a dungeon somewhere and guarded only by devoutly heterosexual men. Nothing less would ever keep him in check.

Giving him a brisk nod of thanks, Danice hefted her briefcase and strode out the front door, never in her life so relieved to see an anonymous black town car waiting for her. She called out to the driver, who jerked awake and started the engine promptly, allowing her to roll up the power window and put a film of dark, protective tinting between herself and that lethal gaze.

But not until the car pulled out of the drive and turned on to the road leading back to the highway did Danice finally breathe a sigh of relief.

If God had any of the mercy in Him that her mom was always talking about, that would be the very last time she ever had to get within thirty feet of McIntyre "Call me Mac" Callahan. The man wore trouble like a double-breasted suit, and that was the last thing Danice needed in her life at the moment.

The very last thing.

Mac watched the car pull away with a smile on his face and a bulge in his jeans. Danice Carter made a tasty little treat. In fact, it had been a long time since he'd met anyone who intrigued him as much as the attorney with the smart mouth and the honey-dark skin. A long, long time.

Glancing down at the business card in his hand, he read the elegantly engraved text with a considering eye. DANICE L. CARTER, ATTORNEY-AT-LAW, worked for the remarkably prestigious and eminently stodgy firm of Parish, Hampton, Uxbridge, and Yorke, a law group so well known, it represented senators, actors, former presidents, corporations, and even the leaders of a few foreign countries, when their concerns landed on American soil.

On a more metaphorical level, it represented law as big business, and wasn't at all the kind of working environment where he pictured Danice Carter making her mark. He could much more readily see her in the kind of small, independent firm that forged a place for itself by waging war on the clients Parish Hampton worked for and pulling out stunning, come-from-behind victories that law schools would lecture on for years to come. The kind of win you could read about in a John Grisham novel, or see acted out in a heartwarming Hollywood blockbuster.

Working for Parish Hampton seemed like the kind of job that would slowly rob a woman like Danice of her spirit. And that, he reflected, would be a shame.

Tucking the card in his pocket, Mac dug out his cell phone. He jogged down the steps of the empty house and made his way to his own car, which he'd pulled around to the garage located behind the side of the house. As entertaining and intriguing as his encounter with Ms. Carter had been, it was time to get back to work. Rosemary Addison was out there somewhere, and he needed to find her.

Before whoever had hired him started to get cranky.

Punching in a familiar number, Mac listened to the line ring as he slid behind the steering wheel.

"Under Belly," a voice grunted.

"Let me talk to Quigley."

"Ain't here."

Mac scowled. "Where is he?"

"I sound like his mommy?"

Considering what some of the female imps he'd met in his life had sounded like, Mac decided not to answer that question. Instead he asked, "Did he leave a message for me? It's Callahan."

The bartender of one of the biggest Other dives in Manhattan grunted again, which amounted to eloquence in his case, and said, "Told me to tell you his boss is gettin' impatient. Said he needs results soon and he'll be checkin' in with you tonight. An' unless you wanna pay me like the guy at Western Union, I'm tellin' both of you to stop usin' me like a damned telegraph office."

Mac bit back his retort, though it wasn't necessary since Hedge had already hung up on him. The golem had never been the most cheerful conversationalist, but then again, most of his customers didn't drop in for conversation. They dropped in to drink, fight, and conduct the sort of business transactions that weren't welcome in most other establishments. A long time ago, Mac had started to wonder if the Under Belly wasn't just *a* pit, but actually the kind of pit that made up one of the levels of the fiendish underworld. He wouldn't really be surprised.

Shoving his phone back in his pocket, he started the car and pointed it west. If his client was already pressuring their go-between for results, Mac had better get back to the city and get back to work. He'd known when a few minutes at his computer had yielded the information about Rosemary Addison's current whereabouts that the case had seemed too easy. Now it looked like he'd been right. Time to start pounding the pavement, knocking on doors, and knocking heads together. It might not be the easiest way to make a living, but Mac had done it before, and frankly, he was damned good at it.

The only thing he had to worry about at the moment was keeping his mind on his job and off Danice Carter's lush little mouth.

Somehow, he knew that would be easier said than done.

Seven

Since she'd wasted her entire day on Thursday traveling to and from Connecticut to an appointment her client hadn't even bothered to keep, Danice found herself more than a little buried in catch-up work on Friday. A Friday that just three days ago she had hoped would yield the infrequent treat of allowing her out of the office by 5 PM.

She should have known better than to hope.

At six forty-five, she sat at her desk with one hand poised over the brief she was reviewing and the other vainly attempting to rub some of the tension out of the muscles at the back of her neck. Neither task seemed to be going at all well.

Her phone rang, the call coming straight through since her assistant had already left for the day. More than an hour ago.

Not that Danice felt bitter about that, or anything. Oh, no.

"Danice Carter," she said, trying to keep the irritation out of her voice, it never being a good idea to make clients think you hated having to talk to them. Even when you did.

"What, in the name of all that is holy, are you still doing at the office? It's nearly seven o'clock!"

The voice was familiar, as was the accusation, but at least Danice didn't have to play nice with this particular caller.

"I'm still here because I have a damned job to do, whether it's seven o'clock or midnight, Corinne. Thanks for asking so nicely."

Her friend grumbled. "Don't take it out on me just because you work for a bunch of fascist slave-drivers. Tonight's Girls' Night. Did you forget?"

Danice rolled her eyes. "No, I didn't forget. I'm just not going to be able to make it. I have too much to do."

"But you can't miss Girls' Night! It's . . . it's . . . it's *sacred*!"

"Corinne, it's an excuse to drink too much wine and talk about sex. I don't think that qualifies as the next thing to a papal inauguration."

"Well, it should."

"Then why don't you call the Vatican and voice your opinion? With a name like Corinne D'Alessandro, I have no doubt the operators in Rome will patch you right through."

There was a brief silence on the line, followed by a low whistle. "Sheesh, Niecie, what the hell crawled up your ass and died? Is something the matter?"

Danice dropped her pen and went back to rubbing her neck. "No, everything's fine. I just have a lot of work to do. Even more than usual. I'm feeling a little stressed right now."

"Then Girls' Night is exactly what you need. And

it's at Ava's place tonight, so you don't even need to worry about Frick and Frack, the monster men, hanging around. It's an Other-Free Zone."

"Dmitri and Graham aren't that bad," she said, chuckling reluctantly, referring to Regina's and Missy's husbands, neither of whom precisely qualified as human.

"Sure, if you like 'em fanged and furry. But since we all know that Ava does not, tonight will be entirely humans only."

"What, isn't Reggie going to be there?"

Corinne paused. "Of course she'll be there. When I said 'humans only' I wasn't talking about her. She was human just last year, after all."

Regina had allowed her husband, a vampire, to change her into one as well when she agreed to marry him. Danice still hadn't figured out how she'd brought herself to do it, but apparently a girl didn't like to think about getting all wrinkled and saggy while her hubby surfed that whole wave of eternal youth.

"I'm sorry, Corinne." Danice sighed. "I'm just not gonna be able to make it. I've got at least another hour or two of work to plow through here, and when I'm done, all I want to do is go home, soak in the tub for a while, and then crawl into bed."

"Ava is not going to be happy to hear that."

Danice grimaced. "Don't threaten me, girlfriend. Besides, right now Queen Ava is the least of my worries."

"Holy shit," Corinne gasped, the sound just faintly exaggerated. "Niecie, what the hell have you gotten yourself into? Do you need help? Do you have to fake your own death? Get a new identity? What?"

Corinne was only half joking, Danice knew. It was

kind of hard to fathom what could worry a person more than getting on Ava Markham's bad side. The woman might be one of the closest friends either she or Corinne had, but that didn't mean they didn't live in fear of her. If Ava had been born a few hundred years earlier, even Genghis Khan would have quaked at the sound of her name.

"I'll be fine," she assured her friend. "I've just got a bit of a caseload overload at the moment. And that thing for Yorke is turning out to be an even bigger pain than I was afraid it would be."

"The girl still hasn't called you back?"

"Nope. I'm starting to think she plans to use me as another way to piss off her grandfather."

"Yeeah, no wonder you're in a mood."

"Wouldn't you be?"

"Good point." This time, Corinne sighed. "Well, if you're sure I can't persuade you to say screw it all and come out tonight, I suppose I'll let you go. I'll even try to cover for you with Ava, but I can't promise anything."

"I wouldn't expect you to."

"And I'll accept that as proof you haven't completely lost your mind yet. Try and keep it that way, okay?"

Danice agreed and hung up the phone a minute later feeling even wearier than she had before it rang. She just couldn't tell if the conversation itself had exhausted her, or if she was regretting missing Girls' Night more than she had expected to. She did enjoy the get-togethers, when she was able to make them. Each of her friends had either a career or a man to keep her busy— Reggie and Missy had both—so setting aside one night every month or so where they could all gather in one room and enjoy one another's company had become an important part of their friendship. Too bad it looked like yet another thing she would have to sacrifice on the altar of a partnership at Parish Hampton.

There were days lately when Danice found herself wondering if it was worth it. She'd known since she was a girl that she wanted to be an attorney, and she'd pursued that goal with the kind of single-minded focus she dedicated to everything she considered important. From the National Merit Scholar Program to Phi Beta Kappa to the top 5 percent of her class at Columbia, she had worked her tail off all her life to ensure that she always stood head and shoulders above the students around her. She didn't want anyone assuming that the girl with the darker skin received special treatment; she wouldn't have tolerated that. But she also didn't intend to be overlooked for a position with the kind of top law firm she had always envisioned.

Parish Hampton had made her short list before she'd finished her first year at Columbia. By the time she'd started her third, all three firms on that list had been courting her, promising her the kind of bonuses and benefits she'd worked so long to achieve. In the end, the offers had been so similar that she'd based her decision more on the prestige of the name than on anything else. She'd agreed to work at Parish Hampton because that's where the best lawyers in New York all wanted to work.

Danice just couldn't be sure that *she* still did.

Groaning, she dropped her pen and raised both hands to rub at the persistent throbbing in her temples. Obviously the headache was beginning to affect her thinking. What the hell could she mean that she wasn't sure she still wanted to work for Parish Hampton? She had always wanted to work for a firm like this, and having achieved that desire, being as close to earning a partnership as she was now, she'd be a raging lunatic even to contemplate giving it up. One more thought like that and she'd be driving herself down to the admitting entrance of the Bellevue psych ward.

Danice blamed it all on Mac Callahan.

Right now she'd blame the crash of the *Hindenburg* on him, if she could just spend a few minutes working out the logistics. As far as she was concerned, he was responsible for everything currently wrong with the universe and a few things that had happened before he'd ever been born. Mostly, though, his sins boiled down to one very simple problem: She couldn't stop thinking about him.

Really, that was the entire issue, boiled down to its thick and flavorful essence. It had been more than twenty-four hours since she'd run down the steps of the Addison house and offered the driver of her town car an extra fifty bucks if he got her back to New York in one piece in less than forty-five minutes. He'd done it, too, even though she thought her spleen might still be somewhere back on one of those ridiculous curves in the Merritt Parkway. And she had done that because of Mac Callahan. Because he was the first man she'd ever met who made her forget her name, rank, and serial number.

Danice would not have called herself a blushing virgin type. Hell, she wasn't sure she even could blush anymore, and she hadn't been a virgin since a rather forgettable experience in her freshman dorm room at Fordham. She might not have had time for what she'd call a real relationship in the last, oh, seven or eight years, but that didn't mean she had denied herself the pleasure of some occasional male companionship.

Why should she? Danice liked men. She liked them a lot. They might not always be the brightest bulbs in the universe, but they entertained her with their inexplicable arrogance and endearing bumbling. She liked the way they viewed things in such linear, black-and-white terms, so that you could always tell what they were thinking. And she liked the way they would occasionally surprise you by actually noticing something you'd been waving in front of their noses for a week or two. She liked the way they couldn't seem to stifle that caveman-ish protective instinct they all had, yet somehow didn't think there was anything wrong with indulging in some of the most ridiculously dangerous behaviors on earth, just for the adrenaline rush.

Men were awesome.

But before Mac Callahan, they'd also been completely forgettable. In Danice's world, men had functioned a lot like handbags. They had their uses, and occasionally a girl could feel totally lost without one, but in general the important question was whether one would hold your cell phone and lipstick, and whether or not it clashed with your shoes.

Somehow, when Mac Callahan had been staring at her, how he looked with her shoes had been the last thing on her mind. She'd been too preoccupied thinking about hands and lips and shoulders and thighs and—

Damn. There she went again.

Danice was a grown woman, for God's sake. She

ought to have more control of her hormones than this. She ought to be able to put Mac Callahan completely out of her mind, and instead she sat here mooning after him like a teenage groupie over the latest Hollywood heartthrob. It downright embarrassed her.

"Enough," she growled at herself, picking up her pen and forcing her attention back to her work. She'd read approximately one sentence farther from where she'd left off to answer Corinne's call when the phone rang again.

While she was tempted to answer with a curt, *No, Ava, I am* not *going to be there tonight,* her common sense prevented her. Knowing her luck—especially over the last few days—the one time she didn't answer the phone in a polite, professional manner would be the one time she found herself talking to an insulted client.

Despite her maudlin thoughts of a few minutes ago, Danice had no intention of losing her job.

"Danice Carter," she answered.

"Hello, Danice Carter. This is Mac Callahan," a voice rumbled in her ear, and for a moment she thought her mind might be playing tricks on her.

"I beg your pardon?" she stammered.

"Mac Callahan," he repeated, sounding more amused than insulted. Of course, in her short experience with him, Mac always sounded amused. "We met yesterday in Connecticut. At the Addison home."

The last thing Danice had required was a reminder of who he was or where they had met. She could still feel that long, lean body pressing hers down into the mattress.

And therein lay the root of her problems.

Or perhaps the root of all evil. She hadn't decided on that yet.

"I remember, Mr. Callahan," she managed, though she had to fight to keep her voice even. *Trust me, I couldn't forget you if I tried,* she thought. *And I have tried.* "I'm just surprised. I wasn't expecting to hear from you. Certainly not so soon."

"I just couldn't stay away," he teased, but he continued before she could voice a protest. Or her astonishment. "And I think I might have some information that's pertinent to Rosemary Addison's current whereabouts."

"You do?" That was enough to quiet the fluttering in Danice's belly, at least temporarily. She grabbed a legal pad from her drawer and flipped to a blank sheet. "What have you heard?"

He paused. "It's not really information I'm comfortable sharing over the phone. I'd like you to meet me somewhere, so I can tell you in person."

Danice felt her eyes narrow. "You want to meet with me," she repeated, her voice laced with the suspicion she couldn't stifle. "I'm fairly certain that's not necessary, Mr. Callahan."

"Mac," he corrected. "And since I'm the one with the information, I think I get to decide whether or not meeting in person to discuss it is necessary. Don't you?"

"Not really."

"Believe me, Danice, I'm not playing a game here. This really is something you need to hear face-to-face."

He sounded sincere enough, but the way he said her name, the way his voice seemed to caress the syllables, made her wary.

"Look, Mr. Callahan, I tried to make it clear to you yesterday morning that I'm not interested in anything more than a professional relationship with you—"

"Whoa, slow down there, Lance," he interrupted, his voice firming, "before you actually manage to insult me. This is not an excuse to try to talk you into bed. Believe me, I'll get to that at some point. But at the moment, I'm being straight with you. I have information that pertains to your missing client, and it's not something I'm going to discuss unless you're sitting in front of me. That's not a come-on; it's the straight truth."

Still, she hesitated. His tone said he meant business, but when he threw in the part about trying to talk her into bed, he jumbled the whole thing up again and she ended up as wary as she'd been before he tried to "reassure" her.

"Mr. Callahan—"

"Mac. And I'm not going to argue with you. I have info I think you want. If you do, you'll meet me at the Courthouse in half an hour."

And he hung up on her.

Danice stared at the receiver in her hand for a long moment before replacing it in the cradle. What should she do now? Should she believe him? And if so, which part should she believe? The one about having information on Rosemary, or the one that confirmed he intended to try to seduce her? Maybe both were true.

She weighed the situation in her mind. On the one hand, he'd sounded perfectly sincere about Rosemary— she blocked his possible sincerity on the other matter from her mind for the moment. On the other, he'd asked her to meet him at the Courthouse, which was a bar only a few blocks from her office, and a bar wasn't the most professional rendezvous point he could have arranged. Of course, it was a bar frequented mainly by lawyers, clerks, and judges, so she supposed it counted more as her territory than as his. That could signal an effort on his part to make her more comfortable with the situation. Then again—

Danice halted her whirlpool of thoughts before they spiraled out of control. She could sit here and debate with herself all night. In the end, the essential truths remained the same: Mac Callahan had information she needed, and if she wanted it now, the only way to get it would be to meet him as he'd requested.

Cursing aloud, she stuffed her paperwork into her briefcase, grabbed her purse, and headed for the door. Better to move fast. Before she could change her mind.

Eight

Mac was betting she'd show. Of course, he'd lost bets before, so what that really meant eluded him. The reality was, he hoped she'd show.

Hoped hard.

The past twenty-four hours had flown by, but not in the most pleasant of ways. Mac was the first to admit that he could be a bit bulldoggish when he was after a certain piece of information, and he'd proven that today. He'd accomplished a lot of digging since last night, and wouldn't you know it but he'd come out of the exercise covered in dirt.

The kind liberally laced with fertilizer.

He sat in a booth at the back of the Courthouse bar, the kind where no one could sneak up on him from behind, but that still afforded him a clear view of the front door and all the people coming and going through it. He didn't expect to see more than an occasional Other pass through, and so far he'd been right about that. He just hoped his luck would hold out for a while longer.

His head turned the minute she came in, as did more than a few others, he noticed. He could hardly blame the men for looking. In her garnet-colored suit and sleek, shoulder-length hairstyle, she looked cool and elegant and sexy as hell. Mac would be astounded if he'd been the only one to notice. On the positive side, though, she didn't acknowledge any of the looks pointed her way. She simply scanned the room with her direct brown gaze until it locked on him. Then she made her way toward him with an unhurried focus.

"It feels like a cliché to say this, but you'd better have something good, Callahan."

Mac watched her slide onto the bench opposite him and read the mix of emotions on her face with an amused eye. "Rough day, Counselor?"

She growled at him.

He chuckled around the mouth of his beer bottle. "Order yourself a drink. You look like you could use it."

"Unlike some people I could mention, I'm working at the moment, and I don't drink while I'm working."

"You have to clock out at some point, sweetheart. Either that or you'll lose your mind."

"Too late," she muttered under her breath as he held up a hand to their waitress.

"Wine? Beer? Or you heading straight for the hard stuff?"

Danice managed a small smile for the waitress. "I'll take a glass of red. Whatever's open." Her expression when she looked back at him did not feature a smile. "There. I'm having a drink. We're having drinks. So why don't you go ahead and tell me what's so blasted sensitive that you can't discuss it over the phone?"

Mac sighed. Her attitude didn't surprise him, but it did disappoint him. At least a little. He knew she had to feel the spark between them; people in Antarctic research stations had to feel it. But he couldn't figure out why she'd want to fight it so hard. He didn't want to fight it. If it hadn't been for those pesky public decency laws enacted by the humans, he'd have not fought it right here on this bar table. Danice, however, looked ready to go twelve rounds. Without gloves.

"Wait for your drink."

She stared at him.

"If it was sensitive enough to keep off the phone, I'm not going to have the waitress overhearing half of it while she drops off your wine. Wait for your drink."

She made a sound a bit like a duck being strangled.

"Why don't you tell me about your day, dear?"

He thought he might have seen a bit of smoke puff out one ear.

"Why would you have us meet in a bar if you didn't want to be overheard?" She enunciated each word with extreme care, as if the choice were between that and barking them out alongside the bullets she was probably imagining putting into his chest. "In case you hadn't noticed, we're not exactly alone here."

"A crowd is the very best place to be alone, Danice. I'd think an intelligent woman like you would know that."

The waitress slid Danice's wineglass onto the table and placed another bottle of beer in front of Mac. She also offered him a wink that made him think his cocktail napkin might turn out to have more than the name of the bar printed on it. He thanked her for the beer and ignored the wink, though he couldn't help but notice that Danice glared at the woman's back as she walked away.

That promised to turn his evening right around.

"All right, she's gone." Danice raised the glass to her lips and glared at him over the rim. "Now spill."

Mac drained his original beer and set the bottle aside, stalling for time. When he reached for the fresh one, Danice whisked it away to her side of the table and held on to it firmly.

"I said, *spill*."

Oh, but where to start? Mac considered.

"I told you I'd been hired to locate Rosemary Addison for a client," he began.

Danice nodded. "Right. But you wouldn't tell me why. Or the name of the client."

"The first was because all I knew about why boiled down to a vague reference to an inheritance or a gift that the client wished to give her," he admitted. "And the second . . . well, the second was because I don't actually know the name of the client."

He watched her eyes widen, then narrow suspiciously.

"You're telling me that you accepted a client and took on a case without knowing who that client is? I'm supposed to believe that?"

"It's the truth. And it's not out of the realm of my experience, or the experience of a lot of investigators. We often take on cases precisely because the client wants the kind of discretion and anonymity they can't be assured of receiving from the authorities." He shrugged. "It doesn't happen every day, but it does happen. So I didn't really think that much of it."

"But you're thinking of it now?" she guessed.

"You might say that."

And now came the hard part.

Mac shifted in his seat and watched Danice carefully. He always found it difficult to tell with humans. How they'd react, and all. Some of them just shrugged, as if the news hadn't come as such a big surprise, while others refused to believe it. They walked away after referring him to Bellevue and ordering him to stay away from them on pain of police intervention. And some got really excited about the whole thing. Way too creepily excited. He didn't think Danice would react the latter way, but he debated flipping a coin between the other two possibilities.

Of course, the only way to know for sure was to just tell her.

He flattened his palms on the table and captured her gaze with his. He needed her to know he was sincere. Even if she laughed in his face and ran out of the bar screaming for a straitjacket, he wanted her to see that he meant what he was about to tell her.

"Danice," he finally began, choosing his words with caution. "First of all, you need to know . . . that there are . . . things out there . . . that aren't exactly . . . human."

She stared at him, her expression blank, and Mac realized after several seconds that he was holding his breath. But he still didn't let it out. Not until she blinked and said, "Yeah, so?"

He bit back a groan. Trust her not to make this easy for him. "I'm not talking about cats and dogs and carrier pigeons. I'm talking about the bogeyman. Vampires and werewolves and werecats. Oh, my."

She took a sip of her wine and shrugged, sliding his beer back toward him. "I know."

She knew?

Mac stared at her, at her gorgeous, expressionless face, at her nonchalant posture, at her hand, steady as a rock on the stem of her glass.

She knew.

He shook his head, trying to clear away the odd buzzing in his ears. "What do you mean, you know?"

"I mean, you're not telling me anything of which I was not already aware. Trust me, I know about The Others."

This time Mac turned to his drink, not because he was thirsty, but because he needed an excuse for not speaking while he tried to reacquaint himself with the laws of the universe. Which way was up, again?

His bottle clanked as he half set, half dropped it back onto the table. "And how, exactly, did you come to know all about The Others?"

"That's really none of your business," she informed him, then pursed her lips and glanced over his shoulder. "But if you must know, I'll just say that a couple of my friends introduced me to the concept last year."

"Introduced you to the concept. What, did they give you a PowerPoint presentation?"

She stared at him.

He stared back. Damned if he'd let himself be intimidated by this woman. Intimidation and sex did not mix, and he still hadn't given up on the idea of sex. Not by a long shot.

Her gaze shifted away from his again. "Regina and Missy ended up meeting Others with whom they developed close personal relationships. Since they're also among my closest friends, it wasn't as if they could keep it secret from me."

That time, she didn't just surprise him; she nearly stopped his heart. Some things were just too strange to be counted as coincidence.

"Regina and Missy," he repeated. "Are you talking about Regina Vidâme and Missy Winters?"

Her eyes widened. "You know them?"

He snorted. "The wives of the former and current heads of the Council of Others? Yeah, I might have heard their names mentioned somewhere."

It might not be polite of him to savor the fact that now she looked like the one who'd been taken aback, but Mac didn't care. It tasted sweet.

"Does that mean that you're . . ." She frowned. "Well, you can't be a vampire. I saw you standing in direct sunlight, and while I know it doesn't make vampires burst into flames like in the movies, I also know that they try to avoid it." She studied him in a way he found both arousing and disconcerting. And a little bit unsettling. "Does that mean you're some kind of shapeshifter? Because, honestly, I wouldn't have pegged you as the type."

Mac couldn't resist. "Oh? And what's the type?"

"Well, you know. All, *Me alpha. You Jane.*"

"I think you've been spending too much time around Graham Winters and the silverback Clan."

"You mean they're not all like that?"

"How would you like it if I asked if all humans liked to start wars for entertainment?"

That made her wince. "Point taken. But you still haven't answered my question."

"What was it?"

She made a face. "If you're not a vampire or a"—she searched for the correct term—"a Lupine, then what are you?"

"That's not a very polite thing to ask an Other, Danice, darling," he scolded. "But I'll let you off the hook this time. As it happens, I am not a full-blooded Other, but I am half Fae."

It looked like she needed a minute to digest that, so he took another sip of beer and waited.

Finally, she squirmed a little in her seat. "Okay, I'm going to assume that when you say you're half Fae, you're not trying to tell me that you're half homosexual. Besides, wouldn't that be bisexual? You're not, right?"

He nearly spewed beer all over her doubtlessly expensive business suit. "Of course not!"

"Okay." She seemed to relax a little at that, which made him wonder if she was relieved to hear he was straight, or just relieved that they apparently still spoke the same language. "Then when you say 'Fae,' you mean like . . . like a fairy?"

"Faerie," he corrected, tweaking her pronunciation just a tiny bit around the vowel sounds. "But yes, that's what I mean."

"You're trying to tell me that you're half fair—er, half Faerie? As in the Fair Folk. As in, *Darby O'Gill and the Little People*?" She shook her head. "Maybe I'm just imagining this whole conversation."

He winced at her characterization of his heritage, even though he'd heard all of it before. Humans really could be so clueless sometimes. "No, those are not Faeries; they're fairy tales. In fact, there's no such thing as a Faerie. Faerie is a place. The people who are native to that place are called the Fae."

"Right. I'm so sorry that I'm not up on the intricacies of the Tinker Bell set." She took a healthy swallow of wine.

"Now you're being deliberately offensive."

"Am I?"

He leveled his gaze at her. "Do I look like someone you should be referring to as 'Tinker Bell'?"

She at least had the decency to blush. It had to be guilt. She hadn't had that much wine.

"You said you're only half Fae."

"I am. My mother was Fae."

"And your father?"

"Human. That makes me a changeling."

"And here I thought I had a complicated ethnic identity," she muttered. After a second, her expression settled into a frown. "Wait, I thought a changeling was part of the fairy-tale crowd. Isn't that when the fairies kidnap a human child and leave some kind of demon-spawn in its place? And then the human family ends up raising the Bad Seed, or something?"

"That's just Hollywood. Changeling means half-blooded Fae. That's it."

She considered him for a moment, then finally, hesitantly, ventured, "So can you, like, do stuff?"

He cocked an eyebrow. "What stuff? You mean magic?"

She looked shocked, as if she really didn't know what she'd meant. "You mean there's such a thing as magic?"

"I thought you said you knew all about The Others? Have you never met a witch?"

"There are witches? Real witches?" she squeaked.

He laughed. "Of course."

"Christ." She rubbed a hand over her eyes. "First of all, I never said I knew 'all about' The Others. I said I was familiar with their existence. But the only ones I've met have been either vampires or were-somethings. I never thought about there being other kinds!"

Mac briefly considered blowing her mind and listing all the types of Others he had encountered during his life—and he hadn't met more than a fraction of all the different varieties that existed. Then he thought better of it. She wouldn't be very helpful if she fell into a catatonic stupor.

Some human minds really did blow when they heard the truth. They overloaded on the information and short-circuited. The effects could last a few minutes or a lifetime, and Mac didn't want to take any chances.

"Trust me," he settled on, as he lifted his beer. "There are other kinds."

"Let's just . . ." She stopped herself, drained her glass, and set it back down with a distinct *click*. "Let's leave that alone for the moment. Please." She drew a deep breath and pressed her hands down on the seat beside her until her shoulders climbed up near her ears. Then she let it out, long and slow. "Can you please just tell me what all of this has to do with Rosemary? We are here to talk about Rosemary, right?"

Mac nodded, feeling a stirring of sympathy. Danice might have known about the existence of Others when she'd started her day, but he doubted she'd envisioned them playing quite this big a role in her life.

"All of the information I collected on Rosemary up

until yesterday indicated she was staying at the Connecticut house and that she'd settled in there for an extended stay," he told her, leaning forward and wrapping both hands around the beer bottle, just to give them something to do. Something other than reaching out and touching the woman who faced him. "I talked to locals in the area and learned she'd had the place cleaned and aired a week before her arrival, and that she'd instructed the housekeeper to make sure the kitchen was stocked for at least a month."

She nodded and motioned for him to continue.

"You don't think it's odd that she would state her intention to stay at the house for at least a month and then suddenly up and relocate without letting anyone know?"

"I don't know Rosemary personally, so I can't hazard a guess as to what's odd for her and what isn't," Danice said. "But I think you'd need to prove she hasn't gone back to the house since we were there before you assign some sort of mysterious significance to the fact that she wasn't there when we were. How do you know she didn't just run into town for something the housekeeper forgot to pick up?"

"Because I'm good at my job, Danice, and I didn't get that way by jumping to conclusions. I'm keeping in touch with a contact in Connecticut, and he's told me that she hasn't been seen at the house since Wednesday evening."

She appeared to have no answer to that.

Mac continued. "Well, you might want to reserve judgment, but I thought it was odd, so I did a little digging."

"On Rosemary?"

"At first. I went back to the club where she supposedly met her mystery lover and asked some more questions. It turns out they're familiar with that routine. It's not the first time someone has come by to ask about a girl no one can find."

Alarm flashed across her face. "What's the supposed to mean? Do you think Rosemary is the victim of a crime? That she was picked up by some serial killer?"

"No, because some of them turned up unharmed. One or two seem to have had alcohol-induced blackouts and forgotten a few days at a time, but if there were really a killer out there, the police would be on it. They'd at least be looking into it. No, I didn't meant to imply I thought Rosemary was a victim. I actually think the other kind of digging I did turned up more promising information."

"On where Rosemary might be?"

He shook his head. "On who hired me to find her."

Now she was starting to look uneasy. "And what did you find out?"

"Nothing good." He paused. "I still don't have a name, but I'm beginning to suspect that whoever wants me to find Rosemary is a member of the Unseelie Court."

Danice stared at him blankly. "The un-what-y what?"

"The Unseelie Court. It's one of the two halves of the kingdom of Faerie. And frankly, it's the half that's even less inclined to look kindly on humans than the Seelie Court."

"Meaning?"

"Meaning they usually don't have the slightest use for humans, and when they do, the humans tend to get the short end of the bargain."

"But what on earth could some Fae person who doesn't even like humans possibly want with Rosemary Addison?"

Mac's mouth tightened. "I was really hoping you'd be able to tell me that."

Nine

This couldn't be happening.

At least, that's what Danice tried telling herself. There was no way that she'd somehow gotten mixed up in some kind of weird business with Fae and Faerie and missing heiresses and her boss's granddaughter disappearing under mysterious circumstances.

And how did she know she couldn't have gotten mixed up in that kind of thing?

Because shit like this did *not* happen to Danice Lynn Carter, scholar, attorney, and overachiever.

Danice was the normal one. The sensible one. She didn't work in advertising like Regina, and she certainly wasn't a vampire like her friend. She hadn't married a werewolf, like Missy. She had never been an internationally famous teenage model, like Ava. Hell, she didn't even have a job as unusual and interesting as Corinne, who was a staff reporter at a local New York tabloid newspaper. Danice was *normal*.

She came from a normal family. Sure, her dad had been born in England to a local woman and a black South African man, and her mom was the product of the forbidden relationship between a Japanese American soldier and the Cuban woman he'd fallen in love with. But that was just details. Silly stories about skin color and ethnic divides. When it came down to it, her dad was an electrician and her mom worked in a beauty salon, and they had raised her and her older sister Daphanie to be ambitious and independent and kindhearted. They went to church on Sundays and paid their taxes and planned to live in their same apartment in Brooklyn until they stopped living altogether. They were *normal*.

So why in the hell was this happening to her?

She really needed another glass of wine.

Her voice sounded hollow in her own ears when she asked, "How in the world should I know what an evil Faerie—sorry, Fae—what an evil *Fae* could possibly want with my boss's granddaughter? I didn't even know what one was half an hour ago. Hell, I'm not sure I do even now."

"But you know her family. Have you ever heard anything about Fae blood in the family tree? A weird aunt no one talks about? Some third cousin who talks to animals? Literally?"

Danice closed her eyes and wished very hard that when she opened them, she'd find herself in her own bed in her own apartment and none of this evening would ever have happened. If she could go back to Tuesday, so much the better. That would mean she would never even have gotten this nightmare assignment from Yorke.

Unfortunately, when she lifted her lids, her eyes focused right on Mac Callahan's gorgeous, yet dreaded face. Damn it.

"Of course not." She sighed. "You're talking as if I'm her best friend or her big sister. I've never met the woman, either. The only things I know about her are the few things her grandfather told me—which mostly consist of how annoying he finds it that she won't bow down whenever he snaps his fingers—and what little I've read in the press. Since I don't normally spend a lot of time on the gossip columns, that's not even very much. I don't see how I can help you."

"How you can help me isn't really what I think either of us needs to be concerned with right now," he said, his voice as grim as his expression. "The reality is that if someone from the Unseelie Court has been sending me on a hunt for Rosemary Addison, there's a good chance they've sent others, too."

Danice felt her stomach clench. "Do you mean others, or *Others*?"

"Truthfully? Both."

"Oh, shit."

"That's been my thought, as well."

She shot him a glare to let him know she wasn't amused.

He pulled a face. "I could be overreacting, but the way I see it, the current situation boils down to one of two scenarios."

"Am I going to like either one of them?"

"Probably not."

She held up a hand to stop him. "In that case, I'm really going to need another glass of wine." She motioned to the waitress.

"I thought you didn't drink while you were working."

"Since it's my work that's driving me to drink, I'm going to make an exception. Do you have a problem with that?"

"Absolutely not. In fact, I think it's a damned fine idea." He lifted his own hand and held up two fingers.

Danice drummed her fingertips on the table while they waited for their drinks. A couple of times, Mac opened his mouth as if he intended to say something, but the expression on her face must have stopped him. Instead, he busied himself peeling the label off his beer bottle.

She was just trying to keep her head from exploding. The ache she'd noticed in her office had grown into a full-blown throbbing of excruciating proportions.

When the waitress dropped off their drinks a moment later, Danice sipped hers while the other woman blatantly brushed her hip and breasts against Mac's side in the process of clearing away their empties. In her current mood, it made Danice want to stab the floozy through the eye with a swizzle stick. Fortunately, she didn't have one on hand, and Mac, to his credit, did his best to ignore the obvious come-on. At least he had enough class not to flirt with one woman while seated at a table with another.

And why should she care who he flirted with?

Danice pinched her eyes shut and wished violently for some painkillers. She had absolutely no claim on Mac Callahan, nor did she intend to stake one. He could flirt with whomever he wanted. Clearly the headache was affecting her thinking.

The waitress finally gave up and left them alone

with one last seductive smile aimed in Mac's direction. Danice ignored it. Along with the twitch in her left eye that seemed to accompany it.

"Okay," she said, clutching her wineglass like a life vest. "What are our two scenarios?"

Mac spun his beer bottle between his palms. "Scenario one: The Fae who hired me also hired someone or something considerably less competent than me to locate Rosemary Addison. She turns out to be an intelligent young woman who caught sight of her other stalker somehow, got spooked, and decided to disappear for a few weeks until this other person gives up and goes away."

"Why do I have the very bad feeling that that was the more positive of the two options?"

"Scenario two: Whoever else my client hired to locate Rosemary is just as good at his job as I am and managed to stay one step ahead of me. He's already gotten Rosemary and instead of informing her that someone wants to speak to her the way I would have done, he's forcibly relocating her to the Unseelie Court to instigate the conversation."

"It's like I'm psychic."

"What?"

"Nothing." She reached for her cell phone, then paused. "You're going to tell me that there's no use calling the police, aren't you?"

"Not if I'm right."

"And if you're wrong?"

"If I'm wrong, we're talking about an adult woman who's had a known disagreement with her family. No one has seen or heard anything suspicious, and she has every right to avoid her appointments if that's what she wants to do. The police are not going to mobilize a task force. They're going to say give her a few more days, maybe a week or two, then if you still insist, maybe they'll agree to file a missing persons report."

"Seriously. I should give tarot readings," she muttered and set her phone carefully down on the table. Mostly that was to keep from throwing it against the wall in a supremely immature gesture of frustration. It wasn't even the immaturity that restrained her; it was the fact that without her cell phone, her life would become entirely impossible. All her important contact information was in there. Otherwise, it would already be on the floor looking like the spare parts from a fourth grader's science project.

She glanced back at Mac. "In either of the scenarios you've mentioned, the fact remains that Rosemary is missing. This leads me to believe that our first priority should be finding her. If we can do that, we'll know exactly what's going on, right?"

"I certainly hope so."

"Appreciate the confidence."

"Well, it's an assumption, but I think we should go with it for the moment."

"So the question is, where do we start looking? You're the private investigator. Do you think you could, you know, pick up her trail? Or something."

His mouth quirked at that, one corner hitching up in a half smile that even in this morass of disaster still managed to make her heart skip a beat. Or two.

Man, she needed help.

"Probably, given enough time. I doubt she's all that

good at the disappearing act," he said. "But the truth is that either way we look at it, this Unseelie client of mine is the key. Either he already has her, or he's trying very hard to get her. When you look at it that way, I think it would be smarter to head right for the source. I need to go to Faerie, find out who the mystery man is, and confront him. That way I can find out what he really wants with Rosemary and get a better idea of where she is all at the same time."

"Do you really think he's just going to tell you what you want to know?" she asked. Then she frowned. "How do you know it's a he?"

"I don't. I'm assuming," he said, waving away her question. "And no, I don't think he's going to invite me in for a glass of Faerie wine and spill his guts. I suspect there might be strong language involved. Probably extreme violence. Adult content, without a doubt. Viewer discretion will be advised."

Danice stared down into her wine. If he kept giving her news like this, she was going to need more than a cheap Merlot to get her through the next few days. Hell, black tar heroin might not be enough.

How in God's name had she gone from thinking clients could get no worse than Henry Hollister and his Goons of Corporate Greed, to a client who might just have been kidnapped by the bogeyman, and who incidentally was the beloved favorite grandchild of an unforgiving boss, in less than forty-eight hours? Really, things like this were not supposed to happen in real life, and certainly not in the real life of Danice L. Carter, Esquire. She was the girl who had it all figured out, the one voted most likely to succeed.

Now she thought she had a good shot of being voted One Whose Life and Career Dangle by a Thread Over the Fiery Pit of Hell.

The new title had better at least come with a damned big plaque.

Before she just gave up and whipped out her scissors, though, Danice intended to do what she always did: battle fate with the tenacity of a bulldog and the futility of a Chihuahua. If her career was destined to go up in flames, she'd be damned if she let anyone else strike the match.

"Okay," she said, pausing for a deep breath and an even deeper drink of wine. "To Faerie it is. When do we leave?"

The stony silence that greeted her innocent question wasn't just thick and pointed; it had personality.

And it was grumpy.

"That depends on what you mean by 'we,' " he said, his expression as hard and forbidding as a sheer rock cliff.

Fortunately, Danice had scaled more than one insurmountable obstacle in her time.

"I subscribe to the usual definition," she replied calmly, her gaze steady and challenging on his. " 'We' is the sum of the two individuals known as 'you' and 'me.' "

"And 'no' is the sum of 'fat chance' and 'over my dead body.' "

Danice tsked him and sipped her wine. "I hate when people put it like that. Murder is such a messy business. It makes much more sense to me to keep things bloodless by coming to some sort of compromise."

"Okay, in that case, how about this? The 'me' of 'we' will go to Faerie and track down my client, while the 'you' of 'we' keeps your pretty little ass right here in Manhattan until I get back to tell you what I learn."

"And how exactly is that a compromise, pray tell?"

"It means that I give up on the part of the plan where I paddle your pretty ass for making such an idiotic suggestion and leave you hogtied in your apartment where I know you'll be safe."

"Honestly, I'm not into the kinky stuff, so that part was never going to happen anyway," she replied calmly. Calmly on the surface, anyway. Underneath her even-keeled exterior, she felt a suspicious tingle in unnamed places over the idea of his hands and her ass making skin-on-skin contact. Although in her mind, there was no paddling involved. More like squeezing, kneading, caressing—

Shaking her head, Danice tore her attention away from that little fantasy and fixed it on the matter at hand with a stern reminder that getting involved with a man like Mac Callahan did not figure into her plans. Her plans included no moves of such obvious self-sabotage.

"I have just as much at stake in getting to the bottom of this entire ludicrous situation as you do," she said. "Maybe more. There is no way I'm going to sit at home wringing my hands and letting a big strong man take care of a problem that could make or break the career I've been building since before I graduated from the eighth grade. I'm not that kind of stupid."

"I don't care what kind of stupid you are," he snapped back, his glare piercing and thunderous. "I'm not going to be responsible for you insulting some boggart and ending up as its dinner. You have no idea what Faerie is like. You wouldn't survive fifteen minutes."

"I legally absolve you of all responsibility. Just give me a couple of minutes to draw up the liability waiver."

Mac thumped his bottle down with a solid *click*. "This is not a joking matter, Danice. I'm deadly serious. Faerie is a dangerous place for natives; for a human, it would be like walking into a dynamite factory holding a lit match."

Danice echoed his gesture, though (she liked to think) with a bit more delicacy. She set her glass down with a *click* and folded her arms on the table between them. "Apparently, no one ever told you that you should never try to argue with an attorney, so I'm going to keep that in mind while I point out to you three very important facts: One, the only way you can possibly stop me from going anywhere I feel I need to go to serve my client is by committing at least one illegal act for which I will surely both prosecute you *and* persecute you; two, I am a big girl with a big brain who is fully capable of taking care of herself; and three, you bear absolutely no resemblance to my father, my boss, a law enforcement professional, or any other figure with either the right or the responsibility to control my actions."

Holding his gaze while she spoke, Danice could see anger, frustration, worry, and heat warring behind those stormy blue eyes. The frustration told her she'd made her point, but it was the heat that made her decide to claim her victory and quit the field of battle before it could spark something truly conflagratory.

Adopting a satisfied and deliberately not-at-all-nervous expression, Danice grabbed her purse and slid out from the suddenly very intimate booth. With her feet planted firmly on the floor, she turned back to Mac and painted a cool expression of challenge on her face. She like to call it her War Mask, the one she donned for opposing counsel, arrogant judges, and hostile witnesses.

"I'd like you to keep all of that in mind as we move forward," she advised Mac, keeping a wary eye out for smoke emerging from his nose or ears. It never hurt to practice caution. "I believe it will make our association that much more pleasant for us both. Have a nice night."

She considered it a dignified exit, one that allowed her to blow out a satisfied breath as she stepped out of the bar and onto the crowded Midtown sidewalk. Unfortunately, the sense of satisfaction lasted only about fifteen seconds. That was how long it took for the hair on the back of her neck to alert her that someone perhaps hadn't planned to let her have the last word.

Her senses rioted an instant before a strong, lean hand curled around her upper arm and pulled her out of the pedestrian traffic, propelling her to the side of the building she'd just exited. She felt the brush of rough brick against her bare skin and wondered abstractedly whether the heat of the night really came from environmental factors, or if it emanated from the stone-faced man looming over her.

His expression warned her that either his head was about to explode, or she had better brace herself for the kind of language that would have sent her mother reaching for the soap. Bracing herself, she prepared to have her hair blown back and her eyebrows singed. When

Mac drew in a deep breath, she made sure to keep her knees soft. Just in case.

Danice watched, fascinated, as he opened his mouth, closed it, and opened it again. Still no sound emerged. The muscle in the side of his jaw, though, was working overtime, and she thought she could probably choreograph a dance number to the pulsing of the vein in his temple. What was he waiting for?

Always an adherent of the philosophy that the best defense is a good offense, Danice opened her mouth to goad him into getting whatever he intended to say off his chest. That way it would be out in the open, and she could pick apart his nonsensical arguments and go back to ignoring his protests. She had it down to a science.

Except that her open mouth turned out to be the opportunity he'd been waiting for.

He descended on her like an invading army, the Visigoths at gates of Rome. Before she could even register the sight of his head swooping down to her, she felt the hard pressure of his mouth on hers and instinctively gasped her surprise.

Mac took advantage with ruthless skill, sweeping into her mouth and claiming every inch for himself. In a heartbeat, Danice felt again all the wary excitement he'd stirred in her when he'd had her pinned to that bed in the Addisons' deserted vacation house. This time, though, she couldn't blame any of the adrenaline that coursed through her on fear. She knew Mac now, at least well enough to know he wouldn't hurt her, so she couldn't pretend he scared her. The shivers he incited beneath her skin stemmed from an entirely different sort of reaction.

The noise of the city faded around them. All Danice could hear was the ragged sound of her breathing, the low rumble of satisfaction that seemed to be issuing from Mac's throat, and the rushing pulse of blood in her ears. All she could taste was the sweet, dark fire that was McIntyre Callahan, and all she could smell was the exotic spicy scent of his skin. He could have transported her to another dimension for all she knew, for all the notice any one of her senses paid to the people moving past them on the busy sidewalks. The nonchalant glances and amused curiosity of the average New Yorker didn't pack nearly a big enough punch to shatter her absorption in Mac's unexpected (and unexpectedly thrilling) embrace.

Frankly, Muhammad Ali, Mike Tyson, and Iron Man probably didn't pack enough punch. The man was a seriously good kisser, even when the kiss spoke as much of frustration and anger as it did of passion.

It took the flash of a camera and the laughter of a group of teenage juvenile delinquents to end the embrace. Or assault. Or earth-shattering revelation, depending on how you wanted to look at it. When Mac finally lifted his head, his eyes had darkened to a thunderous shade of gray and his ragged breathing sounded as if he'd just completed the marathon in under thirty seconds. Danice figured her heart thought it must have attempted the same feat, because she could feel it beating all the way down to the soles of her feet.

She looked into those stormy eyes and scrambled for a quip, a smart-alecky retort that would let him know that she wasn't some swooning virgin in a regency novel to be manipulated with something as casual as a kiss. The only problem was that she needed to catch her breath first to keep herself from swooning.

"This is not something I'm going to argue with you about," he growled, which made her frown. She didn't like it that he could recover his powers of speech before she could. She didn't want him to have that kind of advantage in the battle between them. She didn't want him to have any kind of advantage. "I know Faerie, and you don't. Therefore, you're going to have to trust me on this one. You aren't coming with me."

"Ngh—" Cursing to herself, Danice cleared her throat and tried again. "You can give all the orders you like, Callahan, but that doesn't mean I'm going to listen to them."

Somehow, that retort didn't do anything to smooth the wrinkles of fury that marred his arrogant brow. "You're going to have to listen, whether you like it or not. Or have you forgotten that of the two of us, I'm the only one who knows how to get to Faerie?"

Her eyes narrowed. "You are not the only one, however, with connections, or the ability to ask well-placed questions. You might want to keep that in mind."

"I've got plenty of things on my mind already, pretty little Niecie. Would you like me to demonstrate for you?"

If his purr hadn't given away his game, the way he pinned her back against the rough brick building and angled his hips until the erection behind his jeans rode against her hip would have clued her in. Did he really think she was stupid?

"The only thing you need to demonstrate for me,

Callahan, is that you can think with a part of your anatomy that doesn't get distracted every time a nice pair of tits walks by." Danice kept her gaze level and steady on his, which required a concerted effort to ignore the heat curling in her belly and shooting seductive tendrils down between her thighs. She refused to allow herself to be manipulated with sex. "You aren't responsible for me and you don't get a vote in my decision-making process. If Faerie is where I need to go to help my client, then that's where I'm going. End of story."

He stared down at her for a long tense moment, the heat between them banked but far from extinguished. She could feel it settling down in her gut like embers just waiting for the application of the correct kindling. Behind her hip, she crossed the fingers of her left hand that Mac would realize a busy city street wasn't the right place to apply that kindling.

When he levered himself away from her, putting a much-appreciated foot or so between their bodies, Danice couldn't quite stifle her sigh of relief.

His eyes narrowed at the sound. Then the corner of his mouth quirked upward and he took another step back. "Oh, our story isn't even close to ending, pretty Niecie," he said, eyes gleaming in the reflected light of neon and headlamps. "We have pages and pages still to go."

On that taunting note, he turned away from her and began to stride gracefully down the sidewalk. Scowling, Danice shot out her hand and caught him before he'd gotten far.

"I expect you to tell me when you're leaving, Callahan," she told him, giving him her sternest face. "I intend to go whether or not you approve."

"Save tomorrow's troubles for tomorrow," he told her, his shrug casual, the look in his eyes anything but. "We've plenty of others to deal with first."

"Like what?"

"Why, before we decide who'll be making the trip, fair Danice, we'll need to make plans to take us there."

She eyed him skeptically. She wouldn't put it past him to use some lame trick to keep her from going. "You mean you don't already have it all mapped out?"

He shook his head and glanced down at where her fingers still gripped his arm. She colored and released him.

"It's not the sort of place you'll find on a map," he said, his eyes once again locking with hers. "Just as it's not the sort of place a human should be going."

Danice rolled her eyes. And there it was. One more shot aimed at making her change her attitude. She let it sail past and folded her arms in a decidedly belligerent posture. She couldn't help it. The man made her feel belligerent.

When he wasn't making her feel like she needed to change her panties.

"You keep repeating that, Callahan. Eventually you might run into someone who believes it," she snapped, tearing her mind off the things he did to her body. That train of thought would not serve to bolster her position. "Until then, remember to keep me in the loop. As soon as you decide when and where we're going, I expect you to let me know. Understand?"

Instead of waiting for a reply, Danice shot Mac one last meaningful glare, shouldered her briefcase, and turned on her heel to stride purposefully toward the nearest subway entrance. As far as grand exits went, she figured it was about the best she could do, given the setting and the circumstances.

And the feel of a storm-clouded gaze trailing her all the way to the downward staircase.

Ten

Three days later and the man still hadn't stopped arguing. Danice had to give him points for the strength of his convictions.

"It's out of the question," he repeated. Again. "Not only are humans highly unwelcome in Faerie, but the last person who showed up uninvited to the Unseelie Court ended up . . ." He seemed to suddenly realize what he'd been about to say and cut himself off with an indignant humph. "Well, let's just say he ended up very unpleasantly occupied at the court feast."

Danice rolled her eyes and kept a firm grip on her cell phone as she wove her way through the evening pedestrian traffic toward the entrance to the subway. Luckily, a winning day in court had left her in a very good mood. "Mac, you can threaten and order and argue and try to scare me off all you want, but we already had this argument, and I already told you: I'm coming with you."

Danice very pointedly did not mention the way the last round of the argument had ended. Neither of them had brought it up yet, and she intended to keep it that way for as long as possible. She couldn't afford the distraction promised by the chemistry between them.

Or maybe that was "threatened."

"You don't understand what you're getting into."

"Probably not," she said, exasperated, "but I'm kind of considering that an advantage. I find I think more clearly if I don't go into a situation with preconceived notions that I ought to be intimidated."

"You shouldn't be intimidated, you should be scared shitless!"

"However you want to word it."

She shrugged her briefcase strap higher onto her shoulder and gripped the rail with her free hand as she started down the tunnel steps. In her ear, Mac muttered something she thought might have been in a foreign language. Or maybe two. Either way, she didn't understand it and was pretty sure she didn't want to.

"Look, arguing about this hasn't made either one of us change our minds yet," she pointed out, reaching the subway platform and stepping toward the wall, out of the way of the crowd. "How about I admit that you tried to warn me, you go right on thinking I'm an idiot, and we move on to talking about when we're leaving and how we're going to get there. Have you figured it out yet?"

Danice had learned recently that traveling to the kingdom of Faerie wasn't quite as simple as she had assumed. It apparently involved less chanting and fewer empty British moors than she'd thought and more secret doorways in carefully hidden locations only accessible by those who already knew where they were. Which, as it turned out, Mac didn't.

"My mother dropped me on my dad's doorstep before I was a year old. How am I supposed to remember how to get back?" he'd demanded, rather crankily, when she'd expressed disbelief at his ignorance.

"I may have convinced the contact who hired me to take us across," he said now, though she had to strain to hear him. Somehow the crowd on the platform seemed especially loud tonight.

"That's great! When?"

Not that Danice was anxious, or anything, but she felt fairly certain that the firm's switchboard operator and Celia were both going to quit on her if she asked them to help her dodge one more of Matthew Yorke's calls. He seemed to be getting anxious for an update. One Danice still didn't have to give him. And his version of cranky bothered her more at the moment than Mac's version.

"Maybe tomorrow. We're still negotiating."

Despite the summer warmth, a chilly breeze stirred the air around Danice and she scooted aside, farther from the air-conditioning vent. "When will you know for sure?"

"Maybe tonight. I'm going to threa—I mean, we're meeting again in a few hours."

"All right. Just let me know the minute you hear."

He sighed. "Fine. But I should tell you that Quigley wasn't happy about the news that you want to go on this little trip, either. So we're not actually done arguing yet, you know."

Danice grinned into the phone. "I'm a lawyer. I'm never done arguing."

She cut off the call in the middle of his grumble and shoved her phone into her briefcase with a completely inappropriate feeling of happy anticipation. Inappropriate, because a woman in her situation—hanging on to her job by a thread and contemplating a transdimensional trip to the home of people who didn't sound very nice—had neither the reason nor the right to feel happy. And anticipation because that seemed to be what she felt all the time around Mac Callahan, as if she was just waiting for something spectacular to happen. Like another kiss.

Lord, she was an idiot.

Crossing her arms over her chest, Danice fixed her gaze on the empty train corridor and struggled to wipe the smile off her face. This was no time to moon over any man, let alone one she'd met less than a week ago under far-from-romantic circumstances.

In general, she tried to avoid men who attacked her at first sight, as well as ones who thought public sidewalks to be the appropriate setting for passionate, male-dominant kisses. But something about Mac Callahan just *got* to her. She couldn't understand it, and she sure as heck couldn't describe it, but when she saw him, her heartbeat sped up and her blood pressure skyrocketed, and her stomach became a stopping point on the annual monarch butterfly migration route. She didn't think she could attribute it solely to his looks (although he looked *fine*) or to his charm (which could melt women at fifty paces). Frankly, although she'd gotten a taste of his seductive powers for a few brief moments at the Addisons' summer house, he'd been too concerned over their mutual problems to spend much time charming her. There had been very little charm in his devouring kiss outside the Courthouse.

But the truth was, when she was with Mac, things felt . . . right. The world was more interesting. She felt just like herself, and yet she felt like she'd become part of something else, something bigger and better. She felt more alive.

Which would prove itself really ironic if these Fae of the Unseelie Court wanted to kill her as much as Mac seemed to want her to believe they did. Having never met anyone of that particular persuasion, she admitted to having a little trouble wrapping her mind around the image of a homicidal fairy.

Fae, she corrected herself with a grin. No need to antagonize the little winged buggers.

A glance at her watch told her that the train was running late. No big surprise there, but Danice had been looking forward to soaking in the tub for five or six hours before she tackled her paperwork. It looked like forty-five minutes would be all she'd get, and that would be if she read while she soaked.

For once, the other passengers waiting for the train hadn't begun the ceremonial griping that accompanied all delayed trains. In fact, the drone of their conversations even seemed to have died down, almost grown muffled in the large, concrete tunnel. Or maybe Danice was coming down with a cold and her ears were getting stuffed up. The timing would suck, but that just figured.

Tilting her head to the side, she flexed her jaw to elicit a pop in her ears. Nothing happened. In fact, the noise seemed to fade even more, and the hair on the back of her neck stood up as a shiver of unease crept down her spine. Another gust of cold air blew past her, and Danice suddenly knew that something was wrong.

Very, very wrong.

Newly alert, she looked around her, searching for the source of her unease, but she saw nothing. The platform remained crowded with strangers. Hundreds of people gathered in the space waiting for the train to emerge from the tunnel and carry them away. None of them looked as if they had sensed anything to fear. In fact, none of them looked as if they sensed anything.

The entire crowd faced forward and stood at frozen attention. The sound of their conversation had died completely, and all Danice could hear was the odd buzzing sound that hummed inside her head. She turned to her right and looked toward the stairs she'd walked down earlier, but all she could see was an impenetrable blackness filling the opening. People stood frozen there as well, feet halted in midstep as if time had stopped while they jogged down toward the subway platform.

What in the name of God was going on?

Panic began to well up, leaving a bitter taste on the back of her tongue. This couldn't be happening. None of this could be happening, because it just didn't make sense. Danice might not be a physicist, but she knew that time couldn't stop, that entire crowds of people couldn't freeze in place, and that she was not about to die some horrible death at the damned 59th Street subway station.

She turned and looked deeper into the tunnel, but the blackness had gathered there as well. Both exits had been cut off. Between the blackness and the motionless crowd in front of her, Danice had no place to run. So was she just supposed to stand there and wait for whatever was coming for her? The idea didn't sit well.

Fingers grasping for her cell phone, she began to weave her way carefully through the crowd, looking for other avenues of escape. She had no plan in mind, which annoyed her, but moving felt better than just standing still. Standing still felt too much like tempting fate.

She stepped around a large man in an ill-fitting suit and emerged onto the edge of the platform. In either direction, she saw nothing but stagnant darkness. Until the darkness on the left shifted and moved and began to creep forward.

Eyes wide, she took a step back and caught her shoulder on the corner of a cement pillar. The impact jolted her, but she didn't stop. Not until the darkness stopped moving forward and began to swirl and seethe, coalescing into a thing the size and shape of a tall, slender human. It moved forward again, and a figure emerged to face her.

She backed up another step.

The figure looked like the character of death from an old silent movie. It stood over six feet tall, cloaked and hooded in a black so dark it seemed to suck away the surrounding light. While Danice watched, gloved hands lifted and pushed back the hood until she could make out the vague outline of features set in skin the color of charcoal.

She got the impression of the requisite nose and mouth, but the only thing she could focus on was the eyes. They glowed with an eerie blue-gray light, like gunmetal lit from within. The lids, both upper and lower, were rimmed with red, and red like blood appeared inside its mouth when it parted its lips to speak.

"You will not leave."

Its voice should have hissed or growled or rasped unpleasantly. Based on its appearance, that would only have been fair. Instead, it spoke smoothly, the key even and pleasant, the tone melodious, in an androgynous sort of way. She had no idea if it was male or female, only that the animation in its voice conveyed the slightest hint of malice.

Okay. More than a hint.

Danice took another step backward. "Um, actually, I believe I will."

"You will not leave," it repeated. "I have sought you out to deliver a message. You will stay and hear it."

Oddly enough, the menacing words did indeed make her stop. She frowned. "A message from whom?"

"You involve yourself in matters that do not concern you. This displeases us."

"Us? Is there more than one of you here, or was that the royal we?"

It ignored her. "The Unseelie Court is not your place, and your presence there is not welcome, your interference there even less so."

Danice eyed the figure warily, but for the moment it seemed content to threaten her verbally rather than physically. "Why would you think I'm involved with . . . well, anything? I have no idea who you are."

Or what you are, she thought, but figured it would be healthier to leave that last bit unspoken.

"But I know you, Danice the Carter, and I know what it is that you are seeking. And I know you will not find it."

The shine of those metallic, glowing eyes was beginning to get to her. Or maybe the fact that she was one of only two people conscious and able to move in the 59th Street station during rush hour, and the other one seemed not to like her very much, was making her nervous. Either way, she darted a glance toward the nearest exit, which still didn't look like a viable escape route. Since the thing talking to her had come out of the same kind of black fog, it wasn't something she felt very inclined to venture into.

"Right now, all I'm trying to find is my train," Danice said, turning back to meet that uncanny gaze. "Other than that, I have no idea what you're talking about."

The eyes blazed with eerie gray light. "Do you think you can lie, and I will not know the truth? I am not some mortal creature you can deceive, Danice Carter. I am so much more than that. More than you can ken."

It stepped forward, or maybe glided (glid?) or floated or something. Nothing Danice had ever seen before moved with that sort of grace, and the only thing she'd seen move more lethally was her friend Missy's Lupine husband. Abandoning the process of inching backward step by step, Danice spun around, hung on to the strap of her briefcase, and began to sprint for the door.

She couldn't move all that fast because of the crowd in her way, but she gave up all pretense of good manners and shoved them out of the way whenever she had to. Behind her, she heard a low, growling hiss of rage and felt a gust of icy wind sweep toward her. She didn't bother to look back. Why the hell would she look back? Whenever the girl in the movie looked back, that was when she tripped on a root or a rock or her own damned clumsy feet and fell down in a screaming heap of murder victim. Danice had no intention of becoming a victim of any sort.

But she still reserved the right to scream.

The stairway up to street level was still crowded and still filled with black fog, but it seemed the best of her options, so she headed toward it with grim determination. She drew the line at knocking down a twelve-year-old kid who looked like he was heading home from school, but she drove her shoulder into a huge, doughy mountain of a man in a poorly tailored suit. She expected to feel him sway away from her the way all the others had, but instead the man offered about as much give as one of the cement pillars. He stood fast.

Instinctively, Danice turned her head to look at the man's face. And, oh, how she wished she hadn't. Unlike all the other people in the subway station, this man's face lacked the blank, vacant look and unfocused stare of frozen unconsciousness. The stranger looked right at her, his eyes hazed over and glowing with a sickening gray light. Before she could so much as curse, he reached out and grabbed her by the wrists.

A chill struck the back of her neck, and she knew without looking that the cloaked figure was getting closer. Apparently, it had decided to possess the stranger next to her and ordered him to hold on just to ensure that Danice didn't escape. Well, Danice Carter hadn't grown up in Brooklyn or taken those self-defense courses for nothing. She had no intention of being held.

In a single quick movement, she thrust her hands down and out to dislodge her captor's grip and stomped the tall, chunky heel of her shoe down on his instep.

The man bellowed, and his hold on her loosened but didn't release completely. With a frustrated growl, she brought her knee up between his legs and yanked her hands back so that he rocked toward her, his nose lining up with the swift forward thrust of her forehead.

She could feel his nose break on impact and the shock of the pain finally forced him to release her, one hand flying to his crotch, the other to cover his bleeding face. A trickle of moisture down her skin told Danice that not all the blood had stayed on the stranger. Hoping to God the man didn't have any communicable diseases, she swiped at the wetness even as she stumbled forward toward the stairs.

A hand grasped the back of her summer-weight silk sweater, and even without feeling the slightest brush against her skin Danice knew from the intense cold that raced through her exactly who had dragged her to a stop. The thing was strong, stronger than anything had a right to be, and it gave a satisfied hiss as it lifted her off her feet.

Just as Danice was about to say to hell with public nudity laws and wriggle out of the sweater in order to escape, a rumbling sound caught her attention. A train was nearing the station.

Behind her, the thing with the freaky eyes shrieked along with the high-pitched scream of the train's brakes beginning to slow it down for its stop. Thinking the sound indicated her imminent death, Danice said a hasty prayer, even as she drew breath for one last, vicious fight.

As it turned out, she needn't have bothered.

She felt the rush of hot air and heard the cacophony

of sound that indicated the train's arrival. Immediately she also felt the hard slap of concrete against her knees and palms, since the creature attacking her had opened its hand and released her without warning. Instinctively she reached out to brace herself against the fall and wound up on her hands and knees in the middle of the subway platform just as the spell that had frozen the world around her dissolved. All at once the crowd surged and Danice found herself kicked twice and tripped over once before two sets of hands reached down to help her to her feet.

"Hey, lady, are you all right?"

Danice looked around in confusion, but the cloaked figure had vanished, along with the thick black fog that had filled the exits just a minute ago. Everything looked just the way it should at rush hour on a Monday evening. Everything looked completely normal.

"I'm fine," she mumbled, brushing her hands together and wincing at the sting of scraped skin. "I just—I—I tripped."

The brawny-looking man to her right frowned down at her. "Are you sure? You look like you hit your head or something. You're bleeding."

"No, I'm fine. It's just a bump."

"Hey, maybe you should get someone to take a look at that," the figure on the left suggested. He was an older man with thick gray hair and a concerned frown. "There's a clinic a couple of blocks from here. You want I should walk with you?"

Danice flashed the men a nervous smile, already moving. "Thanks, but I'm fine. I've got to go. Thanks."

She didn't wait for their protests, just broke into the

fastest jog she could manage and fought her way through the crowd to follow the exiting passengers back up the stairs to the street level.

What the hell had just happened? Had some monster she'd never seen before really just tried to kill her? Had she just been warned away from searching for Rosemary Addison and from the Unseelie Court? By whom? By what?

And what would Mac Callahan say when he found out?

Eleven

"Shit."

Danice sighed. "Now you're repeating yourself."

He was, too. Mac had said exactly the same thing thirty minutes ago when he'd spotted the disheveled and slightly bloody attorney hurrying toward the entrance of his office just as he exited the building. He thought he might have repeated it a couple of times in the cab he hustled her into seconds later, and it was quite possible he'd said it again in the elevator on the way up to his apartment a few minutes after that. So really, she shouldn't have been surprised to hear it again while she sat on the edge of his bathtub and watched him clean the small cut on her forehead where the skin had apparently caught a tooth on its way back from its nose-bashing adventure.

"Sorry," he muttered, dabbing the alcohol pad against the stubbornly dried blood. "This isn't coming off easily, and I'm afraid I'll hurt you if I really rub."

"Here, just give it to me." She snatched the pad away from him and scrubbed it roughly over the wound, wincing at the burn of alcohol on torn flesh.

He watched and winced in sympathy.

"Well?" she demanded. "Aren't you going to say anything? I mean, anything other than 'shit,' because I think we've covered that part."

"What do you want me to say?"

She tossed the swab in the trash and scowled at him. "You might start with telling me what the hell it was that attacked me. Then maybe we could move on to discussing exactly why it did so."

"I think why is the easier part." His hands shook as he reached for a tube of antibiotic ointment. He frowned at them until they steadied enough so he could dab some of the gel onto Danice's cut. "It told you it wanted you to stay away from Faerie, right?"

"Yes, but I want to know *why* it wants that. Along with how the hell it knew that I even know Faerie exists."

"You're the one who insisted I had to get Quigley to agree to take you with me."

"Are you saying the guy you've hired to guide us into Faerie has already sold us out to the people there? Before we've even set a date to go, let alone set foot in the damned place?"

"I'm saying he wouldn't have had to." He looked at her. "I don't suppose you're going to want me to put a bandage on your forehead."

She glared.

"I didn't think so," he muttered, tossing the paper packet aside. "Look, I did not run around Manhattan shouting at the top of my lungs that I needed someone to volunteer to take me and Danice L. Carter, attorney-at-law, from the firm of Parish, Hampton, Uxbridge, and Yorke, to Faerie; form a line on the right. But Quigley is a hard one to pin down, and the place where we usually meet is a bar. A public place. You know, the kind with people in it."

Her expression failed to sweeten. "Then someone could have overheard."

"Of course they could have. In fact, they probably did. And it's not like I didn't already explain to you that travel between Faerie and here—from either side—is strongly discouraged."

Danice rose and turned to the sink. He stepped out of her way, but lingered in the door while she scrubbed the dirt and grit from her raw hands.

"You never told me why that is," she pointed out.

"It's always been that way. Or at least, it has been for all recorded history. The stories say that the Fae used to live here rather than in Faerie, but when humans began to spread across the continents and started to shape the earth to suit their own needs, the Fae decided to retreat. They moved across the veil into Faerie and left this world to the humans."

"Great. Another group to view us as the despoilers of Mother Earth. They must get along great with the Lupines."

Mac shrugged and handed her the antibiotic cream. "They stopped paying attention to what happens on this side of the veil a long time ago. They keep in touch with the Council of Others, I think, but mainly just to make sure that the existence of Faerie remains a myth to humans."

He refused to let her fumble with trying to bandage her own hands and briskly accomplished the task himself. Ignoring the way he wanted to hit something when he saw her injuries gave him something else to think about, but it couldn't completely distract him from the sparks of electricity that buzzed through him every time his skin brushed hers. Or from the memory of the kiss he'd pressed on her Friday night. Neither one of them seemed to have the courage to bring up.

She mumbled her thanks and followed him back out to his living room.

The loft Mac rented in SoHo predated the days when lofts became contemporary spaces. His was a holdover from the time when artists had first convinced the owners of empty old industrial buildings that renting them on the cheap to the bohemian set beat letting them sit around collecting dust. The exposed brick and ductwork looked as old as they actually were, but he'd made sure they stayed solid and had lived in the space long enough to make it look and feel like a home. A bachelor's home, but still.

He waved her to a seat on the battered leather sofa in the center of the main space and crossed to the kitchen counter at one end of the room. Without asking, he poured two glasses of wine and handed her one before seating himself next to her.

She accepted without comment. "Have you been warned away from going to Faerie?"

Mac shook his head. "No, why?"

"I'm still trying to figure out what happened to me, and if any travel between here and Faerie is discouraged, like you said, then why was I the one that thing chose to warn off? Actually, it seemed pretty content with the idea of killing me to keep me from making the trip. Is that how these things are normally handled?"

"I doubt it." He thought about the details of the story

she'd told him and struggled to separate his rage at the idea of anyone attacking her from the equation. It wasn't easy, and it left him with a few very unsettling questions. "So did the figure who attacked say that he knew what you were looking for?"

Danice nodded. "Yeah, but he didn't specify what that meant. I thought for a second he might be referring to Rosemary, but that would be impossible. I mean, you haven't told anyone the reason why we want to go to Faerie, right? So he couldn't have known about Rosemary. Or she couldn't. Or it. Oh, how the hell would I know? I still don't even know what the damned thing was."

"Well, I can't tell you specifically, but I'm sure it was Fae. And no, I didn't mention Rosemary to Quigley, but—"

"Wait, how exactly can you be sure it was Fae? I mean, I wondered who else would warn me away from Faerie, but you weren't there to see it."

"I didn't need to be. You said the train scared it away, right?"

"I said I thought it must have," she corrected, "because I couldn't think of anything else that would have stopped it. It certainly wasn't having any trouble kicking my ass, so the idea of a whole new crowd of people must have made it think twice."

Mac shook his head. "It had nothing to do with the passengers on the train; it was the train itself. One of the few remnants of human lore about the Fae that's actually true is the bit about iron. They can't stand it. It's like their kryptonite. It would have been uncomfortable just being near the iron subway tracks, but once the train itself pulled up, that amount of cold iron so close would have been intolerable to it. The fact that the train made it run is all the evidence you need to prove it was Fae."

He watched her digest that news and nod. "Okay, then at least I don't have to worry about some other group of Others out there wanting to see me dead. There's just the one. That's some comfort, I suppose."

"I doubt anyone wants you dead," Mac said, shifting at the way the idea of someone threatening this woman made him want to go out and kill things. "The messenger was probably sent to do just what it did, and that was to warn you off."

"But who sent it?"

"That's what I was going to say before. I didn't mention to Quigley why we wanted to go to Faerie, but I don't think it would take another Sherlock Holmes to put together the inquiries I was making over the last couple of weeks with my sudden request for passage into Faerie. Anyone could put those two facts together and come up with the reason why I'm looking for a guide."

Danice scowled at him. "Rosemary Addison comes from a very powerful family. Weren't you at least a little discreet when you were looking for her?"

He shook his head. "Why should I have been? The more people who knew I was looking for her, the more likely it was that word would trickle back to her and she'd contact me herself, saving me any more work. I had no reason to think anyone meant her any harm."

"You'd been hired by an anonymous client. It could have been Jack the Ripper for all you know!"

Mac gritted his teeth. "The odds were against it. I

told you before, a request for anonymity isn't unheard of in my profession, and it's no reason to assume the client has nefarious purposes. I wasn't asked to do anything illegal or unethical. If I had been, I'd have turned down the job."

Dark brown eyes challenged his statement. "Would you?"

He stiffened at the insult. "Damned straight, I would have. And let me tell you something, Danice Carter." He leaned in close and felt the way she tensed, saw the trickle of unease behind her direct gaze. "If you don't trust me that much, there's no way in hell you should be following me into Faerie. You're talking about a place where you'll be so far out of your depth, even a lifeboat isn't going to save you. I'm the only thing that can. But if you don't follow every single one of my orders without wondering about the motivation behind it, you're going to find yourself on the dinner plate of something a hell of a lot scarier than the messenger you just ran into."

Mac tried to keep his expression harsh and his demeanor unforgiving, but being so close to Danice that he could feel her breath brushing his cheek with each exhale threatened to snap every last thread of his self-control. He'd felt attraction to her the minute he'd set eyes on her, and every second he spent in her company only intensified the sensation. He wanted her so badly his hands shook with it. The fact that this mess with Rosemary Addison stood between them just might kill him if it lasted too much longer. He needed to get his hands on Danice before his head exploded.

Or something even more embarrassing exploded.

He set aside his wineglass and braced his hands on the sofa to push to his feet. One of her hands covered his and froze him in place. Those big, dark eyes had locked on his face, and he found himself wondering how any woman could have eyes that looked as soft and sweet as melted chocolate and yet conveyed such incredible strength and self-assurance. She should have reminded him of a puppy or a deer, or something else cuddly and vulnerable, but instead she presented herself as an exotic warrior queen.

What else could he call her? After all, he had already begun to suspect he'd been conquered.

Her palm pressed against the back of his hand, sending sparks shooting up his arm and straight to his heart. "I think that I do trust you, Mac. I think that if I hadn't, you would have been the last person I went to about tonight. After all, you're not the only one I can ask about questions of magic and mayhem, remember? But when the train came and I was able to leave that station, I didn't go home, or to Reggie or Missy. My first thought was that I had to tell you. To me, that sounds like trust."

"I notice you didn't mention anything about obeying my orders," he pointed out, feeling his mouth quirk with reluctant humor.

"No, because I really hate making promises I'm not a hundred percent certain that I'll be able to keep." She made a face. "I'm not stupid. I realize that you're going into this situation knowing a lot more about where we're going and who we'll be dealing with than I do, so I'm not going to blow you off just for the sake of asserting my independence. I don't have to prove that you're not the boss of me. Which means that I can at least promise not to do anything stupid. How's that?"

"I think it's the best I'm going to get." He smiled.

"I think so, too."

"However," he continued, deciding to press the advantage while he had it, "I think it would make a very nice gesture of mutual trust if you told me why it is that you've been working so hard to get in touch with Rosemary Addison."

He watched her expression shift into a grimace and saw her shake her head.

"I'm sorry, Mac, but you know I can't do that," she said, and she did, to her credit, actually sound regretful. "Attorney–client privilege isn't just a catchphrase to me; I take it seriously. I can't disclose information about my client without her permission."

Mac knew she was only being honest, and he respected her for that. But all the respect in the world didn't make him comfortable about walking into the meeting with Quigley, or into Faerie itself, blind.

"Okay, I get that you can't disclose information, but how about I tell you what I've learned about Ms. Addison and if you don't tell me that it has absolutely nothing to do with your case, I'll be satisfied that I know where we stand. Deal?"

He saw her mull it over, realize that she wouldn't be violating privilege by letting him repeat things he already knew, and nod reluctantly.

"Okay," he said. "Here's what I've heard. Apparently Ms. Addison hooked up with a man a few months ago at a club. They were seen leaving together on a Saturday night, no one heard from Rosemary for a couple of days, and when she did show her face again, she seemed angry and upset over the fact that she hadn't heard from her mystery man after that night."

Danice just let him talk, her expression carefully blank, but she hadn't stopped him yet to tell him he was nuts.

"There are rumors going around that Rosemary tried pretty hard to find the guy again with no luck. Apparently, he made quite an impression.

"Other rumors say that Rosemary herself has been hinting she might have wound up pregnant after her one-night stand, and that she hasn't done the hinting all that quietly. Some people are even saying she's making it public to try to smoke the guy out in the hope that he might want to have something to do with any child he might have fathered."

Danice said not a word.

Mac shook his head and whistled. "That could be really bad news. What if the person who hired me, the one connected with the Unseelie Court, is the father of Rosemary's baby?"

"Would that be so bad?"

"Depending on who it is? It could be fine, but it could also be disastrous. I told you, members of the Unseelie Court as a rule are not generally all that kindly disposed toward humans."

"Well, one of them might have liked Rosemary enough to sleep with her. And if you're right, isn't it a good sign that he was interested enough to listen when

Rosemary started spreading her news around New York? I mean, unless most Fae keep their eye on the society pages of the papers here."

"No, most Fae couldn't care less about human society."

"Oh. Well, can I at least think positively for a while?"

"Maybe." Even to his own ears, Mac sounded unconvinced. "I think the safest bet, though, is to get ourselves to Faerie and find out the truth as soon as possible."

Danice frowned and nodded. "I agree."

The plump line of her lips made him want to trace the seam with his tongue, to nibble on the lush little pillows and explore all the secrets they concealed. His stare must have tipped her off to his train of thought, because her gaze dropped to his mouth and she swayed ever so slightly toward him. The memory of Friday's kiss hovered between them, and Mac craved the opportunity to show her what a kiss without anger could generate between them.

Then again, he wasn't sure if his insurance was adequate for the resulting explosion.

Just before he made the decision that the destruction of all his personal property might be worth it, Danice seemed to jerk herself to her senses.

She pulled back and cleared her throat nervously. "So, uh, when did you and Quigley decide we'd be able to leave?"

Mac stifled a curse and carefully lifted his gaze to her eyes, sternly ordering it to stay put. Any lower than the bridge of her nose, and he tended to get distracted. "We haven't yet. I arranged to meet him tonight, remember?"

Danice looked startled, then winced. "No, I totally forgot. What time is it? Did I make you late? Don't tell me you've missed him."

"No, relax. It's only eight. He won't be expecting me before ten. Quigley's a bit of a night owl."

"Really," she mused, and the light that began to glow in her dark eyes made him very, very nervous. "So, you're meeting tonight to arrange the best time to make the trip, hm? The trip you and I will be making together. It sounds to me like I made a lucky decision when I headed for your office instead of my apartment after the subway thing. Now that I'm here—"

"No," he said, cutting her off. "No way."

"—it would be silly for us not to meet with your friend together."

"Forget it."

"Now, Mac, be reasonable." Her expression was sly enough to turn his wine into vinegar. "It only makes sense that both of us be there for the meeting. That way, we each hear any instructions Quigley has for us, and he gets an idea of who exactly he'll be leading on this little expedition."

"He doesn't need to have an idea of that. We're not trekking through the Bolivian rain forest. He's leading us through a gate. It's not like you have to have special skills and a machete."

She raised a brow. "After that incident tonight, a machete might just make me feel better."

"You see? That's exactly why you don't need to be there," he said. "He's just the type to take offense to remarks like that. You can't go around insulting his countrymen, Danice. It's not polite."

"Oh, don't be a poop. I can be as diplomatic as the Swiss when I need to be, and I promise to be so in two more hours. Which"—she glanced at her watch—"should give us just enough time to grab some dinner beforehand. How do you feel about Chinese?"

Twelve

Mac seemed to feel just fine about Chinese. It was how he felt about bringing Danice to meet with his Fae contact that she guessed had set his teeth on edge. He hadn't said more than three words over dim sum, and he'd spent the entire cab ride into the Village glaring at her as if he'd like to see her stuffed and mounted in an entomological exhibit.

Surprisingly, that didn't make her any more comfortable than when he looked at her as if he'd like to see her wearing nothing but whipped cream and a cherry.

Damn it, girl, she scolded herself, *you need to make up your mind. Do you want him to want you, or not? Because at the moment, nothing is making you happy.*

Danice walked along beside him as he led the way from where the cab had dropped them off to the bar where he'd arranged to meet his contact. Actually, she half jogged, because Mac appeared to be in no mood to make allowances for her shorter stride, and just now she wasn't about to ask him to slow down so she could keep up.

It made her uncomfortable to have him upset with her, and knowing that only served to make her even more uncomfortable. She didn't want Mac Callahan to have the power to affect her moods, but it looked as if that ship had sailed. She really hadn't known him long enough to feel such a connection with him, had she? And even if she had, wouldn't that kind of relationship need to be based on more than a physical attraction? After all, it wasn't as if the two of them had anything in common.

Okay, that wasn't precisely true, she admitted as she jogged around a corner and followed Mac into an alley between two sets of brick row houses. They each worked in fields adjacent to, but not exactly in, law enforcement, and they each had a mind that latched onto puzzles with something akin to rabid fervor. He seemed to enjoy her rather dry sense of humor, and she appreciated his sly charm. And judging by what she'd seen of his apartment, they appeared to have similar tastes in books and music, but how much could that mean? They'd never gotten a chance to discuss those things, or any of the other thousand subjects two people who were interested in each other discussed before they started to really matter to each other.

So, yes, she told herself, she needed to get a grip and calm down and keep her mind focused on the matter at hand. Especially since it was the only thing that she and Mac had ever really discussed—this damned case, and getting to Faerie so they could find Rosemary Addison and wrap up the whole damned mess.

Danice was so wrapped up in her mental debate that she didn't notice when Mac stopped in front of what looked like a steel service-exit door in the side of one of the alley walls. She nearly ran headfirst into the back of him, and had to reach out and grab the wall to keep from doing so. It felt damp and slimy to her touch, and she made a face as she wiped her hand on the leg of her trousers. After the subway, the garment was already doomed.

Before she could ask why he had stopped, Mac lifted a fist and tapped out a complex series of raps on the metal of the door. Without warning, the door swung inward to reveal a set of steps leading down and a sign hanging from the ceiling. In letters that glowed a rather sickly shade of green, it spelled out THE UNDER BELLY. Mac didn't spare it a glance. He just started down the steps and left Danice to scramble after him.

The steps consisted of huge, granite slabs worn down in the center by years and years of traffic moving up and down. The walls began with the same brick that made up the alley outside, but as they descended, the brick changed to rough stones, fitted together so tightly that only the barest traces of mortar showed between them. Unfortunately, the stone displayed the same rancid sheen as the slimy alley walls, so Danice made very certain to keep her hands at her sides and concentrate on her balance.

She followed Mac down to a landing at what she assumed must serve as the basement level to the buildings above. This time their way was blocked by a battered wooden door painted a chipped and peeling black. Mac ignored it and faced the stone of the wall flanking the stairs. He chose a stone somewhere in the vicinity of his navel and demonstrated another elaborate knock. The stones seemed to shudder and waver like an out-of-tune television picture before they thinned and then blinked out of sight, exposing an archway at the top of another flight of stairs.

"Seriously," Danice muttered as they started down once more, "you come to this place for fun? Like, voluntarily?"

"No, I come here for business. And you promised to let me do the talking."

"Yeah, to other people."

He scowled at her over his shoulder. "Well, let me do *all* the talking."

The second stair moved down along a gradual curve instead of at a straight angle like the first. These lower walls also appeared to have been constructed of stone, but here the gaps were larger and looked as if they'd been filled with soil instead of mortar. It served to emphasize the fact that they were truly underground now, stepping farther and farther into the bowels of the earth. The air had begun to smell dank and musky, like the basement of a very old house. No lights hung overhead in this part of the stairwell, but the walls near the top seemed to glow with an eerie phosphorescence. Around the curve in the wall, she could see more natural-looking yellow light and hoped to hell that it signaled the actual bar.

A few steps later and she could hear the low drone of music mixed with conversation. Her first instinct was relief, followed quickly by uncertainty. She thought she was beginning to understand why she'd never heard of this particular bar, and maybe she shouldn't have decided to make her first visit quite so casually.

The bottom of the stair fanned out into a surpris-

ingly small room; at least, Danice was surprised. She
had expected that whoever—or whatever—had created
the bar would have taken advantage of the greater avail-
ability of subsurface real estate in Manhattan to create
an establishment of more generous proportions, but the
Under Belly really appeared to her to be no larger than
your average city dive bar.

Tables occupied most of the space in the center of the
room. In general, they appeared scratched, round, rick-
ety, and in at least two cases singed around the edges.
The utilitarian chairs looked equally battered, and she
thought she saw more than one customer wobbling
due to their uneven legs. Uneven chair legs, that is. She
tried not to stare at any of the patrons long enough to
tell anything about their anatomical legs.

Three booths lined up against the far wall, with two
more along the near wall, at the back where the room
narrowed briefly before opening up again into a space
just large enough for an ancient pool table and two video
games. Yes, even the Under Belly apparently offered
Ms. Pac-Man.

Tucked up underneath the stairs, Danice spotted a
jukebox that blinked and flashed and poured out some
sort of country-sounding song she'd never heard, despite the fact that she could see the electrical cord hanging limply off the back. No one had bothered to plug it
in. Of course, it didn't appear that they needed to.

She flinched a little when Mac grasped her elbow.
Taking a deep breath, she forced herself to relax as he
led them up to the bar set against the shorter wall closest to the stairs. Two ragged figures hunched over the
far end of the scarred wooden surface, seeming to curl

even farther into themselves as Mac and Danice approached. Why they would worry about two fairly normal-looking people when faced with the behemoth behind the bar, Danice couldn't understand.

The bartender appear to Danice to stand at least seven feet tall and probably stretch half that wide, consuming almost every inch of space behind the bar. His head was bald, his arms bare, and his frame heavy with muscle. In fact, he looked as if he might have been carved from solid rock. Literally. His skin was the texture of weathered sandstone and approximately the same color, an earthy reddish brown that might have been pitted and pocked by wind and rain. Danice would not have been entirely surprised if she'd seen sagebrush growing from the side of his head. Looking at him made her think that a part of the Arizona desert had woken up and wandered into the bar and decided to serve drinks.

Despite his hard-edged appearance, though, the man dried a pint glass with surprising dexterity, and while she couldn't vouch for the rest of the room, the bar itself looked meticulously clean and orderly. The liquor bottles set on the shelves in back lined up in perfect alphabetical order, the unlabeled wooden and brass taps gleamed, and the glassware had been sorted by size and shape and glinted with cleanliness. This bartender might have the look of dirt, but he allowed not a speck of it to mar his work space.

Mac ignored the dozen or so patrons in the room and nodded to the bartender instead. "Hello, Hedge."

The huge figure turned at the sound of his name and grunted. "Callahan. Don't want no trouble tonight."

Ponderous, deep lines formed a perpetual scowl on

the bartender's face, but his eyes beneath the heavy brow ridge were clear, moss green, and utterly mild. In fact, if Danice had to guess, she would call their expression almost . . . friendly.

"I don't plan to start any," Mac assured him. "I'm just here to meet with Quigley. That's all."

Hedge nodded. "And your little friend?" His gaze shifted to Danice, and she felt him taking her measure.

"I'm not going to start any trouble, either," she felt compelled to promise him.

The mossy eyes twinkled at her. "You look to me to be the type that inspires trouble, even when you don't start it yourself, little bit."

Danice found herself smiling, much to her own surprise. "I would never be silly enough to encourage that kind of thing, Mr. Hedge. Of course, I can't be held responsible for the actions of the more foolish elements of society."

A low rumble vibrated through the room, more felt than heard. It took Danice a minute to realize it was the sound of Hedge chuckling. She'd thought for a second it might be a small earthquake.

"Looks like you found yourself a live one," the bartender said to Mac. "Man needs to be careful with those."

"Trust me," Mac replied, his hand tightening on Danice's elbow. "I'm well aware. Has Quigley been by yet?"

Hedge shook his head no. Mac just sighed and ordered them drinks, wine for her and a pint of something called "hell hound" for himself. Danice thought it sounded as if she'd gotten the better end of that deal.

He settled them in one of the empty booths, the last

one on the far side of the room, so that they had only one table of neighbors. She took the side facing the room, and had to scoot over to allow him in next to her.

"Sip that slowly," he ordered, setting her glass in front of her, his fingers lingering on the stem. "It's stronger than you think."

Curious, Danice reached out and lifted the glass. Instead of the red wine she normally drank, he'd brought her a white. *White* was entirely the wrong word, though. This liquid was the palest shade of gold she'd ever seen, ever imagined. It looked as if someone had managed to liquefy sunshine and pour it into a glass. When she lifted it for a curious sniff, however, she didn't smell sunshine. She smelled flowers and flames.

Raising the glass to her lips, she sipped carefully and tumbled head-over-heels in lust. With a beverage.

"Oh, my God. What is this?" she breathed, her eyes wide as flavors danced and sang and burst into fire on the surface of her tongue.

"Faerie wine." Mac's eyes flickered from the door to her face, and his mouth quirked. "You like it?"

"Like it? I think I want to be embalmed in it when I die."

He chuckled. "Remember what I said, though. It's strong stuff. Go slow."

Danice nodded and took another sip. She'd never tasted anything like it, not in her entire life. She'd never even conceived of anything like this. It went down as smooth as water, but the path it left behind glowed as if she'd just tossed back hundred-proof whiskey. She racked her brain for the correct words to describe the flavor, but came up empty. Nothing seemed to fit quite right. It reminded her of honey, but it wasn't sweet. Of apples, but it wasn't fruity. Of lemons, but without the acidic bite. The elusive quality threatened to drive her crazy. She needed another taste.

Mac laid his hand over the top of the glass and frowned at her. "Slower. I don't want to have to carry you out of here."

He was saved from her snappish reply by the appearance of the top of a head at the end of the table. Or rather, the tops of two decidedly pointy ears and what appeared to be a tuft of spiky black hair.

"Quigley," Mac said, glowering at someone or something in the vicinity of the hair and ears, which themselves appeared to sport small, dark tufts of hair. Danice could see nothing. "You're late. And since you're approximately two hundred years old, I really have to ask why you still haven't learned to tell time?"

"Don't have a cow, man," the thing practically under the table squeaked. "I'm here, aren't I? Now why don't you buy me a round, and then we can get down to business, heh?"

Thirteen

"*That* is our guide?" Danice hissed a minute later when Quigley tottered back to the bar to order his drink and his booster seat. "You've hired a guide who can't see over the damned table without a booster seat? What the hell, Mac?"

"Sh! Imps have pretty decent hearing, and we don't need him feeling like you've insulted him," Mac scolded. "You really need to get over these human biases of yours, Danice. They'll only get you into trouble."

"I'm not—" Danice cut off her denial and huffed out an indignant breath. "Okay, maybe I'm biased. But can you blame me? When you said you knew someone who could guide us into Faerie, I was picturing someone who'd be able to see over the steering wheel of a compact car!"

"Why? It's not like we're going to be driving to Faerie. Quigley grew up at the Unseelie Court. He's the best guide available who won't demand that we pay him in human infants."

"Infants?" she squeaked.

Mac shushed her again as Quigley approached the table. Taking a tray with three glasses, he set it down, then reached out and grasped the imp by the hand and boosted him up on the bench opposite himself and Danice.

The imp took a moment to settle himself, which gave Danice the chance to take in his appearance and hopefully compose herself before he accused her of staring. Frankly, she thought staring was justified.

Quigley, as it turned out, stood about two and a half feet high at the tips of his ears, which were as red as Santa's suit. The rest of him appeared to be just as vibrant, except where he sported hair or moles, all of which were black. Also black were the nubby little horns that protruded from his forehead a couple of inches above the outer corners of his eyes, along with the claw-like nails on the tips of his pudgy little fingers. He wore his black hair in a Mohawk of modest length and his mustache long enough that he could have tucked the two ends into his belt if he'd felt so inclined. His clothing consisted of what looked like a studded leather dog collar (sized for the average Pomeranian) and a pair of toddler's OshKosh overalls in faded denim. Danice could only assume he'd cut some sort of opening in the back for the pointed tail she saw swishing behind him.

Dear Lord.

When he had the three glasses from the tray he'd brought lined up in a row in front of him, the imp looked up and frowned at her. "What the heck are you lookin' at, lady?"

Danice blinked. Clearly, she hadn't composed herself quite fast enough.

Beneath the table, Mac's fingers dug into her thigh. "Give her a break, Quig. She's never seen an imp before, especially not a greater one. She never thought she'd even get lucky enough to meet a lesser imp. You've rendered her speechless."

"Oh." The imp lifted the first glass, a pint of something that foamed like beer but smelled like swamp water, and knocked it back like a shot of tequila. "That's okay, then." He wiped his mouth on the back of his arm and let out a rollicking belch. "Does she want I should show her my hooves?"

"Uh, some other time," Mac said. "All we want to know is if we're on for tomorrow night."

Quigley's eyes, which looked more like glowing coals to Danice, flared more brightly. "We can do it tomorrow, sure. But it's going to cost you extra."

At her side, Danice felt Mac stiffen.

"We already agreed on a price, Quig. Don't you think it's a little late to change the terms of the deal?"

The imp knocked back his second drink, a glass of the same Faerie wine that after three sips was threatening to leave Danice under the table.

"Terms change as conditions change, ol' pal. The other day, no one was paying much attention to the gate. Tonight things are looking a mite different."

"Are you saying that the gate to Faerie is under surveillance?"

"Keep your voice down," Quigley hissed, looking over his shoulder at the rest of the room, none of whose occupants appeared to Danice to care about their conversation one way or another. "Alls I'm saying is, that when a body knows as many other bodies as I do, sometimes he hears things. Rumbles, like. Nothing anyone comes out and says, but, like, whispers."

Mac's brows drew together, and he leaned across the

table to glare at the imp. "What whispers have you heard, Quigley?"

The imp lifted the third glass, drained half, then set it down with a *click*. Danice eyed the thick black liquid warily. "I ain't heard nothing. Nothing solid, that is. But more people today seem to be dropping the word *Faerie* here and there, is all I'm saying."

Mac sat back with a shrug. "And that's supposed to justify raising the price at the last minute?"

"This isn't the last minute. The last minute will be tomorrow night at one before midnight." Over the rim of his glass, the little black brows wriggled and the glowing eyes brightened a little more. "But if a customer was to make things worth my while, I might not feel any need to entertain last-minute price changes."

Danice looked from Mac to the imp and back a couple of times. Mac had his game face on, his mask showing nothing more than the slightest hint of irritation. But with his hand still on her leg, she could feel the tension in him, and she thought she could sense his unease. In contrast, the imp just looked . . . eager. Danice thought she could almost see the tips of his ears quivering.

She frowned. "What was the original price you agreed on?"

Mac's head whipped around, and he focused his gimlet stare on her. "That's not your concern, Danice."

"Of course it is. I'm half of this expedition. What was the price?"

Quigley's bright, sly gaze slid toward her. "Did someone forget to share the details, then?"

Danice never had been the sort to sit down and shut

up, not even figuratively, and especially not when told to do so. "I think someone did."

The imp giggled. "For shame, McIntyre. You know you should always tell the truth entire." The creature drew out the rhyme with a chortle of glee. "This lady has a right to know that I don't work for anything less than *two* bottles of root beer!"

Danice blinked. "Root beer?"

"And I'm talking the big bottles. Two liters. None of those chintzy single-serve jobs. And no lousy generic brands. I want the good stuff."

Unaware she'd been holding her breath, Danice let it out on a laugh and pushed Mac's shoulder. "Geez, you really had me scared there for a minute. I thought he might actually have asked to be paid in babies. You were acting like we'd have to bargain away our souls for this trip."

Mac bared his teeth and hissed out a warning. "You don't understand," he growled, keeping his voice low and speaking directly into her ear to prevent Quigley from hearing. "To an imp, root beer is like meth and crack and moonshine all rolled into one. Two bottles of root beer are going to send this idiot on a bender that could wipe out half of Manhattan. If he asks for another one, he could take out New Jersey, too."

Danice had to stifle the urge to laugh, but judging by the look on Mac's face, now was not the time. Still, the idea of the little red devil sitting across from her leaving a trail of destruction in his wake made her lips twitch.

"But now I'm thinking maybe this is worth more to the two of you than two bottles," Quigley said, rubbing his hands together greedily. "Now I'm thinking maybe it's worth a little bonus."

"Don't press your luck," Mac bit out. "We agreed on the price. Two two-liters is twice what you'd ordinarily get your hands on in a month. Maybe two."

"But if I get caught smuggling folks across the border, they'll lock me down, Mac." The imp's voice went from greedy to wheedling, with maybe a hint of pathetic thrown in. "Then I won't be any good to anyone. They keep such a close eye on me, I won't be able to think about coming back to *ithir*. That's a big risk I'm taking."

"Two bottles," Mac said firmly, then grimaced. "But I'll throw in that five-disk *1980s Metal Mania* CD collection they've been advertising on TV. And that's my final offer."

"Done!" Quigley squeaked, bouncing in his booster seat. "You drive a hard bargain, Callahan, but you won't be sorry. I'll get you exactly where you need to be. Yes, siree!"

He drained the third drink until only a sludgy black film remained clinging to the inside of the glass, then thunked the empty back on the table and let out a raucous belch. Danice actually jerked back a little in instinctive reaction. It sounded like someone had shot off a cannon.

"We're set then," the imp said, squirming out of his seat and off the bench until his two little hooves clacked on the bare stone floor. "You two meet me tomorrow at midnight on the corner of Sixth and C. We'll go from there. And don't forget my payment."

Danice watched the tips of his ears turn toward the

exit and watched as he scampered up the stairs and out of sight.

She sighed. "Midnight in Alphabet City. My, doesn't that sound like just where I want to be tomorrow?"

Mac eyed her over the rim of his glass. "You can still back out. I'm happy to take care of this on my own, you know."

"Yeah, you might have mentioned that. Once or twice. But you can forget it. I'm going. End of story."

He shrugged, but to Danice the gesture looked far from casual. "Fine. Just don't say I didn't warn you."

She glared.

"Oh, and one more thing." He slid out of the booth and held out a hand to help her rise. "See if you can find something in your closet that costs less than a month's salary on minimum wage and that can stand up to a few bumps and bruises."

"Should we be expecting to be bumped and bruised?" she asked, following him up the stairs. "I thought you were the one who told me it wasn't like we were going to be slogging our way through the Bolivian rain forest?"

"We won't be, but Faerie is an interesting place, and getting there is an interesting journey. You never know what might go wrong."

Why, oh why, did those have to sound so much like famous last words?

Fourteen

Just because Mac was half Fae and had, in fact, been born in Faerie didn't mean he viewed going back as a walk in the park. It felt a hell of a lot more like a trip through a former war zone—it wouldn't be pretty, and chances were a few landmines lurked out of sight, just waiting to blow him and his world sky-high.

Boy, he could hardly wait.

He had offered to meet Danice at her apartment and to escort her to the rendezvous point, but she had brushed the gesture aside and assured him she was perfectly capable of getting herself to Alphabet City all on her own.

"I'm a big girl now, Daddy," she'd teased him, "and you don't need to walk me to school anymore."

He had no doubts about Danice's size or her sense of direction, only about the chances of her running into a mugger who hadn't gotten aboard the gentrification train that continued to sweep across the Lower East Side.

At ten minutes before twelve, Mac planted himself on the corner of East 6th Street and Avenue C and leaned against a lamppost, his gaze scanning his surroundings for any sign of Danice or Quigley. All he saw were a couple of homeless people staggering toward Tompkins

Square Park looking for a place to sleep and a few kids heading for the bars in the East Village. Everything looked normal, if fairly quiet for a Tuesday night. No one and nothing looked out of place, which might have explained why he didn't really notice Danice walking toward him down 6th until she had nearly stopped in front of him.

She didn't look like he'd been expecting.

Mac knew he'd ordered her to dress in simple, practical clothing, but the sight of her in anything other than her chic Urban Attorney Armor still caught him off guard. Obviously, Danice had taken him at his word.

She wore a pair of slim, straight-legged jeans so dark they looked almost black until she stepped into the glow of the street lamp, and a battered, black leather jacket so worn that it didn't reflect even a glimmer of light. A long-sleeved black T-shirt and scuffed, lace-up hiking boots completed the ensemble. She'd even changed her hair, confining the dark strands into two French braids that ended in stubby pigtails just brushing the base of her neck. She looked about twenty years old, as if she'd just wandered down from the student housing NYU had erected a couple of blocks away.

Mac felt like a pervert for wanting to drag her into the shadows and educate her in a way no university could possibly have intended.

"You know, it's nights like these when I almost miss the old Alphabet City," she mused, her voice husky and her mouth curved wryly. "I almost didn't even bother to carry my pepper spray. When I was a teenager, I wouldn't have come down here without an armed guard. And if I'd tried, my parents would have killed me."

Mac faked a cough and hoped it would disguise the way his jaw had been hanging open while he stared at her. He also used the opportunity to surreptitiously check his chin for drool. All clear.

"Any sign of Quigley?" Danice asked.

"Not yet." He tore his eyes from her animated face to glance at his watch. "But it's still a couple of minutes before twelve. And he does have that difficulty with telling time."

She chuckled and eyed the backpack he had slung over one shoulder. "Was I supposed to bring my camping gear? I thought this was going to be more of an in-and-out mission."

"It's Quigley's root beer, and a key to the PO box where I arranged to have his CDs delivered."

Danice nodded and shoved her hands into the pockets of her jacket. Silence descended. Followed closely by awkwardness, with a tinge of discomfort. Mac forced himself to look everywhere but at Danice, afraid that if he gave in to the urge, he'd never stop staring; and while most women appreciated being admired, very few enjoyed having an obsessive stalker.

Quigley's unsubtle "Psssst!" couldn't have come at a better time, but it still took several seconds of peering into the shadows surrounding them before Mac spotted the small demon. The imp crouched behind the painted iron fence that enclosed the stairs to the basement level of the house on the end of 6th Street. Concealed as he was by the darkness, it was the glow of his eyes that finally caught Mac's attention.

Nudging Danice's elbow, Mac jerked his chin toward the creature's hiding place and moved across the sidewalk toward him. "What's with the cloak-and-dagger routine, Quig? Was I supposed to memorize a secret password?"

"Shh!" the imp hissed. "Keep your voice down! And for the stars' sakes, don't use my name. I don't want anyone overhearing. You never know who might be listening. Especially these days."

Danice shot Mac an inquiring look, but he shook his head. "You didn't used to be so paranoid," he told the imp. "What exactly is going on here?"

Quigley waved them forward and ushered them down an abbreviated flight of stairs to what Mac had assumed was the door to a basement apartment. On closer inspection, all he could see was a window covered in burglar bars and the kind of miniature door that had been used for coal deliveries, back in the day when furnaces still ran on the stuff.

"I told you," the imp whispered. "A lot more folks been whispering the word *Faerie* these days, and the way I see it, when folks are talking, other folks are listening. That's all I'm saying. You got my stuff?"

Mac handed over the backpack and heard Quigley's satisfied grunt as he registered the weight.

"Good dealing. Since I trust you, I'm not going to check the bottles, but if you're trying to stiff me, I won't be happy with you, Callahan."

"Don't worry. It's all there," Mac said, keeping his voice low in deference to the imp's obvious paranoia. If the creature didn't let up on craning his head around to check to see if anyone was observing them, he was going to end up replacing that dog collar with a cervical collar.

Danice looked down at Quigley and raised an eyebrow. "So now that you've been paid, how about you tell us how we're going to get into Faerie, little man?"

"Through the Faerie gate," the creature sniffed, scowling at her as if she were truly stupid. "The only way to get into Faerie is through a gate." He looked at Mac. "Doesn't she know anything?"

Before Mac could answer, Danice piped up. "No, I don't. But that's mostly because some people never tell me anything."

Mac ignored her pointed stare. "Just lead us to the gate, Quigley. We're ready to go and all we're doing now is burning moonlight."

Sighing, the imp set the backpack on the ground and shrugged into the shoulder straps. When he settled it into place, it rode approximately four inches off the ground.

"Don't need to lead anywhere," he grunted. "The gate's right there."

"Right where?"

Quigley stabbed an impatient figure at the coal door. "Right there."

Mac groaned. "I really hoped you weren't going to say that."

Danice looked at the small blue door, which stood about twenty inches high by two feet wide, and shook her head. "Are you telling me you expect us to squeeze through that tiny little thing? Quigley, you're out of your mind. You could barely fit through there, let alone Mac and me."

The imp shrugged. "That's the gate. I didn't design it, I just know how to use it, and it's the only one around that I know still works. I heard there used to be one up in Inwood Park somewhere, but it ain't been used in five or six centuries. You two are welcome to try it out, but I'm not taking you through that one. It's this one or nothing."

Danice threw up her hands. "Well, since you put it that way."

Mac just swore. He eyed the narrow opening, mentally comparing measurements between his frame and the door frame. It would be a tight squeeze, if it was even possible. Damn Quigley. Mac should have known it had been too easy to persuade the imp to guide them through the gate, but the miniature demon just couldn't resist the idea of a practical joke. Literally. Imps were inveterate pranksters. Luckily, very few of their pranks ended in death and/or dismemberment.

"Very few," of course, existed a fair distance down the measuring line from "none."

He swore again. "I'm going to have to go through first," he told Danice. "I'm about eighty-five percent sure I can make it through there, but if I can't, I definitely don't want you waiting around in Faerie without me. And I sure as hell don't trust Quigley to take care of you. To tell the truth, I don't trust him to wait for either of us if he goes through first, especially since he already has his hands on the root beer. I'll go first, and if I make it through, you can follow me while Quigley keeps watch outside. Just in case his paranoia actually means something."

Danice nodded. "Sounds good."

"Did you catch that, Quigley?"

"Sure, sure. I'll wait out here while you two go through the gate. That makes sense. I can make sure no one tries to stop you. Or us. I mean, us."

Mac watched the imp through narrowed lids. He did not like the expression flickering in the little monster's coal-bright eyes. "Slight revision," he told Danice, stripping the backpack off Quigley despite the imp's squeaks of protest. "I go through, you pass me the backpack, then you, then Quigley. Just to be sure all three of us actually make it across."

The imp glared at him and muttered something in his native tongue that Mac thought loosely translated into a slur on his parentage and a suggestion for rather improbable ways of keeping himself occupied.

Danice just grinned. "I can handle that."

"Good. Then let's get this show started."

He handed the backpack to Danice and rolled his shoulders to work out the kinks. The next minute or two were not going to be very comfortable for him, so best to just get it over with.

The coal door boasted a sturdy industrial padlock, but it posed no problem to Quigley's larcenous streak. Still grumbling about the unfair aspersions cast on his character by suspicious changelings, he popped the lock in fewer than five seconds, then stood back to make room for Mac.

The toughest part of the maneuver would be his shoulders, Mac decided. If he was going to get stuck, it would be there, where his frame was the broadest, so it made sense to go in headfirst. That way, if he couldn't make it, he should still be able to get enough leverage with his legs to pull himself back out. If he went in feet-first, he could get stuck around the chest, and that would really, really suck.

Out of the corner of his eye, he saw Danice glancing between his shoulders and the door. She looked pretty doubtful. "Do you really think you can make it through there?"

"Not straight on," he admitted, crouching down on the cold bricks of the landing to prop the door open against the wall above it. It hung on a top hinge, so hopefully it would stay in place while he slid through. "Thankfully, I'm a pretty flexible guy. So, here goes."

Blowing out a breath, he sank onto his belly and extended his left arm while pressing his right arm tight against his side and slightly under his body. He needed to angle his shoulders and collarbones so that only one side went through at a time. Otherwise, as he'd told Danice, he'd never get through head-on.

It really was a tight fit, and he faced a couple of seconds of doubt when he had his head and his left shoulder in the tiny space as to whether he'd still be stuck in exactly that spot when the sun rose. The back of his shirt caught on the edge of a nail protruding from the wooden frame, and he felt it gouge a shallow trench between his shoulder blades. He hissed but wriggled forward.

It didn't help that he felt as if he were trying to squeeze himself into the center of a black hole. From the outside, with the door flipped up, he'd peered into the gate and seen nothing but the inky darkness of a coal room, but now that he'd managed to get his head (or the proverbial foot) through the door, he didn't even see that much. The magic that powered this gate had erased all traces of any surroundings and created a portal through nothingness between *ithir*—the mortal human plane— and Faerie. Presumably, once they made it through and took their first few steps, they would see Faerie unfolding around them. Otherwise he was going to have to have a long, hard talk with Quigley. One involving teeth and flying fists.

Also, knowing Quigley, probably fists and flying teeth. When cornered, imps showed a disconcerting tendency to bite.

"How is it going? Are you stuck?"

Mac could hear Danice's voice calling to him, but it sounded remote, as if he'd already traveled a great distance. Which, in a metaphysical sense, he was guessing he had. Still, he slid forward a few more inches to demonstrate that he wasn't quite stuck and managed to wedge himself in to just past his nipples. He could feel the frame of the small space compressing his rib cage, but this was the worst stage, and so far no permanent injuries. That offered a cause for celebration.

With the widest part of his torso firmly wedged in place, Mac exhaled the last bit of air trapped in his lungs and used his legs to shove himself forward to the waist. With that accomplished, he groped around him for something to hold on to and realized that he seemed to have slid from one hard surface onto another. He braced his palms on the ground and pulled the rest of his body through the narrow opening, twisting as he did until he could sit and draw in a deep breath.

"I'm clear!" he shouted back through the door,

hoping the others would be able to hear him. Even if they didn't, though, once they saw him disappear, he figured they'd get the message.

He didn't so much see the backpack appear as he heard it scraping against the window frame and the ground as Danice shoved it through the gate. Instinctively, he pushed himself to his knees with one hand and reached for the backpack with the other. That part posed no problem, but when he attempted to stand up straight, he got about two-thirds of the way there before the back of his head made firm and resounding contact with the ceiling.

"Shit," he said, reaching up to rub the emerging lump.

"Are you okay?" he heard, accompanied by the sound of cloth dragging over ground. "Lord, it's dark in here. Is it midnight in Faerie, too?"

Mac couldn't tell if his eyes were adjusting to the lack of light in the gate or if some sort of magical energy allowed Danice to light up like a beacon for him, but he could see the frown on her face as she dragged herself through the opening and started to push to her feet.

"Careful," he said, extending a hand from his awkwardly stooped frame. "That gate should have a sign above it: LOW CLEARANCE."

Danice felt above her for the ceiling and realized that even she would have to crouch a bit to keep from hitting her head. "Maybe we can place that little tidbit in the suggestion box."

"I don't know what you're complaining about," Quigley hissed, scrambling through the door and then striding up to them with no problem, "but I wish you'd keep your voices down. I already told you, you never know who might be listening." He reached out an imperious hand and glared at Mac. "Now I'd like my payment back, if you please."

"I don't please." Mac's hand tightened on the back-pack's top handle. "We're not out of the gate yet, my friend. As soon as I can see we're actually in Faerie, you'll get your root beer. But not a minute before."

The imp muttered something that once again Mac barely understood and he knew Danice couldn't possibly interpret, for which he gave thanks. The demon had a creative mind and a filthy mouth.

"Fine," the creature snapped, waving them forward. "Follow me. But keep quiet!"

As Mac had suspected, it didn't take long before the inky blackness of the gate began to ease and he could start to make out the shapes of trees and plants all around them. Glancing up, he saw the brilliant twinkling of the stars, and within a few more steps he could see they'd emerged into the middle of a Faerie forest, silver-frosted by the light of the moon and stars.

Beside him, he heard Danice draw an awestruck breath. "Wow. I guess maybe it is midnight in Faerie."

"More like one or two in the morning," the imp hissed, turning to glare at his companions. "Now shut up and hand over the goods."

Mac shook his head. "We still have to get to the court, and I have no desire to wander around the whole of Faerie looking for it, especially not starting in the middle of the night."

He knew the instant the imp smiled that something was about to go wrong. Very, very wrong.

"You don't have to find King Dionnu's court," the imp giggled. "I think it's about to find you!"

With a loud cackle, the tiny demon launched himself forward, hands snagging the backpack, teeth sinking deep into the back of Mac's hand.

Mac heard Danice shout and himself hiss as his grip on the backpack loosened, but the pain of the bite wasn't what made him curse. The cause of that was the drumming of hoofbeats in the distance. The distance that he could tell was already closing rapidly.

Quigley had seized the advantage, ripping the backpack from Mac's grip and disappearing into the thick cover of the forest. Danice turned and began to run after him, but Mac snagged her by the shoulder and shook his head.

"Forget about the imp," he snarled, shoving her in the opposite direction, toward another dense stand of trees. "Run. Now."

Danice tried to shake off his grip, but he didn't budge. He gave her one last chance to take off on her own. When she didn't, he grabbed her wrist and leapt forward, dragging her willy-nilly along behind him.

"Mac, wait!" she cried, too loud, making Mac curse. "What the hell is going on? Why are we running? Where are we going? Would you frickin' talk to me, you insane man?"

"No time! Just run!"

He stepped up the pace, not even slowing when he felt Danice stumble behind him. He simply used his strength and his grip on her arm to swing her back to her feet.

"Mac, what the hell are we running from?"

The hoofbeats reached a branch-snapping crescendo just to their right, and Mac saw the glint of silver manes. Heart sinking, he knew it was too late. He dragged Danice to a halt and positioned her behind him. At the moment, putting his body between hers and the threat was the best he could do.

"Mac, what are we running from?" she repeated, sounding as confused as she was impatient.

"That," he said simply, pointing toward the five tall figures emerging from the forest and closing in around them.

Fifteen

Danice had no idea what the hell was going on, and she didn't like the feeling. Not one bit. She also didn't like that something in this place had sent Mac into a tizzy, or that he was standing between her and it so that she couldn't even see what the matter was.

That second part particularly grated, since Danice made it a policy never to make up her mind to be afraid of something until she'd taken a look at it for herself. Unfortunately, Mac was so much taller than she that she'd have to peer under his arm like a four-year-old if she wanted to catch a glimpse. Damned man.

Just before she gave in and said to hell with her dignity, the "that" Mac had referred to stepped close enough for Danice to see around him, provided she craned her head and torso slightly to the side. What she saw didn't quite match up with what she'd been expecting.

They had to be Fae. Danice could accept no other explanation. Once Mac had explained to her that the natives of Faerie had less in common with Tinker Bell and more in common with the Elves from the *Lord of the Rings* movies, this had been what she'd pictured them looking like. Until she'd met Quigley and learned that he was native to Faerie as well. After that, she'd tried not to think about it much at all. But the figures standing in front of them now were beautiful. Breathtakingly beautiful.

And all obviously female.

Danice frowned.

There appeared to be five of them, each of them easily matching Mac in height (which put them around six feet) and as slim and straight as a supermodel. All had hair long enough to reach their butts, but wore it pulled back or confined in tails or braids. Two had inky hair so black it glinted blue in the moonlight, two were platinum blondes, and one had hair the color of living flames. Each had features more beautiful than the last, and Danice hated all of them on sight.

"Mac," she hissed, poking him in the ribs. Hard. "Who are these people?"

"Not now," he whispered back, somehow managing to make the breath of sound into a firm, granite command.

Danice pinched her lips shut and glared. Both at Mac and at any of the strange women unfortunate enough to stand in her line of sight.

"The question of the moment is who are you," one of the blondes said, speaking as if Danice had addressed her question to the Fae rather than to Mac. "And more important, what you are doing on royal lands without the king's permission."

"Doesn't sound much like a question to me," Danice muttered. "More like a demand from someone with a big stick up her ass."

Mac squeezed her hand tightly. "Shut up, Danice."

"Well?" the blonde prompted. "We are waiting, but do not try our patience."

Danice felt Mac draw a deep breath.

"My name is Callahan, son of Tyra," he announced in a clear voice so the Fae could hear. "And I have business with the Unseelie Court."

"Tyra's son?" one of the brunettes repeated. "Tyra ni Oengus? But the lady I know by that name has no child."

The blonde narrowed her eyes and pointed the tip of a spear in Mac's direction.

A spear? Danice thought, aghast. They were carrying spears? She quickly looked at the others. Only the blonde seemed to have a spear, but all of them wore swords strapped to their sides, and a couple of them appeared to be holding bows and packing arrows as well.

"We do not deal well with liars," the blonde warned, her tone taking on a menacing quality.

"And I do not deal in lies," Mac said, his spine stiffening beneath the hand Danice had instinctively laid there. "I am Tyra's son. She chose not to raise me and sent me to my father as an infant. But that does not alter the fact of my birth, or of her part in it."

"A changeling?" the redhead gasped, looking dumbfounded. Danice decided she liked her the least. "You are changeling and you think to demand admittance before the court?"

"I think the court has admitted far worse influences than me. But since when do the King's Guard decide who is and who isn't admitted to court?"

Danice inferred from that question that these five

women made up the King's Guard, which she found a tad unexpected. Sure, they all carried weapons, but from what Mac had told her of Faerie, she hadn't considered they'd be progressive enough to assign women to be the king's personal bodyguards. Assuming she was right about that being what they were.

"We have always decided who would be allowed near the king," the blonde snapped. "Or rather, the blades of our swords have done so."

That brought a scowl to Danice's face. "Is she threatening us?"

Mac ignored her. "I thought that kind of decision only happened when someone with a blade of their own made an attempt on the king's life. Or have the rules changed so that now you strike first and determine a visitor's purpose after you have killed him?"

"We don't have to kill you," the second blonde said, stepping forward. "We could simply cut out your tongue so that you would cease your prattle. Then the king could determine your purpose later."

"How?" Danice muttered. "By divining the meaning in our entrails?"

"Shhh!"

Danice and the bloodthirsty second blonde ignored him.

"Your idea has merit," the guardswoman said, "but I believe we should cut out *your* tongue and read *his* entrails. I would so hate to miss the screaming."

Danice rolled her eyes and stepped to Mac's side, ignoring his attempts to keep her safely behind him. "Oh, would you at least try for a little originality, girl? That threat was so stale, mold wouldn't even grow there."

"Danice!"

She ignored Mac's bark and stood her ground as the second blonde bared her teeth and made as if to lunge toward her.

"Catrin!" the lead blonde snapped, stretching her arm out to block the other's move. "Do not allow yourself to be provoked. Especially not by this creature. She is no worthy opponent. In fact, I believe she may even be human."

The brunettes gasped and put their heads together, whispering to each other before the one on the left spoke out. "If she is human, we must take her to the king. All humans are to be brought to him, Morag."

"I am aware of that, Sorcha," the first blonde (apparently called Morag) snapped, her eyes never leaving Danice's face. "This one does not look like much of a threat, but we will take her with us all the same."

"Nobody takes me anywhere," Danice protested, but Mac cut her off by the expedient means of covering her mouth with his hand. He even knew enough to cup his palm so that she couldn't bite him to make him let go.

"My companion means that she isn't going anywhere alone," he explained, squeezing her arm with his other hand. "She is my guest in Faerie, and I go wherever she goes."

"Oh, we would not think to part you," Morag assured him, her smile not looking the least bit amused to Danice. Or the least bit pleasant. "You will both be our guests during your stay. Or rather, the guests of the king."

Danice narrowed her eyes at the other woman. Morag

the Fae might have a pretty face, but Danice didn't trust her. She didn't like her, either. Mostly, though, she didn't like the way the other woman said "guest."

But Mac only nodded. "Then you will lead us to the Winter Court?"

"At once, my lord *mac Tyra*." Morag offered him a mocking bow. "Please, allow my sisters to be your guides." At a gesture from their leader, Sorcha and the other brunette stepped around to flank Mac, one on either side. "You may release your human friend. We will care for her just as closely."

Danice stepped away from Mac's grasp. She could feel how reluctant he was to let her go, which was no more reluctant than she was to find herself similarly surrounded by Catrin and the redhead. Just her luck, of course, to get the two members of the group she liked least as her "escorts."

"This way. As we did not expect visitors, we have no extra mounts, so I'm afraid you will have to walk."

Morag led the small group through the forest to a well-worn trail a few yards away. There Danice could see that the flashes of silver she'd noticed earlier had come from the saddles and bridles of the five white horses that stood idly along the edge of the path. Having grown up a city girl, the only thing Danice knew about horses was that they could pull carriages full of tourists around Central Park, unless the weather got too hot, in which case the police would send them back to their barns. She'd certainly never ridden one, and quite frankly she was happy to hear she wouldn't be starting tonight.

While the Fae gathered their mounts, Mac took the opportunity to sidle up to Danice's side and hiss a warning.

"Do me one huge favor," he urged, his eyes on the women. "Keep your mouth shut, okay? These are the personal guards to the king of the Unseelie Court. The fact that they didn't just kill us on sight means we caught them in a good mood, so let's try to keep it that way, huh?"

Before she could reply, the women surrounded them again. Morag swung herself up in the saddle, but the others stayed on the ground, resuming stations one on each side of their captives. There was no way, Danice acknowledged, that they thought of her and Mac as "guests," no matter what had come out of their mouths.

The group moved along the trail and out of the forest, with Morag mounted in the lead, followed by Mac and the brunettes, leading their horses, with Danice and her guards (with their horses) trailing behind. Within ten minutes of beginning the walk, Danice's hunch had been borne out. Instead of taking a friendly stroll, the guardswomen marched her and Mac along like enemy soldiers, keeping a brisk pace and snarling curt orders anytime one of them varied their pace by so much as half a step.

Danice strode along, still irritated by the attitude of the women but trying very hard to keep her fears at bay. She might feel as if she'd just been taken prisoner by the Gestapo, but she hadn't been harmed, and not even threatened that seriously. Surely if they were in any real danger, either they would already be dead, or Mac would have put up more of a fuss before allowing them to be captured. They could at least have made a run for it, or something.

She stared at the back of his head as they marched, wishing for the second time since meeting him that she could read minds like a vampire. It would be pretty handy to be telepathic at the moment, so that she could ask Mac what he thought was going on. If they really were being brought to the Unseelie Court—which is what she guessed they had meant when they mentioned that bit about the Winter Court—that was a good thing, right? After all, that's where they had intended to go all along, and where Mac believed the person who had hired him had originated, she reasoned. Getting there so soon after their arrival would have to be counted as a good thing, wouldn't it?

Danice struggled to hold on to that sense of optimism for the next hour and a half as the King's Guard marched them halfway to California, by the feel of it. She hadn't been allowed to talk to Mac at all, and the two or three questions she'd tried out on her escorts had been met with growls and censoring looks. Not exactly the social type, these girls.

They left the forest behind after the first couple of minutes and spent most of the time on a wide, smooth road that curved endlessly along until it emerged at the edge of what looked to Danice to be either a large castle or a small city. Or maybe both.

She first spotted the high stone walls at least thirty minutes before they got anywhere near their destination. The stones glowed in the moonlight, glinting almost as silver as the fittings on the horses or the tip of Morag's spear. The structure appeared to nestle at the foot of some dark mountains, which Danice thought seemed fitting for the king of the Unseelie Court—beautiful and ominous all at the same time. Her third question had confirmed just where they were heading. The castle, she had been curtly informed, was *Bail Gevhra*—Winter Home—residence of the Unseelie king.

Taking in its medieval appearance, lit by moon- and torchlight, Danice made one fervent wish.

Please, Lord, let the place have indoor plumbing.

As it turned out, Morag did not lead Mac and Danice directly to the king's throne room, or wherever it was that His Majesty received visitors, and she didn't offer to give them the nickel tour. Instead, she escorted her guests directly to the dungeons.

"Is this really how the Winter King treats his guests these days?" Mac asked when Morag used the point of her spear to urge him into a cell after Danice. "What happened to the laws of hospitality?"

"Hospitality is for those who come at the king's invitation," the woman replied, following far enough to block the door with her body and prevent any attempts as escape. As if escape had looked like an option, considering that her four friends stood at her back, their hands on the hilts of their swords. "Do you have one of those?"

Danice saw the muscle in the side of Mac's jaw clench and heard him grit out an angry, "No."

"Then I'm afraid you'll just have to wait until the king is able to make time in his busy schedule to see you." Her smile offered little reassurance.

"And how long is that going to be?"

"Oh, I couldn't hazard a guess," she said sweetly. As sweet as poison, anyway. "But I suppose I could ask for you. Just as soon as he returns from his hunting trip."

Her laugh trailed into the room through the heavy door, which she closed and locked behind her. Even the thud of the bar falling into its rest sounded malicious to Danice, but then again, she might be beginning to take things a little personally. Mac might, too, judging by the curse he let out at the blameless door.

"Oh, one last thing." Morag's smirking face appeared in the small, barred window set in the door just at eye level. "I wish you both a restful sleep. And the sweetest of dreams."

Before Danice could decide or even wonder what that meant, Morag brought a cupped hand up to her face and blew, sending a fine mist of sparkling dust floating into the dungeon cell.

"Fuck! Hold your breath!" Mac shouted, grabbing her by the back of the shirt and hauling her away from the door.

But it was too late.

By the time Danice blinked through the dust and opened her mouth to ask what the hell Mac's problem was, she had already drawn breath and taken the powder into her lungs. Her last thought was to wonder why the room was spinning before she sagged bonelessly into unconsciousness.

Sixteen

He slipped into her dreams like a wraith, but his body felt warm and substantial against her skin. He curled around her, a firm, living blanket pressed against her back, his large frame making her feel tiny and protected as he wrapped his hard arms around her and snuggled her closer.

Danice sighed and stretched a little, arching her back to press her behind against the erection that prodded her. That felt hot and a good bit more than substantial. Her sleep-fogged brain tried to latch onto something about the moment that seemed off, but he distracted her with a soft, rousing kiss, placed just behind her ear where the skin was fragrant and sensitive.

"Mmm."

He matched her murmur with a low rumble that sounded an awful lot like a purr. His tongue flicked over the curve of her jaw, traced its way up to the lobe of her ear and teased for a moment before his teeth closed delicately over the plump flesh. He nibbled, and her murmur became a moan.

The arm around her waist tightened in a brief hug before his hand slipped over bare skin to close around a sleep-soft breast. It firmed against his palm, the nipple drawing into a tight bead and taunting his cupped fingers. They closed around the small nub, squeezing gently, tugging in time to the nibbling at her ear. His other arm shifted, and she felt the scrape of a callused hand over her hip and belly before long, lean fingers cupped possessively over her mound.

She sighed, the sound shivering through the darkness. Sleep still cradled her, drowsy and secure, but the sensation of her lover's touch turned the lazy feeling into a sort of spell, holding her in place, making her unwilling to pull away. She'd much rather get closer. Shifting, she tried to turn over in his arms to face him. His hands tightened to hold her in place, and she frowned.

He shushed her murmur of protest, nipping lightly at the curve of her shoulder. His large hand kneaded her breast, taking her mind off his refusal to allow her to change position. Then the hand between her legs slid down and took her mind off everything else. Strong, lean fingers combed through the small patch of curls and dipped, parting her folds and burying themselves in her wet heat.

Instinct arched her hips toward his touch. Her body burned and ached with need, but he avoided touching her most sensitive flesh. Two fingers eased her apart, finding her opening and rimming it with delicate pressure. A gasp escaped her lips, and she squirmed against him.

His erection pressed hard and hot against her buttocks, and she canted them so the shaft rode the crevice between. She reached up behind her to pull him closer, her fingers tangling in a mass of silky soft hair, surprisingly long and wonderfully thick. He resisted her attempts to guide him, making a soft tsking sound against her ear. His hand lifted from her breast, and he laced their fingers together, holding them together as he shifted, rolling to his back and pulling her over on top of him.

The blankets slid away, cool air caressing her erect nipples, chilling her fevered skin. He insinuated his legs between hers and forced her thighs to spread wide around his. She lay atop him, fully open to his touch, feeling the shift and play of his chest cradling her back. He purred again, the sound rumbling in her ear as he nuzzled it and planted kisses in the sensitive hollow beneath.

"Sweet," he whispered, his breath another caress. The hand between her legs shifted, two fingertips pressing against her opening, sliding easily within. "Soft."

She gasped and arched, trying to draw him deeper inside her, trying to get more of his intoxicating touch.

His mouth curved against her skin, and his fingers thrust suddenly harder inside her. Danice cried out. Her body clenched around the sudden invasion, the ripple of internal muscles making her shudder. She shuddered even more when his fingers twisted, probing deeper, scraping delicately against inner walls.

"Hmm, like that?"

His voice was a dark rumble that made her shiver above him. Or maybe that was his fingers.

"Just like that."

He chuckled, and his fingers pulled away. Her hips followed him, greedy for his touch. He gave it back with three fingers, stretching and filling her until her breath caught in her throat.

"How about like this?"

She could only gasp.

He withdrew, thrust again, establishing a slow, driving rhythm. As in driving Danice right over the edge. Her fingers tightened in his hair, and she braced her heels against the soft mattress to get more leverage. It offered an infuriating lack of resistance, allowing her to sink deeper. She couldn't decide if she should take the opportunity to get away or use it to press closer.

Her lover untangled his fingers from hers and shifted his free hand to close again around her breast, thumb flicking over the distended nipple, and that pretty much decided things for her.

"Please." Her voice was a moan, a plea, a subtle threat.

He chuckled again, but his fingers drove deep into her softness, and his thumb rubbed tight circles around her clit. "Please, what?"

"Don't . . . give me that . . . shit," she growled, yanking hard on his hair. "You know what I want. Come inside me."

She felt his hands still. For a moment, she wondered if he intended to leave her. His hand slid from between her legs, and she cried out, but he just shifted his grip to her sides. He lifted her enough to position himself, then brought her hips down, easing her closer as he pressed slowly and relentlessly inside.

She froze.

Breath halting on a ragged sigh, she stilled every muscle she could to savor the moment of his first penetration. She felt the burning stretch as he eased past her tight entrance, the endless, breathless parting as he tunneled deeper. Time stopped while he made a place for himself inside her, and it didn't move forward until he hilted, every last inch of him gripped snug in her moist heat.

And, oh, but there were a lot of inches.

Her head tipped back against his shoulder, and her eyes flew open in the darkness. The lack of light blinded her, but she didn't need to see when she could feel so damned well.

"This then," he said, voice growling against her ear. "This is what you wanted. Me, inside you."

"Yesssss."

"Then you should give me something I want in return."

Her teeth clenched against the rush of sensation as he guided her hips up off his shaft, then back down to receive his return thrust. "What do you want?"

His fingers tightened, hard enough to leave bruises against her caramel skin. "I want you to scream for me."

He punctuated the demand with a jerk that forced her harder against him and butted the head of his cock against her womb. She didn't scream, but she moaned, and he seemed to take it as a challenge.

Over and over, he lifted her as easily as a rag doll, forcing her to ride his shaft as he pounded his hips up against her bottom. Helplessly, she let him, their position preventing her from taking any sort of control over their primitive mating. All she could do was clench her fingers in his hair and moan, tightening her inner muscles around him on every thrust, milking him relentlessly. But those contractions affected more than her lover. They shuddered through her womb, making her hotter and wetter so that he glided inside her as if he'd been born to be there. She quivered and arched, her free hand closing around her own breast, kneading the flesh and pinching hard around her aching nipple. The rough sensation barely fazed her. It felt like a tickle compared with the driving, digging rhythm between her thighs.

"Not good enough." His voice sounded rougher this time. Control was abandoning him as well. His breath panted, and he, too, sounded as if he spoke through clenched teeth. The thought made her smile smugly. "I said . . ."

His hands shifted, one sliding lower to get a firmer grip on her hip, the other reclaiming its place between her legs.

". . . I want you . . ."

She moaned, the sound high and sharp, almost like a squeal as he spread her folds and found the hard knot of nerves at the top of her slit. She was swollen with arousal and sensitive to the slightest brush of air, let alone the brush of his fingers.

". . . to scream."

His fingers closed around the hard little nub, pinching firmly, and scream she did.

She came like lightning striking, all heat and energy and pyrotechnic glory. Her whole body clenched in a spasm of ecstasy. Her muscles closed hard around his invading length, squeezing until she thought she heard him cry out himself, but then she felt the hot pulse of his release, and she lost what little awareness she'd managed to hold on to. For hours it seemed she balanced on the head of a pin, buffeted by wave after wave of pleasure. Her breath came in gasping pants, roughening a throat already raw from her hoarse cry of completion, and every inch of her trembled as if electricity really did course beneath her skin.

She finally collapsed on top of him, limp and breathless. Her hand had clenched so tightly in his hair that it took a minute to convince the fingers to stop spasming and let go. She heard him grunt and felt the whisper of his breath against her ear as he wrapped his brawny arms around her to cradle her against him. She folded her arms over his, savoring his warmth and the thick ropes of muscle that had enabled him to move her so effortlessly for his pleasure. Fighting back a shiver of remembrance, she turned her head to rest her cheek against his chest and rub kitten-like against his warm skin.

Sleep came back to claim her, and she struggled briefly to fight it off. As comfortable and sated as she felt, she had that nagging feeling in the back of her mind that told her something was out of place. Something she needed to pay attention to . . .

Grunting, her lover stretched his hand over the side of the bed and returned with the forgotten blankets, pulling them up over their still-joined bodies. Danice felt her muscles relax even further and sighed. Maybe whatever she had forgotten wasn't all that important after all.

He turned his head, brushing soft kisses over her forehead and her closed eyelids before he pressed his lips softly to hers in a tender, almost innocent, kiss. "Go to sleep," he murmured, shifting slightly beneath her. "We'll both still be here in the morning."

Well, since he put it that way . . .

Danice gave one last sigh, snuggled back into his embrace, and let sleep claim her. Whatever she needed to do, she could always do it in the morning.

Seventeen

She woke the moment he stirred from their sleepy cuddle. Her eyes flew open and that "something" she hadn't been able to remember last night became the only thought in her frantic mind.

Danice didn't have a lover, but she did have hormones that went haywire every time they spotted a certain half-human hottie. Which meant that all her carefully laid plans about avoiding an entangling sexual encounter with said hottie had gone up in a blaze of lust. Great.

Scrambling off the pile of muscle and testosterone she'd been draped over for the last God-knew-how-many hours, Danice grabbed the sheet to cover herself and turned on the man in her bed. He watched her through wary eyes the color of a stormy sea and sat up, bracing himself with his big hands against the cotton-covered mattress. A waterfall of thick, golden hair cascaded over his shoulders.

Memory came flooding back to her. The last week of relentless stress, the search for Rosemary, the journey to Faerie. The unfortunate experience of being taken captive by a bunch of Amazon warrior women and locked in the stone-walled dungeon of some magical castle. But after that last bit, things started to get a little fuzzy. When the hell had they ended up in bed together? In fact, were they still in the small prison cell she remembered? Had there been a bed in there last night?

And where the hell were her clothes?

"Am I supposed to apologize?" Mac asked, his voice deep and rough with sleep.

"Yes! I mean, no. I mean—" Danice blew a strand of hair out of her eyes and groaned. "Those bitches who locked us in here last night are the ones who ought to apologize. But what do you suppose the chances for that are?"

Mac pushed himself back to lean against the carved wooden headboard. "I'd say . . . not good."

She groaned again. "That's what I figured." She buried her face in her hands. "God, I was really, really trying to avoid this."

A hand settled on her shoulder and rubbed gently. Danice took comfort in the affectionate touch even though she told herself she needed to pull away, to put some distance between them.

"Why would you try to avoid this?" he asked. "I've been fantasizing about it for almost a week now. Since the first time I set eyes on you."

"Me, too," she admitted before she could stop herself. She yanked her hair, hoping the pain would shock some sense into her. "But that's no excuse! I hardly have sex with every guy I think is attractive. I'm supposed to have some self-control."

"Clearly, you do. Like I said, it took me all week to seduce you."

"I don't know if you can call it seduction when you took advantage of me in my sleep."

Mac dropped his hand, his features hardening to a stony mask. "Is that what happened? I took advantage?"

Danice shifted her gaze away uncomfortably. If she were being honest—with herself, as much as with him—she had to say no. The entire encounter had a dream-like feel to it, so that if she'd woken alone, she could have dismissed it as the work of an overactive and over-stimulated imagination. But she knew the truth: Mac might have initiated the sex, but she'd welcomed his advances. She'd been with him all the way.

Shame flooded her. "No. I'm sorry. I shouldn't have said that. I'm as much at fault as you are."

"See, I don't think either one of us is at fault." Mac reached out and seized the hand with which she'd begun picking at the embroidered duvet cover. " 'At fault' implies that we did something wrong, and I hope I'm not alone here when I say that what I felt seemed very, very right."

He lifted her hand to his mouth and brushed his lips against her skin. Danice shivered. The man could turn her mind to mush in about one-point-three seconds, flat.

"I don't mean we committed some kind of sin," she said, sighing, "just that it would have been better for both of us to keep this . . . this thing between us on a more professional level."

He nibbled the tip of her finger, eyeing her over it. "Is that how you view us? As colleagues?"

Danice squirmed. She wanted to attribute it to discomfort, but deep down she knew it had more to do with the fire he was already stoking deep in her belly.

"Well, we are working together to find Rosemary."

"True, but I hoped you had come to think of me as a friend. At the very least."

He scraped his teeth over the skin between her thumb and index finger and nearly made her eyes roll back in her head. When she could finally focus again, she gave him The Look.

"Mac, I have lots of friends. I have never had semiconscious sex while locked in a dungeon on an alternative plane of existence with any of them."

"I think that just shows a lack of imagination."

"Mac!"

Sighing, he reached out and grabbed hold of her, sheet and all, and bundled her up into his lap.

"Look," he said, meeting her mutinous gaze with a level one of his own. "I realize that these are not the ideal circumstances for us to have taken this kind of step, but life happened, as John Lennon said, while we were busy making other plans. Frankly, I was hoping for an actual date first. You know, dinner, some dancing, a little necking outside your apartment. But this is where we ended up, and while it's not precisely what I'd envisioned, I'm not going to pretend I'm sorry it happened."

"You're not sorry that Morag and the Ragettes took us prisoner and locked us in the dungeon?"

He squeezed her tighter. "You know what I mean."

"Yeah, and that's part of the problem. We shouldn't be here talking about sex or us or whether or not we have a relationship. We came to his godforsaken place with a job to do, and instead we're sitting here naked! I do not work naked!"

"And neither do I. But I think the problem here has less to do with us being naked together than it does with your inability to separate from your work."

"You say that like it's a bad thing."

He shook her gently. "That's because it is! We were locked in here overnight, Danice. What work on finding Rosemary were you planning to do? Were you going to check to make sure she wasn't hiding under the bed? Search the bathroom? We were stuck here. I think that by default that gave us permission to put aside business for a couple of hours."

Danice scrambled off his lap, taking her sheet with her. No way would she pace around this room naked in front of Mac. And she really needed to pace.

"That's no excuse for losing control of ourselves. We should at least have been having a discussion. Planning our next steps."

"In the ten seconds before we were knocked out with sleeping dust? Or after, while we were both unconscious?"

She shot him another Look. "Don't be sarcastic. I'm saying that we both have jobs to do, and I, at least, am not the sort of person to forget that. At least, not usually."

"I think that's obvious, given how upset you clearly are. But what I'd like to know is what's really making you so upset? Are you really such a workaholic that putting it aside for a couple of hours to get some sleep throws you into a tizzy? Or are you panicking over the fact that we had sex?"

Danice stared at him while her poor, overloaded brain tried to process his questions and come up with some sort of meaningful response. "Yes!"

Mac nodded slowly. "Okay, so there's more than one issue going on here. I'm glad, because I wouldn't like to think sleeping with me automatically causes a woman to lose control of her rational mind. At least, not once the sex is over."

"Don't joke," Danice groaned, dropping to sit on the small wooden stool in front of the fire. "I'm really not in a laughing mood."

"I can tell. So which did you want to deal with first?"

"Huh?"

"Which issue should we tackle first? Your stress over your job, or your stress over our relationship?"

Danice actually did laugh at that, which was odd, because she'd meant it about not being in the mood for humor. "You might think they're two separate issues, but for me it's all one big problem. I *am* a workaholic, Mac. I always have been. My job is the first priority in my life, so I don't have time for a relationship, even if I wanted one. Right now, all my time and attention are focused on my work. I'm this close to earning a partnership." She held up her thumb and forefinger, pinching them almost together to demonstrate. "I've worked for that for too long to let myself fail now. And I'm especially not going to let myself fail because I screwed up an assignment. So I need to find Rosemary and get her back to New York so I can finish my job."

"Why?"

Danice lifted her head and looked at Mac. Was he crazy? Had he not been listening to a word she said? "I told you, this assignment can make or break my career. If I get this done, that partnership at Parish Hampton is in the bag. I'll have it sewn up. But if I manage to screw this up because I let my attention wander elsewhere, they'll probably boot me out the door without so much as a *Have a nice life*. I can already feel the breeze on my backside."

"But why should that matter? You're a talented woman, Danice. I can't imagine you wouldn't find a position at another firm almost immediately. One that suits you a hell of a lot better than Parish Hampton."

"What's that supposed to mean?"

Mac shrugged. "Just what I said. Frankly, I don't know why you started working for those old boys to begin with."

"Those 'old boys' happen to be the most prestigious firm in Manhattan." She knew her tone probably sounded condescending, but she couldn't understand why he was questioning this.

"Sure, the most prestigious and the most conservative. The one about which all the greedy, dishonest lawyer jokes are written."

Danice drew herself up and glared at him. "I can't believe you'd stoop to throwing that kind of stereotype at my head. Do you really see me as greedy and dishonest?"

"No, which is why I never thought you belonged at Parish Hampton. You're too good for them, Niecie." He threw back the duvet and left the bed, striding toward her with a complete lack of modesty. "Tell me, why did you want to be a lawyer to begin with?"

Her jaw dropped. "Mac, you're naked!"

He shrugged and crouched in front of her. "If you're embarrassed, close your eyes." He took her hands in his. "Now, why did you decide to become a lawyer?"

Danice squeezed her eyes shut, but the damage was done. She could picture him, every inch of him, perfectly in her mind, from his tousled blond hair to his long bare feet. And all the delicious inches in between.

She swallowed hard and struggled to remember the question.

He squeezed her hands. "Why, Danice?"

She gave a self-conscious shrug. "Because I knew I'd be good at it. Because I like puzzles. And because I wanted to help people."

"Exactly. And instead of helping the people who need help the most, you're stuck chasing around heiresses whose families don't want to see their names get a little muddy. You could be doing so much more than that."

Danice opened her eyes, frowning. "That's sounding a little self-righteous, there, McIntyre. I don't think you get to judge my job or my decisions based on one roll in the hay."

"That's not what I'm basing anything on. And you know perfectly well that that's not all there is between us. You might want to tell yourself we're still strangers, but the truth is that I know you, Danice Carter, and I know that this job isn't making you happy. And neither will that partnership you keep trying to convince yourself you want."

"I do want it! I've worked hard for it, damn it, and I deserve it!"

She pulled her hands from his and stood, looking around for somewhere else to go. There wasn't anyplace. For a few minutes, she had forgotten that she was essentially trapped in a jail cell. As far as these things went, she supposed they could have been worse. In fact, considering some of the historical novels she had read over the years, she would say they could have been a lot worse.

Sure, the cell had walls about two feet thick, judging by what she had seen as they entered the castle, and the door looked to be about six inches thick, made from solid wood and banded together with metal straps about as fragile as tank armor. And yes, the one tiny window had bars blocking out any hope of escape, but at least it looked clean. And she could see no skeletons of former residents hanging from the wall by rusted manacles, so it had that going for it as well.

In fact, considering that a large fireplace took up most of one wall and a fire actually burned in its grate—blocked, of course, by a metal screen bolted solidly into the stone wall—the place could almost be considered cozy. As long as someone continued to stoke the fire from the opposite side of the wall and no members of the rodent family scurried out from under the bed, Danice figured she could have been kept prisoner in places far worse.

Of course, none of that mattered when she had this burning need to get away from Mac and his ridiculous theories about her and her future and what it would take to make her happy. Damn him! Her work *did* make her happy. She got a rush every time she won, every time she settled a case to her client's advantage, and every time she found the answer she'd been looking for, the precedent that proved her point and got her the win. She loved that!

And so what if there were moments when she wondered if the clients she was winning for really deserved it? She wasn't there to make value judgments; she was there to win cases. Her job might not include a lot of moral victories, but it wasn't like she was defending murderers and getting them off to walk the streets. She dealt with business and contract law, and God knew that if she didn't defend the interests of big corporations, there were a thousand other attorneys exactly like her, just waiting to step in and take her place. Someone would earn a partnership off the work she did for Parish Hampton, so why the hell shouldn't it be her?

"I never said you didn't deserve it," Mac said softly, dragging her attention back to him and away from her internal dialogue. "I just wondered whether or not you really, truly wanted it?"

Danice folded her arms across her chest in a posture she knew was defensive. She told herself it was just because she was cold in the stone-walled room. "That's not really your concern, now, is it?"

Before Mac could answer, Danice heard the sound of the bar outside the cell being lifted, and both she and Mac turned to face the exit just as the door swung open and the most beautiful woman Danice had ever seen glided into the room.

"Callahan, my darling boy! It has been too, too long since we've seen each other. Tell me where you've been! What you've been doing with yourself!"

The woman reached out and placed a hand on each of Mac's cheeks, pulling him toward her for a welcoming kiss. The gesture made both Mac and Danice stiffen, although Danice did notice that there was at least no passion in the gesture. It looked as perfunctory as a handshake.

Mac, however, did not look to be in a very friendly mood.

"Don't pretend to be interested in what I've been doing now. It's a little late for that, don't you think? And you should know exactly where I've been, shouldn't you? Since you're the one who left me there. Mother."

Eighteen

Tyra ni Oengus looked not a day older than the last time Mac had laid eyes on her. And considering he'd still been an infant at the time, that was saying something.

Or it would have said something, if Tyra were human, but as Mac could easily attest, his mother suffered from not a drop of humanity in her admittedly royal blood. If she had normal human feelings, she might have felt some regret at abandoning her only son to his father's care and never sparing him another thought. Luckily for Mac, his father had loved him enough for any child.

Unluckily, his Fae memory had never managed to dim the sight of Tyra's face, no matter how he tried. Over the years, he'd tried to file it away as his cross to bear, a strange quirk of his mixed heritage. He hadn't expected the welling of rage that threatened to overcome him the next time he saw that face, thirty-four years later.

"Oh, Callahan, my darling, don't say you're angry with me," Tyra pouted, the expression enhancing rather than detracting from her beauty. "It's been so long. Surely you can learn to forgive me."

He gripped her wrists and forced her hands from his

face. He couldn't bear her touch a second longer. "I wouldn't count on that, Mother."

Behind him, he heard a choking sound. He turned to see an expression of wild disbelief on Danice's face.

"Mother?" she sputtered. "This is your *mother*?" She clutched the sheet tighter around her, and Mac thought he detected a faint flush of rose coloring her skin from her collarbone to her hairline. She fixed him with a pointed stare and hissed, "Mac, you're not wearing any clothes!"

Mac glanced down at his nude body. He'd forgotten about that. Looking from Danice to his mother, he shrugged. "It's not as if either of you has never seen a naked man before."

Tyra laughed, the sound like chiming bells, while Danice sounded as if a dying frog had taken up residence in her throat. He didn't have to debate over which rang more like music in his ears.

"Mac, she's. Your. Mother!"

Mac shook his head. Sometimes he forgot how prudish human women could be. He reached for his jeans, which had been tossed to the floor sometime overnight, and stepped into them.

"Is that better?" he asked, buttoning up the fly.

"Marginally," she growled.

"Callahan, darling," Tyra interrupted, stepping forward to eye Danice with blatant speculation. "Aren't you going to introduce me to your friend?"

"Frankly, I'd rather not."

"Callahan!" Tyra scolded.

Danice just gasped out an affronted, "Mac!"

Mac frowned at her. "Don't look like that, Niecie. It

has nothing to do with you. I just don't like my mother very much, and I see no reason to inflict her company on you. You've had a rough enough morning as it is."

Tyra appeared to ignore the insult. "Oh, it isn't morning yet, my love. It's still at least an hour before dawn, but I was only just informed of your presence here at court, so of course I came to see you immediately."

"Of course," Mac drawled.

Tyra turned to Danice. "How are you, my darling girl? Did my son say your name was Nee Cee?"

"Danice," she corrected. "Danice Carter. I'm, ah, pleased to meet you."

Mac stepped between the two women before Danice could offer to shake hands. "And now that we all know each other, why don't you tell me what you want, *Mother*?"

He couldn't stop himself from emphasizing the title. It was one Tyra had never wanted, but he'd be damned if he'd let her pretend their relationship was anything else. At least not to his face. Besides, Tyra ni Oengus was notoriously vain. It would rankle to be constantly reminded of her adult son, despite her immortality. Even the Fae disliked growing old, and they especially feared the loss of their looks.

"Why, to see you, of course." She batted her lashes at him. They grew thick and long around eyes the color of stormy seas, dark despite the bright gold of her hair. He had inherited her coloring, but not, he liked to think, any of her spirit. "How could I resist the chance to lay eyes on my darling boy after so many years?"

"You've managed well enough before now."

Danice drew in a sharp breath, but Tyra only laughed.

"Oh, you're still angry with me, aren't you? You dear boy." Tyra laid a hand on his arm, her skin pale and glowing like moonlight, her long, slender fingers decorated with shining silver and glittering jewels. "Of course you are. But only tell me what I can do to make your feel better? Anything you'd like! You have only to ask."

Instinct and logic urged Mac to refuse, to inform her that she had nothing to offer to him that would interest him in the least. She had lost her chance to make up to him decades ago, and now he wanted nothing to do with her.

He didn't, but Danice's hand at his back reminded him of where he was, and why he'd come. Maybe his mother could prove useful at last. For the first time in either of their lives.

"Maybe you *can* help, Mother," he said, folding his arms over his chest and meeting her calculating gaze. She stood nearly as tall as he did, so he had a good view of the woman behind the bright Fae facade. "Danice and I came to Winter Home in the hope of making contact with someone, which we can't very well do from this cell in Dionnu's dungeon. If you could have us freed and gain us permission to talk to whomever we need to talk to, it would go a long way toward . . . softening my feelings toward you."

Mac watched the cold intellect in his mother's eyes as she processed his request. He doubted that she cared much one way or the other how he felt about her, but she wouldn't want the rest of court to see how little her son cared for her. It would be one thing if she were seen to reject him; after all, he was just a mutt. A half-human mistake. The evidence of a night of poor judgment on her part. At least, that was how the Fae would see it. But if he publically renounced her, that would be a different matter entirely. The Fae were convinced of their own superiority. They would not take kindly to a human looking down on one of their own. So how much did Tyra want to preserve her reputation?

And could she possibly get anything else out of making things easier for him while Mac and Danice were in Faerie?

Because that, Mac knew, would be the bottom line. How would helping Mac end up helping Tyra?

He watched her eyes narrow for an instant as she made her decision. Then they opened again, wide and guileless. Provided you didn't look just a little too closely.

"Of course, my darling boy," Tyra gushed, smiling like some kind of benevolent goddess granting a boon to her mortal subject. Which probably summed up at least part of how she viewed it. "Consider it done! In fact, I will arrange that tonight's feast be held in your honor. Nothing but the best for my dearest Callahan."

"Right." Not like she was laying it on a little thick, or anything.

"But first, let me see to the essentials. You and your companion can hardly be seen looking less than your best." She waved her hands at them to follow her and led the way out of the cell and down the corridor to a flight of stairs. The guards outside the door uttered not a word of protest.

Danice, on the other hand, tried to rip his arm off when he attempted to lead her from the room.

"Are you crazy?" she hissed, clutching the bedsheet to her chest like an armored breastplate. "It was bad enough for your mother to see me like this, but there is no way on God's earth or this one that I am going to parade my naked ass around this castle for the whole world to see!"

Mac felt his mouth twitch. "But it's such a pretty ass." He held up his hands and took a step back when it looked as if she might rip his heart out with her bare hands. Clearly, she wasn't amused. Nor was she kidding about her self-consciousness.

He leaned his head out the door. "Mother?"

Tyra stopped halfway down the hall and raised an eyebrow. "What is it, dearest?"

"Danice doesn't feel comfortable walking through the palace without her clothes," he explained, raising his voice to carry above her snarl. "You'll have to give us a moment for her to dress."

"Oh." Tyra displayed the normal reaction of the Fae when confronted with human modesty—complete lack of understanding. "Well, there's no need for that. As I said, there will be a feast tonight, and I doubt either of you dressed in anything remotely suitable. Did you?"

Mac thought about what constituted "suitable" for a feast into Winter Home's great hall, and shook his head.

"I thought not," Tyra said. "So it would be silly to waste time dressing in your old clothes. I'll have new ones sent to your room."

Considering the matter settled, the Fae woman turned to continue to the stairs.

Mac sighed. "Mother. That's all well and good, but it doesn't change the fact that at the moment, Danice is not dressed and doesn't want to be seen on the way to wherever it is we're going."

"Oh. Well, why didn't you say that in the first place, silly darling?" Tyra laughed. "That is easy enough to handle."

And with a clap of her hands, the sidhe woman magicked all three of them out of the dungeons and into a sumptuously appointed guest chamber somewhere on the grounds of the enormous castle.

"There. Is that better?" she demanded, her animated expression clearly indicating that she would not understand if either of them said no. "You darlings can stay right here. There's a private bathing room just through that door there, and I'll have suitable clothing sent up immediately. And I'll also make sure that no one disturbs you, if you two feel the need for more . . . sleep."

Her sly look and smirking smile possessed all the subtlety of a cricket bat to the side of the head. Mac felt Danice stiffen beside him. He reached out to take her hands, squeezing her fingers tightly.

"That's fine, Mother. We'll see you this evening, then."

Tyra smiled wider, the expression reminding Mac of a fox in the door of a henhouse. "Of course you will, darling boy. And I assure you, I'm already looking forward to the pleasure."

Then she gave another clap of her hands and disappeared from sight.

Mac turned and watched as Danice sank to the edge of the bed, still holding on to the sheet like a security blanket. She looked exhausted and numb, or maybe that was forlorn. Either way, he didn't like it.

"So, uh, that was my mother," he said dumbly, shoving his hands into the pockets of his jeans. "We don't get

along very well. We haven't really spent any time together since I was a baby."

"You're kidding."

She didn't even bother to look at him.

"I'm sorry she just barged in on us like that. I never
expected we'd run into her while we were here. I honestly don't know what made her decide to come looking
for me when she heard the Guard had locked us up."

At least that made her lift her chin and look at him.
"Do you really think that your mother is our biggest
problem at the moment?"

He struggled to read her expression. "You did seem
kind of upset about meeting her."

"No, actually, if you'll remember, I was upset before
she waltzed in on us having an argument," she pointed
out. "While naked."

She really did sound upset about the nudity thing.
Mac made a mental note to remember that in the future. He preferred not to see her upset. Though, at the
moment, just being in the same room with him seemed
to be enough to upset her.

"I wouldn't really call it arguing," he hedged. "We
were having a discussion."

"You were questioning my moral integrity."

"No, I wasn't!" Mac scrambled to remember what
he'd said that could have given her that idea. "I was
questioning whether or not you were happy at your job!
I didn't say a single word about your integrity." He
stepped toward her, instinctively wanting to put his arms
around her and know she couldn't just up and disappear
on him.

"Danice, I think you're probably the most moral

person I've ever met," he assured her, reaching out tentatively to grasp her shoulders. She didn't exactly step into his embrace, but neither did she jerk away and order him to keep his hands off her. At the moment he'd take what he could get. "I never intended to make you think I doubted that. I just wanted you to think for a minute about what your job is really worth to you."

She stared at a spot on his shoulder, studiously avoiding his gaze. "Whatever it's worth to me isn't the point right now. I said I would do a job, and I don't walk out on that kind of promise. When I say I'll do something, I do it."

"And I don't doubt that for a second," he said. "But just stop and think for a minute. That incredible determination of yours has landed you in a bit of a tough spot, don't you think? I mean, what was your assignment originally? To interview Rosemary and get the information you need to file your boss's lawsuits, right? Where in that description does it say you had to track her down to another dimension and put yourself in danger by following her there?"

Danice jerked herself from his grip and glared at him. "You're the one who told me you thought she might be being held captive here! When I heard that, was I supposed to throw up my hands and walk away? Oh sorry, but she's out of my jurisdiction now. She's someone else's problem!"

Mac tried to think of something to say, but it seemed like every time he opened his mouth, exactly the wrong thing came out, at least by Danice's standards. Before he could decide on the safest tactic, she closed her eyes and blew out a huge breath, her shoulders collapsing as the tension drained out of her.

"You know what? I'm sorry," she said, hitching her blanket up higher and offering him a wry half smile. "I shouldn't be yelling at you. Especially since I'm not really sure why I am. You haven't done anything to deserve it. It—" She sighed and shook her head. "I'm just going to put it down to stress. I think I'm under just a little too much stress right now."

Mac saw the confusion and embarrassment warring in her eyes and felt himself melt. He wanted to be able to wrap her up in tissue paper and put her on a shelf somewhere to keep her safe. And he admired the hell out of the fact that he knew if he tried, she'd knee him in the balls and take care of things her own damned self. That was just the woman Danice was. It was the reason why he knew very well she needed to come along with him to look for Rosemary. The essence of Danice would allow nothing less.

"Don't apologize," he murmured, wrapping his arms around her and snuggling her close. "I'm the one who started the argument, and I don't know what I was thinking. You're a big girl. You're more than capable of deciding what makes you happy and going out and getting it. So, I'm sorry, too."

He took it as evidence of how stressed out Danice really was that she was sniffling when she pulled back to smile up at him. The smile she gave him sagged a little in one corner, but it was a smile. He'd take it.

"I didn't think I'd have any trouble with this," she confessed, leaning her head against his shoulder and sneaking her arms around his back. "I told myself it was nothing. After all, I knew about all this Others stuff; I've known for almost a year. If I could take vampires and werewolves and shapeshifters and all the rest of it, what did I have to be nervous about with some little ol' fairies?" She huffed a kind of a half laugh. "Then I crawled through that itty, bitty space, got taken captive by a horde of supermodels with bad attitudes, got magically forced into sleep, fell into bed with a man I've known for a week, and woke up to find myself face-to-face with his estranged mother. You know what, Mac? I think this particular mighty has finally done fallen."

Mac smoothed his hand over the tangle of her hair. He had a vague recollection of freeing it from its braids last night, and he loved the thick, heavy feel of it in his hands. He stroked it as he tried to digest being lumped in with the events that had set off her temper earlier.

"I admit we haven't known each other for a long time," he finally said, "but I hope you're not feeling all that bad about the falling-into-bed part. After all, you didn't land alone. I fell right along with you."

She pulled back and smiled up at him. "Don't worry, Mac. That particular fall was the one enjoyable part of this whole experience. I'm just—" She wrinkled her nose and made a face at herself. "I just still need a little time to process . . . everything."

He leaned down and pressed a kiss to her forehead. Something inside him shifted in dissatisfaction with her answer. From the beginning, he'd acknowledged that this woman called to him in a way he'd never experienced before, but now he wondered if there might be even more to his feelings than that magnetic attraction. It had upset him to have her meet his mother, to see what kind of woman he had come from, to expose her to the Fae's instinctive machinations. Would he have cared about that if he weren't already a little . . . a little *in love* with this woman?

And if that was the case, then why would he be satisfied with being the best part of a bad experience? He wouldn't be. He would want to know that she felt the same way about him that he did about her. No way could he settle for any less.

He smoothed the frown from his expression as he felt her shift and pull away from him.

"You know what else I need right now?" she asked, her grin turning teasing. Mac shook his head. "A shower. I feel like a red-hot mess. Didn't your mother say there was a bathroom around here?"

Mac summoned a leer and grabbed one end of her sheet, tugging playfully. "Yes, but the Fae aren't much for showers. They're more a long, leisurely, sensual soak in the tub sort. Which I'll be happy to demonstrate for you. Right this way, madam."

Danice laughed and hurried ahead of him through the door he indicated. Mac followed more slowly, forcing the uncertainties from his mind. At the moment, he would much rather concentrate on more pleasant thoughts.

And, he decided, as he joined Danice in the bathing room and shut the door behind him, turning those very pleasant thoughts into even more pleasant actions.

Nineteen

If there was one area other than the law at which Danice excelled, it was the fine art of denial. Even she, however, had to strive for new heights of achievement in order to pretend that the events of the previous night and earlier that morning had not, in fact, actually happened. It took every ounce of her God-given talent, but she'd be damned if she didn't pull it off.

"This is what your mother considers suitable?" she asked Mac with a laugh after they were dressed and preparing to leave their room. She swept a hand over the flowing gown of blues and greens—accented with sapphires, if you could believe it—that Tyra had sent for her to wear during the day. Apparently, another outfit would be provided for the feast later that evening. "What does she think we have planned for today? Entertaining the sultan of Dubai?"

Mac smoothed a self-conscious hand over his midnight-blue silk shirt and shrugged. "To my mother, these are probably considered what you wear to dig around in the garden. *Down to earth* has never been a phrase widely used to describe her."

Danice stifled a snort. "I'd never have guessed. And I suppose she goes hiking in these shoes." She hitched up her skirts to admire the delicate silver slippers she wore to match.

"If it ever occurred to her to go hiking, I have no doubt that's exactly what she would wear."

She laughed. "By the way, we haven't had time to sit down yet and go over our game plan."

"Game plan?"

"Yeah, you know. How we're going to go about finding out who hired you and seeing if he got someone else to bring Rosemary to him." She made a face. "Somehow after our reception last night, I'm guessing just strolling up to people and asking if they've seen a stray human around—other than me—wouldn't be the best strategy."

"Well, my original plan involved beating the information out of Quigley—"

"Surprisingly, I'm no longer nearly as opposed to that idea as I suspect I would have been forty-eight hours ago."

"—but since that no longer appears to be possible, I'm afraid the choices become somewhat limited."

"In what way?"

"You're right about the fact that questioning random Fae would be more likely to get us thrown back into the dungeon than to further our investigations," he said with a grimace. "The Fae are a suspicious lot, and the Unseelie Court are more suspicious than most. Probably because of all the intrigue and power grabbing that goes on around here. If word got back to the king that a changeling and a human were poking their noses into court business, we would be thinking positively if all we expected was incarceration and torture."

Danice winced. "Doesn't sound like the king around here has much of a sense of humor."

"Oh, as much as your average serial killer, I think."

"Fun."

"Yeah, so canvassing the neighborhoods, so to speak, is out."

"Then what else can we try?"

She could practically see Mac wrestling with his answer, his reluctance to share the obvious idea.

"Come on, spit it out. As long as it doesn't involve locking me away somewhere safe while you beat your manly chest for clues, I promise to give it a fair hearing."

Mac winced. "It's not that. It has nothing to do with you. I was just hoping not to have to go there."

"Where is there?"

"I might not have grown up in Faerie, but I do have relatives here," he admitted cautiously. "Not all of them are quite as bad as Tyra."

"Meaning?"

"Meaning, there may be one or two willing to point us in the right direction without asking us to sign away our souls in exchange."

"Wow," Danice breathed, studying his expression carefully. "You really don't like these people much, do you?"

"It's not a matter of liking or disliking them," he said. "The issue is that I don't trust them." He must have read the confusion in her face, because he sighed and seemed to brace himself for what he was about to say. "Look, the Fae are fundamentally different from humans. I don't know if it's a result of the immortality, or if it's just some fatal design flaw, but they—most of them, anyway—they don't think in human terms. With the Fae, right and wrong are not absolutes. There's no black and white here. For them, everything is just one of a billion shades of gray. They don't share that human sense of conscience."

"Are you telling me that these people are evil?" she asked, fighting back the welling panic. "That we just got ourselves trapped in some kind of devil's lair?"

"No, of course not. I never meant to make you think that. It's not that they all go around looking to harm everyone they come across. It's more like . . ." He paused and frowned thoughtfully. "It's more like the Fae take self-interest to the next level. The Fae are just . . . inherently selfish. They judge the world by what it can give them, by how they can achieve pleasure, or status, or amusement. Especially here at the Winter Court. I'm not trying to tell you that everyone you meet here will be out to get you; just that they probably will all be out to help themselves first."

Danice opened her mouth to issue her usual smart-mouthed retort. Like how maybe she should give up her plans to build a vacation home here. Something stopped her, though. She looked into Mac's face, and she could see his unease. She could see how uncomfortable it made him to tell her all this, and for the first time, she wondered about what it meant to him to be linked to this place by blood and nothing else.

She tilted her head as she gazed up at him. "Is that what your mother is like?"

He barked out a short laugh. "Oh, my mother is a prime example. She could be the poster child for the Fae sense of morality. But she's not really important. I'm just telling you this so that you'll understand that just because I introduce someone to you as family, it doesn't mean that person will necessarily be on our side, okay? In Faerie, you always have to watch what you say, no matter who you're talking to. Even if you think that person is your best friend."

Danice shrugged and reached out to take his hand, the first time she'd reached out to him since they got to this mixed-up place. She laced their fingers together and smiled up at him, letting the tiniest fraction of her feelings for him—the ones she refused to allow herself to think about—to shine through.

"Don't worry," she said, squeezing his hand. "I promise that the only person I'll trust here in Faerie is you."

He raised her hand to his lips. "I think I'm going to be glad that you've decided to trust me at all."

"I've always trusted you," she blurted out, surprised to find it felt like the truth. She hadn't realized that over the past few days, she'd come to rely on Mac completely, for everything from advice about what to do next, to guidance on how to take those next steps. Admittedly, they might have ended up in a bit of a predicament here in Faerie, but even now, she knew in her bones that she could rely on him. That, even if he couldn't get both of them out of the situation, he'd stay by her side for as long as she was in it. And really, what more could she ask of him? Of anyone?

"I do trust you," she repeated, more definitely this time. "So lead on, MacDuff. Which of your favorite aunts or uncles should we go see first?"

Mac reached out to pull open the chamber door, and

whatever he'd been about to suggest never managed to make it past his lips. And what made it past Danice's lips really wasn't something she felt comfortable sharing. Frankly, if it hadn't been for shock, she liked to think she never would have said it at all.

Standing just on the other side of the door, Morag and her Unmerry Women ranged across the exit in a wall of smug dislike. The head of the King's Guard even had the audacity to shake her finger at the two of them like a scolding schoolmarm.

"Ah-ah," the Fae woman tutted. "Lady Tyra might have moved the two of you to a more comfortable room, but don't mistake the fact that both of you are still prisoners of the king. At least until he says otherwise."

Danice frowned. "But Tyra arranged to have us released and to gain us the right to move around Faerie however we needed to accomplish our work."

Mac cursed beneath his breath. "Correction: She promised those things. That doesn't mean she actually got them done. Or even remembered to bother trying." He looked at Danice, his expression apologetic. "I'm sorry, but it would be just like her to decide how she wanted things to be and then completely forget to inform anyone else—like the king or the King's Guard—of her plans."

"That's hardly your fault," she assured him, turning back to Morag. "But I'm sure there must be a way to clear this all up. I don't think either of us is really enough of a threat to anyone to justify keeping us as prisoners."

"I'm afraid that's not your decision, human."

To Danice, the guardswoman sounded about as regretful as Ted Bundy.

"Then tell me whose decision it is, and we can go talk to them."

Morag's smile widened. As a direct consequence, Danice's stomach dropped. It was not a pleasant smile.

"As it happens," the Fae said, "that is precisely the reason we're here. The Guard has come to escort you both to meet just the official with that kind of authority. You've been summoned to an audience."

Oh, yeah. *Not pleasant* didn't even begin to cover this.

Danice turned her head to look up at Mac. His face looked as if it had been sculpted in marble, all hard planes and sharp edges. If she had to make a wager at the moment, she would have laid every last cent in her bank accounts that his stomach had taken a similar plunge to hers. Both of them currently rested about one floor below the rest of their bodies.

Even before she opened her mouth to ask the question, Danice feared she already knew the answer.

"An audience with whom?"

Mac's voice answered, his tone tight and clipped as it formed exactly the words Danice had not wanted to hear.

"With the king."

Twenty

Having never before traveled with an armed guard, Danice could see that in other circumstances, she might have enjoyed the experience. In this case, she wanted to give every single one of said guards the wedgie of her life. Too bad they all carried enough weaponry to make rebel insurgents look like Girl Scouts.

Mac had remained curiously silent on the trip through a mind-numbing number of identical corridors, his eyes straight ahead as he marched in time to their improvised chain-less gang. Again, Danice spent most of her time wishing she could read his mind. She had begun to understand that Mac's veneer of charm really was a mask he wore to prevent anyone from seeing the deeper feelings that lay beneath. She knew now that when everything was normal, the man could chat like a magpie, but when he went silent, it really was time to worry.

For her own part, Danice kept quiet by default. The only member of the present company she was willing to exchange more than barbed insults with was the one who'd clammed up tighter than the CIA, so instead she concentrated on taking in the scenery. Until the guards escorted them into the throne room. At that point, she simply lost the ability to speak.

She had never seen anything like it.

Hell, she'd never imagined anything like it, and Danice had a first-rate imagination.

First of all, the room was enormous; the New York Giants could easily host home games inside the walls. With room for fans to gather and watch. Maybe even to tailgate. She would never have guessed at the size before the doors opened. After all, they looked a lot like the doors to the room Tyra had put her and Mac in, if more elaborately decorated. They stood about eight feet high in a corridor whose ceilings—like those of all the others they had passed through—went up maybe twelve to fifteen feet. Not until they stepped through and into the vast chamber did the space soar (easily two additional stories) into the air before losing itself in darkness. For all Danice knew, the thing could rise another ten stories above that. She could only say that the proportions of the place seemed designed to make anyone who entered it feel like an insignificant speck in a universe beyond ken.

Which, she imagined, was precisely the idea.

The room wasn't just larger than Danice had expected, it also presented a vastly different image from what she had pictured. When Morag had informed them they would be having an audience with the king, she had pictured something out of Buckingham Palace, or maybe Versailles. (Okay, she'd never been to either of those places, but she'd seen pictures of the homes of royalty before, and they didn't look like this.) She'd expected elaborate moldings and gilded furniture and portraits of ancestors so ugly that you wondered how they'd ever managed to reproduce. But the Unseelie throne room looked nothing like that.

It could have been a cave. For a wild moment, Danice wondered if she'd forgotten descending a stairway or five on the walk from their room, but she knew she hadn't. They couldn't possibly be underground, but the arch of natural rock walls overhead, the pillars bearing more than a slight resemblance to stalagmites, the uneven surface of the floor, all of those things painted a convincing enough picture to make her doubt her own senses. She could even swear that she heard the squeaking and chirping of bats from the darkness hanging over them.

Torches mounted on the pillars and walls at slightly-too-distant intervals provided a wan light, elevating the atmosphere from inky to dim. Enough light to see by, but not enough to move without caution. Overhead, chandeliers (real ones, the kind filled with candles, not light-bulbs, and made of metal, not crystal) seemed to float in midair, offering marginally more flickering illumination. Actually, Danice admitted to herself, she guessed they really were floating in midair, since she could see nothing supporting them from either above or below, and they were, after all, in Faerie. Here, she reminded herself, magic just happened.

Surprise had halted her steps just inside the door as she turned her head this way and that trying to take in the scene. Morag and her gal pals, though, seemed disinclined to allow either of their prisoners time to gawk. A hand in the middle of her back shoved Danice forward, sending her stumbling her first few steps into the room. When she turned around to glare, the self-satisfied smirk on Catrin's face left little doubt of the assault's origin.

Glaring back, Danice flipped her middle finger at the woman. It might not mean anything in Faerie, but it gave Danice a sense of personal satisfaction. At least temporarily.

At first, as they made their way into the chamber, Danice thought it must be empty. The king, she assumed, wanted to keep them waiting to remind them of his authority, and so that they would be suitably alert when he decided to make his grand entrance. It was a tactic the senior partners used often on newer and younger members of the staff. But when they passed the first set of pillars, she peered toward the far end of the room and saw what looked like a huge, flat-topped boulder positioned in the middle of the central space. On it, she could make out several objects like chairs, two large ones in the center, flanked on each side by a smaller one, more like a stool than a chair. The ones in the center undoubtedly functioned as thrones.

They walked closer, Danice silent as she tried to absorb the sights and sounds around her, Mac for reasons of his own. Ones she really wished he would share with her. They'd become oddly close in the short period of their acquaintance, but she wanted to remind him that that didn't mean she knew everything he did. For instance, she had no idea what to expect here; she knew nothing about the customs of Faerie, let alone the customs pertaining to the nobility of Faerie. Knowing her luck, she'd wish the king a good morning and not find

out until she watched her own head roll off the guillo-
tine that doing so was considered a grave insult at the
Unseelie Court.

In other words, it would really help if he would talk
to her just now.

Danice glared in Mac's direction, and either it had
no impact on him at all, or he had just decided to ignore it. Since that didn't work, she moved on to clearing her throat. Pointedly.

And again.

"Cease making that disgusting noise, human," Catrin barked from just over Danice's right shoulder.
"You'll offend the king's ears. And even if you don't,
you're offending mine."

Danice ignored her.

"Mac," she hissed, leaning slightly toward him. "Now
would be a really good time to fill me in on our game
plan. You know, for dealing with the king?"

He didn't even glance at her. "We don't have one."

"Say huh?"

Mac stared straight ahead, his eyes already locked
on the figure lounging in the left-hand throne. "We
don't have a game plan for this. We were going to avoid
the king, remember?"

"Yes, well, that strategy seems fraught with problems right about now. So how about plan B?"

"Plan B was to run like hell for the nearest gate back
to the city."

Danice let her head fall backward so she stared up
into the ceiling and groaned. "So then, we're just going
to stand here like we're screwed and not worry about it?"

"Oh, I'm going to worry about it," he assured her,

gaze focused straight ahead. "But we are just screwed. Sorry."

"Great. There go my visions of you as a dashing romantic hero."

"Yeah. Sorry about that."

The guardswomen continued to prod them forward, Morag leading the way to the odd natural dais at the end of the room. The closer they came to the thrones, the better a look Danice got at the figure seated there, and the more her skin began to crawl.

She couldn't define precisely why, but something about the Unseelie king made the tiny hairs on the back of her neck stand up. Not to mention the ones on her arms. Hell, if she didn't wax religiously, she'd bet the hair on her legs would stand up, too. And this reflex had very little to do with the kind of electricity she felt every time she got near Mac; this was the kind of thing she imagined a rabbit felt when it looked into the eyes of a predator. Being in the presence of this particular Fae gave Danice a very keen sense of her own mortality.

Nothing about his outward appearance could explain the blaring of her internal alarms. He dressed all in black, from the shimmering material of his tunic-like shirt, to the leathery sheen of his trousers, but Danice was from Manhattan where black was practically a uniform. The king—Dionnu, she thought Mac had called him—was an incredibly handsome man, with the kind of unearthly beauty Danice was coming to expect from the Fae. Human models and actors might have beauty that could take a person's breath away. Mac had that; just looking at him sometimes made Danice want to jump on him. But the Fae took perfection of form to a whole new level.

Every one of their features matched its mate with perfect symmetry. Every patch of skin looked smoother, every woman more feminine, every man more stunning. Even their hair and eye colors were somehow *more*. The Fae weren't just blonds or brunettes; their hair was silver or gold, jet or mahogany.

Dionnu had hair as black as obsidian and skin as pale and rich as cream. Despite his lazy seated pose, Danice estimated he stood over six feet tall, with the kind of lean, deceptive strength of a long-distance runner. His dark hair curled in loose waves over his collar, framing the perfection of his face, from the high, noble brow to the sharply defined jaw and slightly pointed chin. He possessed a strong nose and two blades for cheekbones that only served to draw attention to a mouth almost hypnotic in its sensuality. He appeared no more than thirty, younger even than Mac, except for his eyes.

His eyes were ancient, black, and empty, like the eyes of a snake. Or like looking down into an endless pit. Or up into the dark, blank nothingness above his throne. The longer Danice looked into those eyes, the colder she could feel herself growing. A shiver finally shook through her, and the reflexive motion knocked her gaze away from him.

Dionnu saw it, and the corner of his mouth quirked in amusement. The amusement of a Roman emperor watching his lions feast on martyred Christians. Immediately he dismissed her and turned his stare on Mac.

"My guards informed me I had uninvited guests in my castle, but I thought they told me one of you was a half-breed," he drawled, his eyes raking over Mac's steady form. "I suppose I expected something a little more obviously . . . special."

Mac didn't utter a word. He gazed back at the king, his eyes steady and his back straight. Danice didn't know how he did it, how he could bear to look into those eyes. She had to settle for watching a spot over the Fae's left shoulder, though she was glad when he spoke to Mac, because then she had an excuse to look at the change-ling instead. That quieted some of the voices in her head, the ones screaming at her to run.

"Who did you say this mutt belonged to?" Dionnu asked Morag, his tone casual, his gaze never moving from Mac's face.

"Didn't she tell you, Your Majesty?" a feminine, uncomfortably familiar voice asked from somewhere in the darkness behind the throne. "The boy is my son. A bit of a youthful indiscretion on my part."

A shadow parted from the others and shifted forward until the light hit it and Danice recognized the face of Mac's mother. Tyra wore blue, the color of midnight, shot through with silver thread and spangled with glittering jewels so that it appeared as if she'd wrapped herself in the night sky. Her golden hair had been pulled back to cascade in shimmering waves behind her, and atop her shining head she wore a small circlet of silver, intricately worked to appear like a crown of snowflakes upon her brow.

She moved to stand beside Dionnu's throne, pressing herself against the side and wrapping her arms around the top corner as if to embrace it, or the man it seated.

Dionnu turned his head to smirk at her and held out

a cool, elegant hand. "Really, my sweet. I thought you had better taste than to consort with a human. Just look what it got you—a mongrel brat. And a troublemaking one, at that."

Tyra placed her hand in the king's, and Danice wondered that their skin didn't clink together like ice cubes. Even when Dionnu brushed a kiss over the back of the woman's fingers, there was no warmth in the gesture. Oh, it gave the appearance of intimacy between them, which is what she supposed he wanted, but Danice didn't see any sparks there. Ambition and greed apparently could attract two people together into a kind of icy passion. Just the thought of it brought on another shiver.

She snuck a glance at Mac, who watched the couple above them with a coolly remote expression of his own. She couldn't tell what he was thinking, but she could see the tic of the muscle in his jaw and knew he must be fighting back some strong emotion. She wanted to reach out to him, but thought better of it. The king would likely read it as a sign of weakness, and that was the last thing she would willingly convey to this man.

"Tell me, my star," Dionnu continued, looking back at Mac. "What do you call it?"

"Then or now?"

Mac finally spoke, and Danice felt a surge of pride at his steady voice and the tone of utter boredom he managed to convey. Unlike Dionnu, though, his disinterest came encased not in ice but in obvious disdain.

"Now, I believe she's taken to calling me Callahan," he continued, "which is my father's name. But in the beginning she didn't bother to call me anything. Whoever dropped me off on my father's doorstep—and I hesitate to assume she performed such a meaningless task herself—left a note with what my father thought must be my name, so he adapted it as best he could for me to use. Too bad I was legally McIntyre by the time I realized that all the note had said was that I was the son or daughter of Tyra. 'Mac. Ni. Tyra.' One or the other. I doubt she bothered to check."

Danice listened to the king's laughter while sickness welled up in her stomach. That was how Mac had come by his unusual name? She'd assumed it must be a family name—something passed down from a previous generation, a connection to a beloved or revered ancestor. Not a misreading of the callousness of the woman who had abandoned him. It boggled her mind that any woman could be so heartless that she didn't even bother to communicate the sex of her own child to the father on whose doorstep she had dropped him.

Thankful that the folds of her dress concealed the way her hands had clenched into fists, Danice concentrated on battling back the urge to hop up onto the stone platform and smack the pretty right off Tyra's face. Only the knowledge that the guards surrounding her would probably interpret her actions as a threat to their king and gut her before she even got close managed to stop her. And still, her fingers itched to dish out some punishment.

"My father calls me Mac, though," he said, a hint of pride creeping into his voice. "And since I'm happy to be *his* son, I call myself Mac Callahan. I don't care in the slightest what you call me. Neither of you means enough to me for me to be bothered."

"Now, don't be grumpy, my darling boy," Tyra chided.

"If you're mean to me, I might decide not to plead your case in front of His Majesty. And he can be so severe on those caught trespassing on his lands. What was it that happened to the last one, my love?"

"Oh, let's don't waste time threatening the children, my sweet," Dionnu said, waving his hand in dismissal. "After all, these miscreants are not the only game in town. My hunters are standing by, eager to resume the chase for the prey who slipped past us yesterday."

Somehow, Danice got the impression that the "prey" Dionnu hunted didn't run on four feet and grow antlers. The longer she stood in the presence of the king and his mistress, the more she began to understand and even appreciate Mac's attitude toward his mother.

No, actually, the Fae female didn't even deserve that title. Toward the woman who had given him birth. And honestly, Danice thought even that was giving the creature too much credit.

"Let us get right to the point." Dionnu dropped Tyra's hand and leaned forward on his throne, bracing his elbows on his knees and steepling his fingers together beneath his chin. "By what right have you intruded on my court, McIntyre Callahan? What business could you possibly have in Faerie, a place you have never had claim to before?"

Mac answered calmly, his impassive expression never shifting. "I never intended to intrude on your court. I was brought here along with my companion against our will. Your guardswomen discovered us in the forest and took us prisoner, although I confess that none of what I know of Faerie convinces me they had any right. I was under the impression that until the hinge swings at Samhain, the rule of law rightly belongs to Mab and the Summer Throne."

That last statement seemed to affect Dionnu like a slap to the face. At the sound of the name, one that meant little to Danice, his lips curled and his hands fisted and he hissed like a Hollywood vampire just doused with holy water. Beside him, Tyra stepped forward, rage twisting her features for a split second before she schooled them again into a mask of haughty amusement.

"That was very naughty of you, my dearest son, to tease our king in such a way." Her tone stayed light, but her eyes flashed like silver-blue blades in the dim light. If the blades had been real, Mac would be bleeding from a thousand precise wounds. "Even someone as ignorant as you should know that name is not to be mentioned in this palace. You will teach your little whore some very bad manners."

Before Mac could react to the slur on her character, Danice made a great show of shrugging the insult off, taking her cue from her companion. "I'm not worried about any manners I pick up from Mac. I'm perfectly capable of telling a good influence from a bad one."

This time, she pointedly met a Fae's eyes, and she saw the seething rage beneath Tyra's pretty, poisonous surface.

Dionnu regained control, though his knuckles still looked white where his hands clutched the arms of his throne. "How quaint, half-breed. It appears the human wishes to champion you. Perhaps I should direct my questions to her instead. I'm certain I could have any number of amusing ways to persuade her to share with me."

For the first time, the king turned his basilisk stare on Danice, and while she didn't turn to stone, she almost wished she had. The feel of his gaze on her was like having thousands of creepy, slimy crawling things moving under her skin. Her stomach turned, and she had to fight not to gag. She had a feeling throwing up in front of the royal person would not do anything to help her situation.

Danice turned her face away, unable to even look at the monster in Faerie form. It was like gazing on the face of the devil, concentrated evil in pretty, perfect clothes. Her gaze fell on Mac, and though he didn't look at her, she could feel the concern radiating off him, concern and anger and frustration. He must know (hell, even she knew, and she knew as much about the Fae as she did about particle physics) that attacking a creature as powerful as the Unseelie king would be an act of suicide. But the urge was there. Danice could read it in every tense muscle, and it made her ache a little bit inside.

"I doubt my business here could be of any interest to you," Mac said tightly. Danice could hear the strain in his voice. "I'm trying to locate a missing human, and I had reason to believe that the one who hired me to do so is Fae. I came here to find either my client or the human."

"As if a sidhe would require the services of someone like you to locate one puny human," Tyra scoffed. She looked as if she would like to say more, but Dionnu waved her to silence.

"Ah, so you did intend to disturb my court," Dionnu concluded silkily, his anger back under control. "Just not me, I would assume."

"I intended to do my job. Nothing more."

"Is that so?" Dionnu's eyes narrowed for a moment. When he spoke again, his mouth curved into a smile that threatened to overwhelm Danice's control over her gag reflex. "Do you know, I believe I am feeling uncharacteristically magnanimous today? McIntyre Callahan, I insist that you not exert yourself over this trivial matter of a missing human. Instead, you and your . . . friend will enjoy my hospitality and rest. I will undertake myself to locate the human. Consider it a gift to one who might have been my subject."

Tyra looked stunned at the offer. Mac looked suspicious.

Danice just swallowed hard.

"Morag," Dionnu called, snapping the guardswoman to attention. "You will recall that yesterday, my hunting party set itself on the trail of a stranger wandering through the woods north of the palace. My hounds insisted the creature was human, but I myself believed no human would be foolish enough to wander unprotected across my lands. Surely, I told myself, it must be one of Mab's little minions thinking to play a trick on me."

Danice struggled to piece together his meaning. While she didn't know all the ins and outs of Faerie politics, she had a hunch that Mab must be the ruler of the Seelie Court, the other half of Fae society. In comicbook parlance, she thought Mab must qualify as Dionnu's archnemesis. None of that, however, concerned her much.

What concerned Danice at the moment—a concern that deepened when she glanced at Mac and caught the flicker of alarm in his expression just before he stamped it out—was what exactly it might be that Dionnu had been hunting.

Or rather, whom he'd been hunting. And whom he intended to hunt again.

Could that be where Rosemary had gone? Had she not been kidnapped at all but traveled to Faerie and eluded capture all this time when Danice and Mac hadn't lasted five minutes? How would that even be possible? And why would the girl have come here?

For an instant Danice felt her heart stop. She wanted answers to those questions, but at the moment she figured a more pressing concern would be how to keep the girl alive.

"Send word to the master of the hounds that I will rejoin him shortly," the king ordered Morag, his gaze still fixed on Mac. "I think it's time to resume the hunt. Peigi, you and the others can escort my guests back to the chambers where they spent the night. I fear they could not have gotten enough sleep and will need more rest."

Dionnu turned to go, but Tyra stepped forward and held out an imperious hand. "Sorcha, your bow," she commanded. "I feel the need to do a little hunting myself. I will join His Majesty at the hounds."

"No, you will not." The king didn't bother turning around or even looking at Tyra. He dismissed her as easily as he had his servants. "I'm not in the mood for your company, my dear. While I enjoyed our evening together, I'm afraid the light of day does little to highlight your charms."

Ouch.

Danice felt herself wincing at the harsh smackdown. As much as she hated Tyra for all she'd done to Mac, it was hard not to feel the slightest bit of sympathy for a woman so brutally and publically rebuffed by a lover.

Dionnu strode away toward the back of the dais, disappearing into the shadows, not bothering with a single glance back at the woman he'd just rejected. Peigi (which, it turned out was the name of the second brunette) and the other guards seized Danice and Mac by the elbows and turned them, shoving them back toward the exit. As she marched along, prodded by the mean-spirited Catrin, Danice chanced one last look back over her shoulder.

There, on the dais, Tyra stood alone, as straight and tall as a statue. Her dress shimmered like the night sky, but her eyes shone even brighter. Whether the light glinted off tears or fury, Danice couldn't tell, but either way, a shudder raced down her spine until the doors to the throne room closed behind them, shielding them from the immortal woman's gaze.

Twenty-one

"So much for our luxury accommodations upstairs," Danice sighed, plopping back on the bed in the small dungeon cell and trying not to think too much about what had happened there just the night before. Unfortunately, while her mind might bow to her self-control, her body seemed to have a memory all its own. Every time she inhaled a whiff of Mac's scent, it suffered Vietnam-intensity flashbacks of sensation.

Mac didn't look up from his pacing. The moment the guards had bolted the door behind them, he'd begun to stalk the perimeter of the room, his gaze fixed on the stone floor and walls.

"Never trust a promise from a Faerie," he told her. "Especially not when she happens to be my mother."

"Yeah, I'm beginning to understand that. Not to put too fine a point on it, but as it turns out, she's a really big bitch."

He looked up and grimaced. "I hate to say I told you so, but . . ."

Danice allowed him another minute to pace before she cleared her throat. "Um, not to throw you off your rhythm or anything, but it appears to me that we have a bit of a problem here."

He stopped in front of the fireplace and turned to face her. "You could say that."

"I mean, I'm not the expert on Faerie, and the subtext in that throne room was so thick, you could cut it with a switchblade. Which, by the way, I kind of expected to happen at any minute. But unless I'm completely off the mark here, it sounds to me like Dionnu took just a wee bit too much interest in Rosemary and that she was what he intended to go out and hunt tonight."

Mac's mouth thinned into a very fine line. "You're not off the mark. In fact, you've pretty much nailed it."

"Right." Danice sighed. "In that case, I was thinking it might be a good idea for us to get out of our jail cell here and find her before he does. I mean, I can't see him hunting her down just to invite her back to his place for a cup of coffee."

"No, I don't think that's what he has in mind."

"Then what are we going to do?"

Mac bowed his head and clasped his hands behind his back in a thoughtful pose. Personally, Danice didn't think they had time for extended contemplation, but since she was flat out of ideas about how to get out of the kind of prison that looked like it could have contained the man in the iron mask for thirty or forty years, she felt a little bad about nagging him.

As it turned out, she didn't have to bother. After less than a minute, he heaved a really big sigh and lifted his head, his gaze locking on hers. His eyes held an intense expression that made Danice simultaneously wary and very, very hot. She felt as if tongues of fire had leapt from his eyes to her skin.

When he remained silent, she shifted self-consciously and shook her head. "What?"

He appeared the slightest bit uncomfortable, as if he feared her reaction to what he was about to say. Frankly, unless he suddenly announced that he'd decided to defect and join Dionnu in a lifetime of malevolence, Danice couldn't fathom what he might say to make their situation any worse.

"Mac, what is it?"

"Since I think we can safely assume that this time, Tyra is not likely to ride to our rescue and have us released from this prison again, I'm afraid it looks to me like we're left with only one choice."

"Which is?"

He unclasped his hands from behind his back and gestured at their surroundings. "This room is not someplace we can break out of or dig out of or trick our way out of. I heard Peigi tell Catrin and Sorcha to stand guard outside the door until she and Ailis, the redhead, came to relieve them. Thankfully the door is thick enough that they at least shouldn't be able to hear us talking, but I don't think they're taking any chances with us."

Danice waved her hand impatiently. "Yeah, I know all this already."

"What I'm trying to say is that the only way out of this room is going to be magic."

She sat back and crossed her arms over her chest. "Well, since I'm human, and you're only half Fae, I'd say that really sucks. So I hope to hell you're holding back some kind of good news."

"That depends on how you want to look at it." Mac

ran a hand over his hair, almost as if he felt nervous. "The thing is that I'm not just half Fae. Since Tyra is— regrettably—my mother, that makes me half sidhe."

Danice blinked. "Does that mean something?"

"The sidhe are the noble race of Faerie. They're the most powerful of the Fae. Hence Dionnu being king, and my mother one of the higher members of the court. It also means that they get their magic in a different way than most other Fae. They raise power through passion."

"Huh?"

"I think I told you that most of the Fae tap into the energy around them to do magic. Well, the sidhe some- times do that for the little things, too, but to work really powerful magic, they generally use sexual energy. A kiss can work for small things, but major magic requires actual sex."

Danice felt her eyes go wide. "Are you trying to tell me—"

"That I think I might be able to figure a way out of here, but I'm going to need your help," he confirmed, looking strained and uncomfortable. "I need to have sex with you. You know. Again."

Mac had never experienced this level of discomfort in his life. This was not the way he wanted his relation- ship with Danice to progress. The first time they had made love, she'd reacted afterward as if it had been some kind of ghastly mistake, as if she'd had too much to drink and would forever associate waking up next to him with the nausea of a bad hangover. That wasn't how he wanted her to think of him.

Things had not improved with the interference of his

mother, a figure he firmly believed had never improved a situation in her life. Where Tyra went, exacerbation followed, kind of like the pharaoh's plagues. Then there had been the king, threatening not only their lives, but that of Rosemary as well. And to top it all off, the only thing he could think of to get them out of their predicament was to turn sex not into an expression of their mutual attraction and the deepening feelings he had for her, but a mechanical act akin to charging a cell phone.

How romantic.

He almost couldn't bear to look at her. Mac didn't want to see the look of distaste and disappointment she would wear. He didn't want her to see him as the same kind of user that his mother and her lover were. From the beginning, he'd wanted her to think well of him, but that had been when all he'd felt for her was that sizzling attraction. Now there was too much more. He didn't think he could stand to have her hating him.

Waiting for her response, braced against the inevitable rejection, he held his breath. Man, if she thought the tension in the throne room had been bad, he couldn't imagine what she made of this. His muscles felt tighter than the head on a snare drum.

"Right," she said, her voice sounding oddly strained. "Well, as much as I hate to admit it, I've fallen for worse pickup lines." She blew out a breath. "So, does it need to involve something special? I mean, we're not talking anything kinky, are we?"

Mac didn't believe he'd heard her correctly. His head snapped up, and his jaw dropped open, and he couldn't swear that he hadn't uttered something embarrassing, along the lines of, "Wha-huh-say-uh-di-uh-wha?"

In fact, he was pretty sure that was exactly what he said.

Danice gave him a lopsided smile and a tight shrug. "We need to find a way out of here, right? I mean, unless you're hiding some explosives in your pants or something—"

She stopped abruptly, her cheeks flaring with the kind of crimson color he'd only ever seen on the extremely fair-skinned. He could almost feel the heat radiating off her face. Somehow it comforted him to know she felt as awkward about this as he did.

She cleared her throat. "I mean, I don't see how we can escape from this cell through normal means. You said it yourself. So if you really think this will give us a way out . . . I mean, I'm pretty confident you're not the kind of sleaze who would make this up just to get into my pants. Figuratively speaking. Especially since you've already been there and done that."

Didn't she realize that in the last week it had become his driving ambition in life to repeat that experience as often as possible?

Mac forced his expression to remain neutral and nodded.

"Then if this is what we need to do, I say we do it." Her words sounded definite, but her tone remained a tiny bit shaky. "I mean, if that's what you want to do?"

If he wanted to? Was she really asking if he wanted to make love to her? If he wanted to lose himself again inside all her honeyed heat? What would she want to know next? Whether he intended to continue having a heartbeat?

Mac concentrated on taking deep breaths. And on

not jumping on her like a starving man on cheesecake. He didn't want to scare her into changing her mind.

Slowly, he took a step toward her, then another. She watched him with those chocolate cat's eyes, her lips soft and slightly parted. He could almost taste them already, the tart, rich, spicy flavor of Danice. She drew him like a magnet, not just her body but her *herness*. The amazing essence of being Danice—strong, smart, calm, and competent. And so sexy he thought he might burst into flames without ever getting close enough to touch her.

He halted in front of her and lifted a hand to tuck a lock of hair behind her ear. His thumb brushed the high arc of her cheekbone and he felt the rush of her breath against his wrist. Even that was nearly enough to have him shaking.

"Um, do you have something in mind?" she asked, even as her head moved into his touch, like a kitten seeking to be stroked.

Oh, so many things, he thought, watching her hungrily. He wanted to take her in every conceivable way, in every position, in every location. He wanted to drown in her, to glut himself, to have her so often that he forgot what it felt like to live in a body separate from hers. He wanted to sate himself with her, even though the idea seemed impossible. He couldn't imagine this gnawing hunger ever truly leaving him. It might fade, but it would always return and demand to be fed.

She must have read his answer in his eyes, because her skin pinked again, and she bumped him scoldingly with her knee. "I meant, did you have something magical in mind? A certain kind of spell," she hastily clarified when he began to smile.

His hand slid around to cup the back of her head, drawing her toward him. His fingers tangled in the heavy thickness of her hair, holding her in place.

"I'm considering a couple of options," he breathed, brushing his lips across her cheeks. "I could try a charm on the guards, control their minds until they believe they've been instructed to set us free."

Danice nodded, the movement sluggish and uncoordinated. Already, the same heat raging through him had begun its drugging effect on her. He felt her eyelids drift shut. He feathered kisses over those, too, and then followed the line of her cheekbone across to the tip of her nose.

"Or maybe I could rearrange the walls, so that the stones in the outer wall moved to fill in the fireplace and left an opening for us to escape through."

His lips drifted down to hers, hovering for a moment, drawing in the breath she expelled, tasting her on the hot, humid air. She moaned softly.

"Or then again, maybe I could just move us, the way we moved this morning. We would just disappear from here and reappear somewhere outside."

Slowly, painfully slowly, he let his lips descend to the corner of her mouth, let them brush against the satin of her skin. His tongue snuck out to taste her, just the barest touch, until she strained upward, seeking a firmer pressure.

"It all depends," he murmured, his voice deep and low, another kind of dark caress, "on how much power we can raise."

Danice's eyes fluttered open, and a small frown creased the area between her brows. "Is that what this is about?" she asked hoarsely, pulling back until she could focus her gaze on his. "Is that the reason for the seduction scene? The reason for teasing me? Because it will raise more power?"

That was probably the last thing Mac had expected to hear. He felt his eyebrows lift in surprise. Could she honestly believe even a degree of the heat between them was anything but organic and honest? Did she think he was putting on some kind of act? Drawing out the moment for any reason other than the pleasure it gave him to anticipate the utter perfection of the moment when their bodies joined and the world dissolved around them?

He searched her gaze for a moment, saw the ghost of suspicion, but recognized beneath it the same passion he knew shone in himself. Her mind might harbor a few lingering doubts, but her body knew as well as his that they had been made for each other, formed and shaped to give each other pleasure.

Mac let his mouth curve in an expression he knew would appear anything but reassuring. He would look to her like the big, bad wolf himself, all dressed in Grandmother's nightclothes and more than ready to feast on unsuspecting little Red. He watched her eyes widen as she took in the grin he knew made him appear positively devilish.

"Is that was this is about? You think the fact that I want to savor the scent of you, the taste of you, the feel of you, is because of the power we can raise together?" he purred, wrapping his free arm around her waist and using it to press her closer, close enough to feel her trembling all along the length of him. "Because I'd be more than glad to show you how wrong you are about that."

He loomed over her, blocking out the light, filling her vision and allowing his hair to fall like a curtain around them. She shivered at the silky, soft brush of it against her skin, and he could feel heat racing through her. Her back arched and flexed, pressing her closer of its own volition. He didn't know if she'd intended the movement or not, but he heard when she bit back a groan.

His mouth quirked. "I'd enjoy showing you, Danice." He used the arm around her waist to lift her onto the mattress, sliding her back until he could press her gently into the soft cushion of silk and down.

Mac settled his weight on top of her, bracing his forearms against the mattress and brushing her hair aside so he could cup her head in his palms. He wanted to surround her, to consume her, really. To press her so tightly against him that he simply dissolved into her softness. All they needed was one body. They could live happily, could only survive, he was sure, as one body.

He aligned their figures with a sinuous movement that nearly made his eyes roll back in his head. She felt so soft and perfect beneath him, even concealed as they both were by far too many layers of fabric. He tilted his hips against her, pressing his erection against her soft belly until he swore the heat would sear her through the barrier of silk.

Lowering his head, he pressed his mouth to hers and pushed forward like a conquering army. He let himself sink into her, savoring every soft sigh, every melting acceptance, every tentative welcome. His tongue searched out every hill and crevice, every last secret, reclaiming the terrain he'd made his the night before. She moved restlessly beneath him, struggling to free her arms from the trap of their bodies so she could wrap them around him and pull him even closer.

Goddess, he needed to get closer.

All at once, the clothing that separated them became an intolerable interference. He was scowling when he pulled back, hating the idea of leaving her even for as long as it would take to strip them both naked. Which in the circumstances he figured he could manage in forty-seven seconds, flat. He felt the rapid rise and fall of her chest as she struggled for breath, saw the doubt begin to creep back into her eyes and knew he couldn't let that happen.

Reaching out with his inner senses, he searched the atmosphere around them until he found the pulsing heat of the power just their need for each other had already raised. Pulling the barest seed of it to him, Mac caught her gaze and winked, and in an instant the garments between them disappeared. They blinked out of existence as if they had never been, leaving nothing separating his skin from hers.

"I promise you, Danice, this is about more than power," he murmured, loving the way her skin flushed and softened and her eyes went all hazy and unfocused with desire. "But the power can come in very handy. Don't you think?"

Twenty-two

Danice gasped, but her legs shifted instinctively, parting just enough to allow his erection to nestle against the warmth between her thighs. She could feel exactly how genuine was his need for her, and the thought threatened to drive her crazy.

She closed her eyes when he lowered his head, moaned when his tongue stroked over the curve of her jaw, danced down the side of her throat, and flicked over her collarbone. Then he set teeth to skin and started nibbling, and a violent shudder quaked through her.

"The power is nice, and you'll be glad of it later," he assured her, stroking his hands along her sides, following the dip and rise of her curves, making her ache for more intimate contact. "But power is the least of the reasons why I want you. In fact, I would love to show you all the reasons I want you, Danice, but I'm afraid the task would take me a very long time."

His lips curved against her skin, feathered over lush curves, and invaded sensitive hollows.

"I'd like to show you how incredible it is that our bodies fit together so perfectly, every inch and angle in precise alignment. I'd like to show you how the heat we generate in each other could warm the surface of the earth during the coldest part of night. I'd like to show you that nothing else will ever feel as perfect as your skin against mine."

Danice arched her head back and moaned. The man had the voice of a snake charmer, low and rhythmic and relentless, vibrating through her belly and thighs and up into the deepest, hottest part of her.

"But I'd also like to show you why you should appreciate the power we create together, not because of what we can do with it, but because of the way it feels building inside you."

He nipped the side of her neck, then laved the small sting with the flat of his tongue as Danice struggled for breath.

"I want to show you the difference between a man and a changeling. The way subtle magic can make your skin come alive with feeling, or the way it can amplify each sensation until your nerves scream for respite."

His hands shifted, stroked over her shoulders and beneath her body to cup her hips and urge them higher against him. "I want to teach you how to hear the voices of a thousand choirs of the Fae singing songs of ecstasy and want."

His tongue flicked across her nipple, and the nub immediately swelled and tightened for him. Between her legs, another nub began to swell, this one coated in the thick, sweet honey of her need. "I want you to know that for the Fae, arousal is not a biological imperative, but a spiritual one. I don't need you because I'm hard; I'm hard because I need you."

His thighs urged her legs to part, and Danice gave

up pretending to protest. She spread her legs in wide welcome and wrapped her calves around his lean waist. She hooked her ankles together behind his back and fisted both hands in his hair, pulling the length of it forward over his shoulders. The scent wrapped around her as surely as his body did, redolent of sandalwood and clove, moss and man. She brought a handful to her face, breathing in the scent of him before rubbing the strands against her cheeks like a yard of living silk. He chuckled, but she decided he could laugh at her all he wanted. She was too far gone to care.

Mac's chuckle rumbled into a moan when she rubbed the sole of one foot high against his inner thigh, and became a growl when she untangled one hand from his hair and closed it over one firm cheek of his behind. She raked her fingernail lightly over the inner curve, and he shuddered, yanking her hard against him and positioning himself so his cock knocked against her entrance, trembling for a chance to be inside her. She could almost hear the way he gritted his teeth in a desperate bid for self-control, and it gave her a small sense of satisfaction. At least she wasn't the only one in this bed who would kill right now for the sensation of his hard length sinking to her eager depths.

Arching her hips to take the very tip of his shaft inside her, Danice opened her eyes into narrow slits and looked up at Mac with clear demand. "If you want to do all those things to me," she said, her voice raw and low with need, "why don't you stop talking about them and start doing them!"

Digging her heels into the small of his back, she

clenched her hands in his hair and thrust her hips up toward him, hard and fast, forcing him deep into the very heart of her.

"Lady!"

His hoarse shout sounded as if it had been ripped from his throat, but it didn't sound much like a protest. The way he threw back his head and braced her for the quick shove of his hips didn't feel like a protest, either. It felt like heaven as he forced every last inch of himself deep, filling her until she thought she could feel him nudging against her heart.

"More." She breathed the plea, barely a whisper, but he answered with a slow, intense rhythm that wound her tighter and tighter with every driving thrust. Her hands abandoned his hair and gripped his shoulders for support. She could feel the mattress shaking beneath her and the slick sheen of sweat coating his muscles and hers. She expected to see sparks where their bodies rubbed together, especially where the base of his shaft massaged her clit on each stroke. When he grunted and adjusted his position to slide a fraction deeper, her eyes flew open, and she swore she did see sparks.

She cried out, and he grunted an answer.

Her chest felt squeezed tight. She struggled just to breathe, struggled not to lose herself in the intensity of the sensations. She felt as if her very identity, her soul, her essence, were dissolving and being drawn from her into the hot space above them. She swore she could feel the power building, not just within her, but around her. This was more than the tension coiling in her womb, more than the clawing need for orgasm; this was raw energy, the stuff that moved the planets through the heavens and the earth on its axis and fed the spark of life into all the creatures under the stars.

This was creation, distilled into the purest, most intense haze of shifting, swirling magic.

And it had come from inside Danice.

From within her and the man above her, around her, inside her. The knowledge exploded inside her mind, blinding her, deafening her. For an instant she felt as if she had seen the heart of the universe and watched it beating in time with her own.

Pleasure returned her to consciousness.

The shock of it, the knowledge of it, of being there at the edge of the precipice waiting to dive in and let it consume her, pulled her back. Her body arched beneath Mac's, her lungs expanding to draw in one last, desperate gulp of air. She clung to him, their skin sliding and slipping under sheening films of heat and moisture. He felt like the only solid anchor in a vortex of power and pleasure, and yet she knew that in another moment, even he would dissolve, and they would each become a single, united atom in the explosive charge of power.

His breath soughed in her ear, rough and hoarse. His body strained against her as he gave himself up to the inevitable ending.

"Agh!"

"God!"

He roared.

She screamed.

The world imploded around them, a star collapsing in on itself in a cosmic burst of immeasurable intensity. His big body tightened above her, and Danice bucked and quivered in the vastness of eternity, her own muscles spasming, body clenching to milk the last drop of liquid heat he poured inside her.

His weight settled on top of her in a hard, sweaty heap, but she surprised herself by not caring in the least. Frankly, she didn't think she was capable of caring. She wasn't even sure she still existed. At least, not as the same person she'd been before. Not only had the universe shifted around her, but Danice had shifted inside herself, and in that moment it was all too fresh for her to make the slightest bit of sense out of it.

Drawing in a shuddering breath, she decided not to try. She couldn't think about this yet, couldn't think about what had changed. Right now she needed to pretend—to herself, if that's what it took—that everything was fine; nothing had changed and the world still made sense and Danice Carter was still an up-and-coming lawyer from Brooklyn with some odd friends and a wonderful family.

And the most amazing lover ever to grace a set of sheets.

She felt herself grin at her own thoughts. But hey, when she was right, she was right.

McIntyre Callahan had just—quite literally—rocked her world. The man might be part of the weirdest experience of her life, but he made a damned good blanket. She could have fallen asleep right there, if not for the nagging thought that there was still something she had to do. Something other than get up to pee to stave off the otherwise inevitable UTI.

Romance, she mourned silently, would forever be sacrificed on the altar of cold, anatomical reality.

Groaning, she mustered every last ounce of her

strength and lifted a hand just far enough to poke Mac in the hip.

"Nngh."

She frowned. That had hardly been helpful.

She poked again.

"N-nngh."

Damn it. He was making her do this the hard way.

She frowned as she tried to force the synapses in her brain to resume firing in the proper sequence for speech. And it was exactly as exhausting as she'd feared it would be.

"Wa'n't there s'mething we're s'pposed to do?" she managed to ask, though the words came out kind of garbled due to the fact that her face was pressed into the shoulder of the man on top of her.

Mac grunted again. Then he drew a massive breath and let it out in a gust that could have caused a tsunami in another part of the world. Or at least, it could have in the human world.

"Did it," he muttered, not sounding pleased that she had required a verbal response. "Now 'm gonna sleep."

"Oh. Okay."

Reassured, Danice let her eyes drift shut and her consciousness float away toward dreamland.

For about a minute and a half. That was how long it took her brain to reboot far enough to tell her what they had been supposed to do.

Her eyelids flew open and gazed at the night sky visible beyond Mac's right shoulder. Enough adrenaline spiked through her to give her the strength to shove her arms hard against his chest.

"Mac, where the hell did you put us?"

"With any luck?" he muttered against her shoulder, where his face was currently buried. "Far enough away from the castle that we won't immediately be spotted and recaptured. Because if we are, it's going to take me at least three or four years before my heart will be strong enough to try that again."

She shoved again, which made him grunt but didn't budge him an inch. "Well, would you take a look around, please, because I have no idea where we are, but my personal fantasies do not include finding myself in a compromising position in the middle of the Faerie equivalent of Yankee Stadium."

"Don't worry. The Fae don't have stadiums. They're not much for team sports. Or for teams, really." With a groan that indicated the expenditure of a great deal of effort, Mac finally lifted his head high enough to peer at their surroundings. Two seconds later he dropped it right back into place. "You're fine. We're in the middle of the forest. No one can see us."

"Good, then you have time to get us some clothes before anyone does."

She could feel his scowl against her skin. "I just told you no one could see us."

"Yeah, at the moment. But did you forget that even as we speak, the king, his hunting party, one unknown individual who may or may not be the one we've been searching for for the past week, and who knows who else, are currently running around this forest trying to find either each other or a way out? And I, for one, would like to have some *pants* on if any of them stumble across us."

One last shove (and, she could admit, likely Mac's

own conscience) finally managed to roll his weight off to the side, allowing Danice to draw breath. And shiver. After all, it was the middle of the night. In a forest. In other words, it was damned chilly.

Mac heaved a gusty sigh and blinked up at the stars peeping through the canopy of leaves. "You know, it seems somewhat impractical that the sidhe method for raising large amounts of magical energy should leave you with so little physical energy that you can barely manage to use it."

Danice sat up and wrapped her arms over her chest. She glared down at him through narrowed eyes. "You're not going to tell me you can't get us clothes, are you? I mean, you made them disappear, earlier. It would be totally unfair for you to tell me you can make clothes *dis*-appear, but you can't actually manage to make them *re*-appear."

"No, no. I got it." With a negligent wave of his hand, Danice felt the warmth of her own jeans, top, and leather jacket surrounding her in their familiar comfort. She blew out a relieved breath. "Thanks. That helps a lot."

Mac heaved himself to his feet, wearing the same jeans and shirt he'd left Manhattan in as well. Holding out his hand, he helped her to her feet and brushed a kiss against her forehead. "Don't thank me. It's actually quite a bit harder to make things appear than it is to make things disappear, so I really couldn't have done it without you."

He stepped back and this time took a good look at the small clearing in the trees where his attempt at sidhe magic had landed them. "You know, here's a small problem, though. I was so concerned with getting us out of

Dionnu's little guest room, I didn't really stop to consider how we would find Rosemary once we did escape. I don't suppose you have any ideas."

Danice refused to give in to the rush of helplessness that beat against the back of her mind. That and the panic. She didn't have time for either of those emotions at the moment. She had not come this far and gone through all this shit to give up or give in now. Not when the end of this entire miserable experience felt so damned close.

She looked around her and frowned in thought. "If we were in Manhattan, I'd use my cell phone and start by calling her cell. Her grandfather gave me the number, and even if she didn't answer, he said he'd registered it with a GPS company so he could track her." She made a face. "Which, come to think of it, makes me understand a little bit better why she felt compelled to run from the old bastard."

Mac stared at her, an odd look on his face.

"What?" she demanded, when he remained silent. His intense expression made her a little nervous.

"Did you bring your phone with you last night? I didn't see you bring a purse."

"Do you really think I would have carried a purse to a midnight rendezvous I knew was intended to culminate in a transdimensional excursion?" She shook her head. Men could be so clueless, even the smart ones. "But of course I brought my cell. I always carry it. In my pocket, when I have one. Which, considering what I'm wearing, I obviously do."

He made an impatient gesture. "Check and see if it's

still there. Sometimes modern electronics don't react well to passing through the veil."

Danice cursed under her breath and unzipped the jacket pocket where she'd stored the small device. "You'd better be joking with me. My whole *life* is on this phone. If it's toast, I'm going to be blaming you. Personally." Her fingers brushed against the familiar heavy shape and she sighed with relief. "It's here."

"Give it to me."

"Why?" She handed it over, but she was confused as to why he'd want the thing. "I wouldn't have thought installing cell towers was a big priority over here. It won't get any reception."

"Don't be so sure."

Danice watched while he powered the phone up and stared intently at the screen. She could feel his anticipation and what felt like excitement rising in him, but she had no idea what he could be thinking. She'd seen no evidence of technology of any kind during her short time in Faerie—no computers, no phones, no televisions or satellite receivers. Even the plumbing in the bathroom where they'd cleaned up that morning had seemed to work by magic. They had faucets and toilets, but no pipes. Water just appeared silently on command, and God knew what happened when you flushed, because Danice certainly didn't.

It took a minute for the phone to settle into working mode, but Danice knew the second it did, just by watching Mac's face. When he handed the little device back to her, he was grinning smugly.

"Take a look at that, sweetheart."

"Look at what?" But her eyes were already on the main screen, looking for something unusual. "It looks the same as it always does."

"Exactly." His tone dripped with satisfaction.

She made a noncommittal gesture. "And?"

"And how many service bars do you see there?"

Danice looked back at the screen, and her eyes widened. "It says I have full service. How is that even possible? Faerie doesn't actually have cellular network towers, does it?"

He shook his head, still grinning. "Nope, but they have something just as good: ley lines."

Twenty-three

Danice just blinked at him. "Huh?"

"Ley lines," he repeated. "Think of longitude and latitude lines, invisible straight lines that circle the earth and intersect at different spots. Ley lines are a kind of similar concept on a magical level. They're invisible lines of magic, only instead of all moving in the same direction, parallel, at regular intervals, from pole to pole, ley lines move across Faerie between points of particular magical significance. Between ancient monuments and sacred groves or streams. Things like that."

Danice tried to absorb what he was saying, and while she thought she grasped the concept, she wasn't quite sure why he felt it was important. "Okay, but what does that have to do with cell phones?"

"Magic is just a form of energy," he said. He sounded like a scientist trying to explain his latest invention; he really wanted her to understand, and he was trying to contain his excitement long enough to explain clearly. His voice held impatience, not with her, but with the fact that he had to resort to something as slow and tedious as speech to tell her about it. "Just like electricity is energy and light is energy and sound is energy. And cellular waves are energy. Frankly, the ley lines carry so much more energy than a cell tower can emit that it's kind of ridiculous to compare the two. But obviously, the ley lines here in Faerie are allowing the cell signal to travel along them the way they would over the air to a cell tower."

Danice shook her head in disbelief. "Oh, obviously." It seemed too weird to believe that magic would operate on such a mundane, human level as cell service.

"Go ahead," he urged. "I'll bet you. Cash money. Try calling Rosemary. Right now."

She stared down at the phone, her thumb hovering over the list of pre-programmed numbers. She didn't want to do it. Well, she did, but she didn't. She wanted to find Rosemary so she could go home, so she could put this horrible assignment behind her and get on with the life she was supposed to be living. But at the moment, while the possibility existed that Mac was right, that this would all work and make that possible, she couldn't quite bear to take that step that might prove him wrong. Until she pressed the button, she could believe him. If the call went through, the belief would be justified; but if it failed, the option would be gone. Right now, *having* options felt a lot more important to her than exercising them.

"Niecie," Mac prompted, breaking through the inertia of her indecision. "Make the call."

Taking a deep breath, Danice highlighted the correct number and pressed the SEND button. She held that breath while she brought the phone to her ear.

"Well?"

"It's ringing," she admitted, crossing her fingers. Inside her boots, she also crossed her toes. Just for a little something extra.

"H-hello?"

For a moment, shock paralyzed Danice's vocal cords. She opened her mouth, but nothing came out.

"Hello?" the familiar feminine voice repeated. "Is anyone there?"

"R-rosemary?" she finally managed. "Rosemary Addison? Is that you?"

"Hello? Who is this?" Rosemary demanded, her voice quivering. "Whoever this is, help me, please! I need help."

With shaking hands, Danice pressed the SPEAKER-PHONE button and lifted her gaze to Mac's. She held the phone out between them.

"Rosemary, this is Danice Carter," she said, raising her voice slightly to be sure the speaker picked her up. "I work for your grandfather, and I've been trying to find you for a week now. Where are you?"

"I don't know," the young woman said, her voice breaking as she obviously fought back tears. "I-I was following someone. I just wanted to talk to him, but he disappeared through this weird cave and I went in after him, but when I managed to make it through to the other side, he was gone and I didn't recognize anything! Before, I was in a park, but when I got out, I was in the middle of this forest. I kept walking and walking, thinking I'd get back to part of the park I recognized, but I don't think I'm in the same place. Nothing here is normal, and I just want to go home!"

She broke down crying.

Mac swore softly, a sentiment with which Danice heartily agreed. It sounded to her as if Rosemary Addison really had managed to find her way into Faerie, probably through simple accident. But however she'd found her way there, now she was trapped, and Dionnu and his hunting party were out there looking for her with a significant head start over Mac and Danice.

Mac leaned closer to the phone. "Rosemary, my name is Mac Callahan, and I'm a private investigator. I've been helping Ms. Carter look for you. We think we might know your general location, but we need you to help us find you. Look around you right now and tell us what you see."

Rosemary drew in a quivering breath. "Um, it's dark out now, so it's hard to see anything except the trees. I told you, I'm in the middle of the forest. Everything looks the same to me!"

"I know you're scared, Rosemary, but this is important," Danice said, trying to make her voice soothing. It would have been easier had she felt a little calmer herself. "Just describe what you see. How far away is the closest tree? Are you sitting under one? Are there any rocks nearby?"

"I'm, uh, I'm sitting on a rock. A huge one, like a boulder, but it's flat on top, and it was warm when I first sat down. Now it's getting cold. And I guess this is like a . . . a clearing, or something? The trees are all around the edges, like, maybe ten feet away in front of me. But they're closer behind the rock. Like only two or three feet."

Danice watched Mac's face, to see if any of this made sense to him. Then she remembered that he hadn't grown up here, so he probably didn't know any more about the geography of Faerie than she did. She leaned away from the phone and whispered, "This isn't going to get us anywhere. I say we activate the GPS function and see if that works as well as the phone does out here."

Mac held up a finger to tell her to wait a minute. "Rosemary, was it still light when you found the clearing and sat on that rock?"

There was a slight hesitation. "A little I guess. But it was getting dark again, and I'd been walking all day. I walked half of yesterday, too, without anything to eat, and I'm hungry, and I was tired. I needed to rest! I wasn't finding anything anyway. I think I've been walking in circles the whole time."

"It's okay," he hurried to assure her, hearing the whining note in her voice. He must have guessed, like Danice, that the girl was near her breaking point. The last thing they needed was for her to start screaming or sobbing loud enough to lead Dionnu to her. They had to find her first. "You absolutely did the right thing. You needed to rest, and staying in one place will make it easier for us to find you. I just want to know if you saw the trees while there was still enough light to see the bark."

"I-I suppose," Rosemary sniffled.

"Okay, then can you tell me what the trees looked like? Were they rough and dark, or was the bark silvery and kind of smooth?"

Danice frowned, seeing the look of intense concentration on Mac's face. His questions were making it sound like he had a specific location in mind. Could he actually know where Rosemary was right now?

"Silver," the girl answered. "They were definitely silver. In fact, whenever the moonlight hits them, they look almost shiny. It . . . it's actually kind of pretty, I guess."

Mac touched Danice's hand. "I think I know where you are, Rosemary. I've heard of a place like that before. I'm not exactly sure of the way to get there, but I'll find it. Don't worry. We may have to try tracing your phone, so don't turn it off, okay?"

"O-okay."

Mac covered the phone's mouthpiece with his hand and kept his voice low as he looked at Danice with excitement in his features. "There's a sacred grove of trees to the northwest of the castle. It's a species of tree native to Faerie with smooth bark, almost like birch trees, but they're enormous, and the bark is distinctly silver and actually reflects moon- and starlight. And there's a giant, natural stone altar at the western edge of the grove."

Danice felt the same excitement sweep through her. "Oh, my God, that sounds exactly like what she described."

He nodded. "I'm certain that's where she is, but I've only heard of the place. I've never been there. I do know that the reason it's a sacred space is because it's one of only three places in Faerie where seven ley lines converge in one spot. If the GPS can point us anywhere, it should be able to point us there."

Excitement took on a tinge of worry. "That seems like an awfully big chance to take when we don't know if the GPS will really work. I have to end the call with Rosemary in order to activate the tracking function."

He hesitated only a second. "We can always call her back, right?"

"I guess."

"What's going on?" Rosemary asked, the fear in her

voice rising once more. "Are you there? Are you still there? Hello?"

"We're here, Rosemary," Mac assured her, "but we are going to have to try to use GPS to track your cell phone. To do that, we're going to have to hang up with you."

"No!"

"Rosemary, it will be the fastest way to find you. I promise."

"No! What if you get lost?"

"We'll be following the GPS signal. We won't get lost."

"But you might. Maybe the trees will block the signal, and then I'll die out here all alone."

Danice felt a twinge of impatience. "Rosemary, if we lose the signal, we'll call you right back. I promise."

"If you lose the signal, how can you call back?"

Mac grabbed the phone impatiently. "It's a different signal. Rosemary, we can't find you unless we hang up. But I promise we will. We're not going to stop looking for you, okay? We'll see you just as soon as we can."

He pressed the END button before the distraught young woman could offer any further protest. Danice winced in sympathy. True, Rosemary was bordering on hysterical, but if Danice had been in her shoes, in Faerie, lost and all alone, she couldn't guarantee that she would have acted with any greater composure.

Mac handed her the phone. "Activate the tracking function. We need to get moving. There's always the possibility that Dionnu could have been close enough to one or the other of us to have overheard that conversation."

"Great, because I wasn't feeling any pressure before."

Danice thumbed through the menu, searching for the correct application. "Cross your fingers, why don't you? Just in case."

Danice herself would have crossed Baghdad naked at this point if she thought it would help.

The phone's screen went black for a second, and Danice felt her heart stutter. Then a digital map appeared with a compass at the bottom and seven blue lines intersecting at one particular spot in the top right corner. Superimposed over the point where they met was a blinking green dot. In the middle of the screen, another dot blinked orange.

She caught her breath and pointed at the orange dot. "I think that's us."

"Definitely." He traced a finger toward the location of the grove. "It doesn't look like we're too far. Stop and listen for a minute. Tell me if you hear anything."

Danice drew her brows together and concentrated on the sounds of the forest. She heard insects and silence and an occasional birdcall. The kinds of things you'd expect to hear outdoors at night. She was about to ask what she was listening for when another noise caught her attention. It was faint, but constant, a kind of whooshing sound, like air from a fan, or . . .

"Is that water? Like a river? Rapids, maybe?"

"It's a waterfall." Mac tapped the screen slightly below and to the left of their dot. "Right here, see? Which means we're facing almost in the right direction. We just need to head that way." He pointed and turned to set off.

Danice grabbed his arm. "Wait, how can you be sure? I can hear the waterfall, but I can't tell exactly where it's coming from, other than behind us."

"I'm half Fae. I can hear it. Trust me."

She looked up at him for half a second and nodded. "I already do. Let's go."

They took off at a walk that quickly shifted into a jog. It was a compromise between moving quickly and making so much noise they might as well announce their presence with a heraldic trumpet. They didn't want to give away their presence to Dionnu if he was nearby, but hopefully his party of Fae, hounds, and horses would make sufficient noise on its own to provide at least some cover. Danice still watched her feet, though, and tried to find the clearest spots for her boots to land, the ones without too many fallen leaves or brittle twigs waiting to snap sharply in the still night air.

She kept one eye on Mac and one on the screen of her phone. It reassured her to see their orange dot moving slowly toward the green one. At least Mac had chosen the correct direction, and it comforted her to see the distance between the two points closing. But when this was all over, Danice swore she would never again go anywhere without sidewalks and taxicabs. And that was a solemn vow.

Mac didn't seem bothered by the rough going, and he made significantly less noise than she did moving across the uneven ground. His long strides also gave him an advantage in speed, even though she knew he was holding back to allow her to keep up. And that just rankled. After all, she didn't run her ass off (literally some months) at the gym every day so that she could be left in the dust by a man when the moment called for speed. She didn't care how long his sexy legs were.

The longer they ran and the closer their dot came to

the convergence of the blue ley lines, the faster they moved, until Mac began to pull ahead. Danice briefly considered calling out to him to stop, but at that point she was less worried about the noise factor of a shout and more worried about conserving her breath. They'd been running for at least twenty minutes, and twenty minutes over uneven ground while trying not to make noise and staring intently at a cell phone screen, she was discovering, took a lot more energy than twenty minutes on a nice, even treadmill while listening to an iPod and watching closed captioning on CNN.

When she looked up and peered into the woods ahead of them, Danice thought she saw an opening in the trees. Then she spotted a flicker of moonlight, and she poured on a new burst of speed of her own. That looked a lot like a tree with reflective silver bark to her.

Mac reached the clearing first, his long legs eating up the last few yards of ground before he broke through the inner ring of tree trunks and into the open air. Danice jogged up behind him and stepped around a tree to see a large, flat stone, like one of the fallen lintels of Stonehenge. Atop it, a lone figure quickly uncurled itself from a crouching position and stood.

"Wh-who's there?" Rosemary asked, and Danice felt such a surge of relief she actually felt her knees tremble a little.

"It's Mac and Danice," Mac said, striding calmly forward to stand at the front of the enormous altar. "It's all right now, Rosemary. I promised we would find you, and we did."

The girl choked on a sob and threw herself at Mac, knocking a grunt from him as she dove off the rock and landed hard against his chest. He wrapped his arms around her—out of reflex, Danice assured herself—and set her gently down in front of him.

"Are you okay?" he asked kindly. "Are you hurt at all?"

Rosemary threw her arms up and wailed, "Do I look okay to you?"

Danice scanned the girl from head to toe and raised an eyebrow. First of all, she couldn't think of Rosemary Addison as anything other than a girl, no matter how old she was. Her recent behavior branded her as a child—refusing to confide in her family about the man who had fathered her child, breaking appointments at the last minute, running off to another dimension without informing anyone of her plans.

Second, the girl barely looked worse for the wear. Her skintight skinny jeans and cropped denim jacket had a couple of dirt marks here and there, and her trendy little booties had been scuffed beyond repair, but Danice couldn't detect a single drop of blood anywhere on her. Her highlighted blond hair was mussed into disarray, but her skin looked smooth, tanned, and unmarked. As far as Danice could tell, Rosemary hadn't even had to sacrifice a fingernail on her excellent adventure.

Rosemary clearly disagreed. And she did so loudly.

"I'm a mess," she sobbed, her pretty, aristocratic features wrinkling up unattractively as she worked herself into a frenzy. "I'm dirty and I'm tired and I'm hungry! My hair is a mess, my clothes are stained, my shoes are ruined, and I stubbed my toes on one of those stupid silver trees! And I just want to go ho-o-o-ooooome!"

She threw herself back into Mac's arms and continued

to cry, pressing her face against his shoulder and clinging tighter than a barnacle. Mac threw Danice a helpless and slightly panicked look over the girl's shoulder, to which Danice responded with an exaggerated shrug.

His expression morphed into one promising revenge as he patted Rosemary awkwardly on the back. "Aw, you don't have to cry. Sh. Please, stop it. We'll have you back home in no time. I promise. Just hush. Come on."

"I want my mother," Rosemary hiccuped, weeping like a three-year-old who had missed her nap. To Danice, she looked a heck of a lot more like a toddler than a mother-to-be.

At the thought, her eyes narrowed.

"Rosemary," she began quietly, then sighed and repeated herself loudly enough to be heard over the other woman's racket. "Rosemary, your grandfather told me that you said you're almost four months' pregnant."

Rosemary turned her head and sniffled in Danice's direction. "So?"

"So those jeans look awfully tight. Are they uncomfortable for you? We want to make sure both you and the baby are okay after what you went through."

The young woman pulled away from Mac and folded her arms over her chest in a defensive posture. She sniffled a couple of times, but the waterworks appeared to have stopped. Rather abruptly.

"There is no stupid baby," Rosemary snapped. "There never was. I'm not pregnant. I just said that because I was so mad at him!"

Danice felt a wave of mingled satisfaction and fury. As soon as she'd actually seen Rosemary, the pregnancy story had struck her as fishy. The girl was as skinny as an actress. She should definitely have begun to show at this stage. Especially in clothes like that, so the satisfaction was for having guessed correctly. The fury came from the understanding that everything Danice had gone through for the last week, from the drive to Connecticut to the threats from her boss, the attack in the subway, and the imprisonment in Dionnu's dungeon, had resulted from this spoiled girl's inability to tell the truth.

"So mad at who?" Mac demanded, frowning at her. "Who made you angry? And why would that be a reason to lie about being pregnant?"

"Pregnant? Did I hear you correctly, McIntyre Callahan?" a voice asked from the shadows behind them.

Danice recognized it without turning, and while she wasn't happy, she could hardly be surprised that Dionnu had managed to find them. After all, he'd had a head start of at least a couple of hours and a pack of trained hounds to work with.

No, what surprised Danice was the look of recognition and chagrin on Rosemary Addison's face as the girl gazed past her toward the intruder. Rosemary Addison had already met the king of the Unseelie Court.

"Is someone expecting a blessed event?"

Twenty-four

Mac stiffened at the sound of Dionnu's voice. He'd been hoping they would manage to stay another step ahead of the king's hunting party. He hadn't possessed a lot of confidence about it, but he had hoped. Now it looked as if they would have to count on Dionnu's total disinterest in humans to convince him not to care when Mac, Danice, and Rosemary promised to leave Faerie immediately and never come back.

Mac turned to face the intrusion and felt a surge of relief that Dionnu appeared to have left his huntsmen and hounds out in the forest. He recalled hearing tales of the sacred grove and thought there were stories about animals being unwilling to cross its boundaries, so that might explain the Fae's lonely appearance. The Faerie king stood at the edge of the clearing, his black clothing swallowing any light the trees cast in his direction. He looked like a slice of night, with his dark clothes and dark hair and the dark, empty pits of his eyes. Only his pale, smooth skin reflected back any hint of light.

Mac heard a gasp behind him and felt Rosemary grab on and cling to his back, using him as a shield between herself and Dionnu. Beside him, Danice pulled back her shoulders and faced the threat squarely.

And right there, he realized, was every reason he would ever need to account for why he'd fallen ass-over-ears in love with this woman.

He stepped closer to her and let his hand brush against hers as they stood together against the king.

"It's not your concern," Mac said firmly. "We've found what we're looking for, and we'll be happy to get out of your hair as soon as you point the way back to the closest gate to *ithir*."

"Not so fast," Dionnu purred, the very mildness of his tone setting Mac on high alert. "I think I should meet this person who caused so much havoc in my kingdom. Let me see her."

The king stepped forward, and out of the darkness behind him a shadow peeled away to glide toward his side. Not a huntsman, Mac could see, although the size and shape appeared Fae. The figure wore a hooded cloak pulled low over its face, but as soon as Mac saw the midnight fabric in the reflected glow of the silvery trees, he guessed who it would be.

The hand that shot out to grab Dionnu's forearm was slim and white and obviously feminine. Its mate reached up and swept Tyra's hood back to expose her bright golden hair.

"My love, surely you have no interest in a human," the sidhe woman mocked, her laughter brittle. "Let's be done with the worthless creatures and send them back to the mortal world where they belong."

Dionnu cast her a haughty, disdainful glance. "I thought I told you to remain at the castle, Tyra. Return there before I become angry with you."

Even in the darkness, Mac could make out the flash

of rage quickly suppressed in his mother's eyes. She attempted to laugh off the order, but a hint of desperation colored the sound.

"Angry? Dionnu, my love, I am not one of the peasantry for you to order about. The blood in my veins is as noble as yours, and I will not be dismissed like a servant."

Dionnu ignored her and beckoned to Rosemary. "Come forward, child," he coaxed, his voice like oiled black satin, dark and viscous. "I won't harm you. I just want to see you. There's almost something familiar about you."

Mac looked over his shoulder and saw Rosemary's reluctance. "You don't have to talk to him, but no matter what, I said we'd get you home, and we will. Remember that."

The girl nodded and released half of her death grip on the back of his shirt. Still holding tight with one hand, she stepped out from his shadow and moved forward. Mac noticed, however, that she remained between him and Danice, as if appointing them her bodyguards.

Dionnu studied her for a moment, his expression tightening. "What is your name, human?"

Mac felt Rosemary tense and heard her suck in her breath.

"You don't remember?" she demanded, her mood suddenly shifting from terrified and traumatized, to angry and indignant. "I can't believe you don't even remember my name, you disgusting pig! I spent an entire weekend in your bed, and you have the nerve to look at me like you've never even seen me before? You fucking bastard!"

Oh, shit.

Mac's world suddenly shifted as missing puzzle pieces slotted themselves into place. The father of the baby Rosemary had pretended to be having, the reason Danice had been dragged into this mess, wasn't some random club kid, some boy from the wrong side of the tracks whom her parents would dislike because he might be a fortune hunter. She had actually had an affair with the king of the Winter Court.

Was she *brain-dead*?

Mac had never heard of such stupidity in his life.

"What weekend was this?" Dionnu asked, not sounding at all fazed by the insults. "I'm afraid you're going to have to be more specific for me."

"You want specific?" Rosemary spat. "Try the weekend after Easter. The last day of April. Or had you already picked up some cheap whore that Saturday night, and I was just round two? Should I feel honored that I actually rated enough for a room at the Plaza and the whole damned night? Or maybe it wasn't even that you thought I was that pretty. Maybe you just went back to the bar and saw it was almost midnight and you needed one more bimbo so you could cut a last notch in your belt before the end of the month."

At that the girl dissolved into loud sobs interspersed with shouts of anger and hatred, none of which were coherent enough for Mac to translate. Apparently, Dionnu and Tyra had heard enough, though, because Tyra let out a scream of her own, this one a cry of rage, while Dionnu uttered a Fae curse laced with excitement.

"You were my Bealtaine treat, weren't you?" he demanded, stepping forward, his stare intent on the girl's face. "What was your name? Something plebeian. Natural. A flower? Lily?" he sounded as if he was talking to himself, but it was loud enough for Mac to hear. "No, not Lily. Not Daisy, either. Rose, I think. Or something like Rose."

That at least shut Rosemary up. She stopped crying and sniffled, watching the king warily.

"Rosemary," Dionnu finally purred. "Not a flower, but an herb. Now I remember. You were in that dance club, the one with all the purple lights. Yes, now I remember. And did I hear you say something about being with child?"

Mac swore and tugged Rosemary back, stepping in front of her to block her from Dionnu's gaze.

Wow, just when he'd thought they were on the verge of solving this whole problem, it turned out to be a thousand times worse than his worst nightmares. For years, Dionnu had been looking to get himself an heir to ensure no part of his kingdom could be annexed by Mab if he were to be killed. He also had made it known he wanted a son in his own image so that he would have an ally who might eventually be powerful enough to help him move against the queen's throne. Dionnu's ultimate ambition had always been to rule over the whole of Faerie.

The king narrowed his gaze on Mac. "This is none of your concern, half-breed," he snarled. "This is between the girl and me. Step aside."

"I don't think so."

"Rosemary," the king barked, holding out his hand. "Come here and tell me if you are carrying my child. If it is so, I will reward you in ways you cannot even begin to imagine."

"Dionnu!" Tyra's shout rang like breaking glass through the clearing. "I demand that you leave that human alone. She is worthless. Even if she is carrying someone's brat, there is no way of being sure it's yours. She might be lying, trying to trap you into giving her anything she wants."

"If she carries my child, a child sired on Bealtaine night, she shall *have* everything she wants," he retorted, not even bothering to look at his erstwhile lover. "Do you know what power would be contained within a child conceived on that night? It could prove to be my greatest weapon against that bitch Mab."

Mac had always thought Dionnu's eyes looked evil, a dark, hollow reflection of his soul, but now he saw a touch of madness there as well. It made the hair on the back of his neck stand up, and he thought he saw Danice shudder out of the corner of his eye. Even Rosemary had begun to look slightly uncomfortable. She shrank closer to Mac and took a half step back, away from the Fae king's grasp.

"No! I will not allow this!" Tyra punctuated her outburst with a stomp of her dainty foot. Mac knew it wasn't her physical but her magical power that made the forest shake beneath that tiny impact. "Dionnu, you will not do this. You will leave this girl alone and forget about her. I will not allow you to bring her to court and install her above me, as if she meant something. You cannot treat me that way. I am your mate."

The king turned on her, his mouth curved in a sneer.

"You were a diversion, Tyra, nothing more. Unfortunately, you seem unwilling to recognize that I no longer find you amusing."

Tyra drew breath and seemed almost to expand with the rage filling her. Her cloak blew back as if pushed by a strong wind, and the same unsettled currents rustled the leaves and trees until it sounded to Mac as if the forest beyond the grove whispered and gossiped in anticipation of a scene. He had no doubt that his mother could create a huge one, but he didn't want Rosemary or Danice caught in the crossfire. He began to scan the area around them, looking for an escape route.

Come to think of it, he didn't want to get caught in that crossfire, either.

A rustle of movement at ground level to his right caught his attention. He peered toward the tree line but saw nothing.

"I will not allow you to treat me with such disrespect," Tyra hissed, moonlight painting her features with an unearthly glow. "I am not one of the human whores you use and cast aside on a regular basis. Or did you think I was ignorant of them? I hope you realize that you never made your little trips to that bordello the humans call Manhattan on your own. I always had you watched. I know the identity of every whore you've ever taken, and I must say you have been a busy boy. Luckily you have the attention span of a boy, so I only ever had to eliminate one or two. A few I merely visited. It's a child's trick to tamper with the memory of a human. They forgot you readily enough, once I finished with them. Once I'd made them pay. Didn't you know how easily I could do that? And I could have killed them all, taken from you even those little pleasures you seemed to so enjoy. Did you think I lacked the power?"

Dionnu shrugged negligently. "I confess, I never thought of your concern one way or the other."

"Oh, I could have destroyed them all," she continued, as if the king had never spoken. "I've always known about your little human sluts, and I've taken great care to ensure none of them ever posed any real threat to my plans. Even before I lured you to my bed, I knew. I've known everything about you for ages, Dionnu Fair-Face. I knew you before you wed with the Summer Queen, and I knew you while you fought like two hungry wolves over who would rule your marriage. How do you think I just happened to be there, the first sight to welcome you back to your hall after Mab threw you out of her palace? I was watching you even then."

Mac felt his eyes widen involuntarily. If his mother was telling the truth, she had been virtually stalking the Unseelie king for centuries. What she described was nothing like love. It bore not the slightest resemblance to what he felt for Danice, nor what he'd seen any committed mate feel for their partner. No, what his mother described amounted to an obsession.

To madness.

Dionnu wore his mask of unrelieved boredom, but Mac thought he could detect the glitter of anger in those soulless eyes. "And when you were taking your own human lover? When you were bearing his son? Did you think of me then, my pathetic little Tyra?"

"Not of you, you arrogant piece of filth." Tyra laughed, a sharp, bitter sound containing little amusement. "My only thought from the beginning was of your power. I said that I watched you, not that I ever cared for you. My interest had always been in the power you represent. I knew you would never succeed in wresting the Summer Throne from Mab. Only a fool would try to move against her, and you have always been a fool. A fool so hungry for the light half of the year that you have never been able to appreciate the power of the dark."

Dionnu's eyes blazed, and he took a threatening step toward her. "A fool is one who contents himself with half a loaf when the tastiest bits lie just out of his reach."

"You will starve to death reaching for the tasty bits. That has always been your trouble—your greed. Greed and the inability to recognize the worth of what you already held in your hand."

"I hope you do not refer to yourself when you speak of what I already held in my hand." Dionnu's voice cut with the cold bit of a winter wind. "Because you never meant any more to me than a moment's pleasure."

"Never meant more? Never meant more when you would have launched a doomed army against Mab in a war you could never win, had I not talked you out of it?" Tyra sneered. "Never meant more when I counseled you to patience all the times when Mab taunted you with her missives, trying to goad you into the sort of foolish action that would have cost you your own throne? Is that what you would have me believe?"

"It is only the truth."

Mac felt a jab to his side and looked down to find Danice's elbow resting against his ribs.

"Uh, I don't think Tyra is going to like hearing that very much," she murmured. "What are the chances we can slip away while she and Dionnu are . . . keeping each other occupied? Do you have enough juice left to magic us far enough away that we can make a run for it?"

He shook his head, peering into the darkness once more. He could swear he heard something rustling just beyond the trees. He hoped like hell it wasn't one of Dionnu's huntsmen coming to see what was holding up the king. He had a feeling it wouldn't be. He thought he was beginning to understand how Tyra had gathered her intelligence on Dionnu's activities on the human side of the veil. She had paid a spy to watch her lover and report on his activities. Probably even to hire native talent if she ever lost track of a particular woman she wanted to keep tabs on.

"No way," he whispered back. "That was big magic for me, even in Faerie where magic goes farther than back home. I had enough left to dress us, and maybe enough to light a path or something, but teleportation is definitely beyond me."

"Okay. Then we need to think of something else. I have a feeling things could get violent around here at any minute."

Mac was only surprised the violence hadn't already started.

And then it seemed Fate heard Danice's words and took them as a personal challenge.

"Fine then. But know this, Dionnu of the Winter Court," Tyra bit out, her form visibly shaking with anger and barely suppressed power, "I will not be cast aside like refuse from your plate. If you wish to tell me that I meant so little to you, I will give myself a meaning by taking away something that means the world to you.

Something the means your very future. You will watch your human whore and her misbegotten brat die!"

A million things happened in the space of a ragged heartbeat. Tyra turned, her rage booming in the air of the grove like a thunderclap. She raised her hands and pointed them toward Rosemary. Dionnu screamed out in fury and denial. Rosemary screamed in fear until Mac thought his eardrum would burst at the volume. The persistent rustling in the underbrush stopped because its source, which turned out to be Quigley, screamed his own denial and threw himself at Tyra's legs, and Danice threw herself toward Rosemary, knocking the girl out of the vengeful sidhe's line of fire.

And placing herself directly in its path.

Twenty-five

Danice came to several realizations in the frozen instant after Tyra shouted her death threat into the chill night air. First, she realized that hell really did have no fury like a woman scorned. Second, she realized that while never before had she thought any man worth that kind of explosive reaction, Mac might just have changed her mind. Because if she ever found out that he had screwed around on her with another woman, she would cut off the man's balls and hang them from her Christmas tree.

And finally, Danice realized that somewhere deep down inside her, in a place she hadn't even realized existed, something like a streak of heroism had been lurking, waiting for this moment to strip her of all sanity and make her throw herself in front of a proverbial bullet for the sake of a person she didn't even really like.

Christ, who would have thought?

Obviously, Danice didn't think. If she had, logic would have told her that Rosemary Addison had brought all this trouble on herself; that the girl was spoiled and selfish and irresponsible, and thought she could manipulate the world into doing whatever she wanted by twisting the truth and throwing tantrums when she didn't get her way. But for all that, she didn't deserve to die, and that was the only thing in Danice's mind when she threw herself on top of the other woman and knocked her to the ground.

And then she waited for oblivion.

It didn't come.

Confused, Danice shook her head to clear away the ringing that had resulted from so many decibels of screaming and shouting and magical thundering going on right next to her. It almost sounded as if not all the shouting had stopped. In fact, one particular voice seemed even louder than before, as if someone was screaming directly into her ear.

After a minute, she realized someone was. Or rather, Rosemary was, and she didn't sound happy. In fact, she sounded as if she was yelling at Danice to get off her and to stop being such a bitch and trying to ruin her clothes out of spite and jealousy.

Danice shook her head again and used her arms to lever herself off the other woman and onto her knees. From there, she managed to make it to her feet, but the assault on her ears only continued. Rosemary lay on the ground yelling and wailing like a toddler in the midst of a tantrum, but that wasn't the only source of sound. Turning, Danice saw Mac and Quigley struggling to subdue Tyra. Quigley had wrapped himself around the sidhe's legs to hold her in place, while Mac struggled to pin her arms to her sides.

Dionnu had surveyed the scene and probably decided it bored him, because he turned his attention away from the wrestling figures and fixed his gaze on Rosemary. Striding across the clearing, he reached out his hand.

"Come," he said, ignoring Danice and speaking only to the hysterical young woman. "I promise that no harm will befall you. I will protect you from all evil. If you wish, I will have Tyra ni Oengus hunted down like a doe and fed to my dogs. You will see I can be very generous to someone who pleases me."

To Danice's surprise, Rosemary made what was likely the only intelligent decision of her life and shrank away from the king's pale hand.

"N-no," she stuttered, shaking her head emphatically. "I don't want to go with you. I don't like you anymore at all. You're not the man I remember from that night. He was gorgeous and kind and charming. He made me feel like a queen. Yo-you're nothing like him."

Dionnu frowned at her, his impatience written on his face. "Don't be ridiculous. I told you I remember you, and I assure you, I remember very few of the humans I fuck. If you have conceived a child, it is mine, and it will be raised as my heir. Now, come. Take my hand."

"No. I told you, I just want to go home." Rosemary reached out and grabbed Danice's ankle. "Mac said he'd take me home. You can't let him take me. I want to go home! Now!"

Danice looked from Rosemary to Dionnu and back and burst out laughing. She knew it was inappropriate— and probably a sign of temporary insanity, given the situation—but she couldn't help herself. Danice stood five-foot-four in her stocking feet and weighed 142 pounds of average human; Dionnu, king of the Winter Court of Faerie was at least a foot taller and fifty pounds heavier, and he was the frickin' King. Of. Faerie. He could probably strike her dead with a lightning bolt just by snapping his fingers. Even if Danice wanted to physically stop him from doing something, how the hell did Rosemary think she was going to manage it?

"Rosemary," Dionnu snapped, beginning to grow impatient. "You will come with me now. The human has no business interfering, even if I were inclined to allow it. I will not have anyone coming between me and my heir."

That made Danice laugh even harder, but at least it gave her an idea of how to kill Dionnu's interest in carrying Rosemary off into the sunset.

She quickly got ahold of herself and cleared her throat.

"Uh, I hate to break this to you, Dionnu," she said, fighting back a smile, "but your heir is a figment of your imagination. It doesn't exist. Rosemary was never pregnant. If you'd overheard even another five seconds of the conversation we were having before you walked into the grove, you would have heard her telling Mac and I exactly that. There is no baby."

Dionnu turned his empty, black eyes on Danice, which easily chased away the remnants of her laughter. Looking into those eyes killed any desire she had to laugh.

"What did you say, human?"

Danice shifted warily, feeling her skin start to crawl. She thought that might be a really bad sign.

"I said that Rosemary is not having your baby. She is not pregnant. It was just a story she told a few people in New York when she was trying to get your attention and piss off her family."

Beside her, Rosemary made a protesting noise and

dug her fingernails into Danice's jeans. Danice kicked her leg free and reached down to drag the girl to her feet. For God's sake, what the hell was she glaring at Danice for? Had she really expected that Danice would lie for her? Make up some story to keep the king from knowing what an immature little brat she had been? The last time Danice had read through them, neither her current job description nor the one for a senior partner had made any mention of being quite that big a patsy.

Even if one of them had, Danice wasn't in the mood. Her job could go hang.

Dionnu's icy gaze traveled from one woman to the other while his eyebrows climbed toward his hair line. "Are you telling me that this human child thought she could trap me into a relationship with her by presenting me with a false claim of pregnancy? That she let it be known I had fathered a child on her in order to draw my attention?"

"Pretty much," Danice said.

Rosemary glared at her, but remained silent.

"And what did she think would happen when I discovered the truth? Did she think I would not care that I had been deceived? Did she think there would be no consequences for her lie? For making a mockery of me before her people and mine?"

"If you're asking me, I'd have to say that I'm not certain she thought at all. I kind of hope that she didn't. Mostly because I don't like to think of any woman being that stupid. It contributes to the misogyny of the backward and ill-informed."

For a moment, Danice held her breath. She knew she could have phrased things with significantly more diplomacy, but exhaustion and exasperation had hijacked her tongue. If the Unseelie king felt inclined to smite anyone tonight, she had just provided him with the perfect excuse. Again, she wondered what had happened to the thoughtful, calm, and well-spoken attorney she had worked so hard for the last ten years to become.

"What the hell?"

Danice heard Mac curse and recognized the urgency in his voice. That wasn't his surprised-and-dismayed tone; it was his duck-fast-because-the-shit-is-hitting-the-fan tone. She whirled around to where Mac, Quigley, and Tyra had struggled seconds before. Now only Mac and Quigley stood there, Quigley looking grumpy and confused, Mac looking furious and worried.

Her heart dropped into her stomach.

"Danice!"

She heard the warning and jumped instinctively to the right, knocking Rosemary down for a second time and just missing the cause of her own funeral. The blade Tyra had aimed at her heart glanced off her upper arm instead. It still hurt like a mother. Danice felt the lethally sharp silver slice through skin and muscle, but it took several minutes for the pain to hit. It wasn't until she stumbled to her knees and clamped her hand over the bloody wound that she felt the searing ache.

Later—much, much later—she realized that she owed her life to the Unseelie king. In the moment, all she could do was stare up at the maddened Fae woman while her shock-addled mind tried to reconcile the memory that Tyra could perform magic and must have teleported herself out of Mac and Quigley's grip to the space directly behind Danice. And then the sidhe had tried to kill her.

Why would Tyra try to kill her? Of all the people in the grove at that moment, Danice would have thought she was the only one the crazy bitch had no good reason to want to see dead. Dionnu was the one who had cheated on her, and Rosemary was the one he had slept with, the one who had lied about having his baby. Mac was the son she had abandoned, the one who'd come back to stir up all this trouble. Even Quigley, her supposed loyal spy—or so Danice assumed from the woman's earlier rant—had attacked her to keep her from killing Rosemary. So why the hell had she decided to stab Danice, of all people?

Maybe it had been a fleeting whim, because now that Danice had fallen to the ground and knocked Rosemary out of the way, Tyra turned her attention on Dionnu.

"It gladdens my heart to know that you won't have the comfort of a child to carry on your name," the Fae hissed, baring her teeth and throwing her knife to the ground. "Now you will have nothing to take with you when I burn the black heart from your chest!"

She launched herself at Dionnu, and Danice supposed it could have been the shock and pain distorting her vision, but she could have sworn the woman went for the king's throat like a lioness. It looked almost like she wanted to tear his jugular vein open with her teeth.

Just the thought made Danice shiver.

"Get away from me, you pitiful nothing!" Dionnu grunted and caught his attacker by the neck, holding her away from him while she shrieked and clawed like an animal. The nails of one hand caught him across the cheek, opening up two long, angry furrows in his skin. Blood welled to the surface. Tyra cackled with maniacal glee.

"Oh, my God, that lady is crazy," Rosemary muttered, sounding more awed and excited than afraid. She pushed herself into a sitting position and stared at the struggling figures as if she were watching a stage production.

In other circumstances, Danice might have pointed out the tackiness of the behavior, but at the moment she was just glad the fight kept the girl distracted enough not to whine again about being knocked down. Danice was also busy worrying that Mac would try to barge through the two combatants to get to her, since their struggles had positioned them directly between them. Judging by the look on his face, she really was afraid he might try it.

"You deserve to die in agony," Tyra gurgled, her voice distorted from the pressure on her throat. "I tell you now, you will."

For the first time since they had come to Faerie—for the first time ever, unless Danice missed her guess—fear flickered across the king's beautiful features.

"Shut up, you bitch," he growled, tightening his grip.

A smile of perfect madness curved the woman's lips, even as her face began to turn blue and violet.

"A *geis* on you, Dionnu mac Lir. I curse you." The words sounded faint and broken as she struggled to speak through the lethal pressure on her vocal cords. "You will meet your death at the hands of a woman.

One of your blood, but not of your spirit. In the end, a far greater power than your own will destroy you."

"Enough!"

The very forest seemed to tremble at the king's furious roar. Leaves rustled, branches snapped, and in the darkness a fox screamed, its cry like a woman in distress.

"Enough of you, Tyra ni Oengus." Dionnu freed the hand he had been using to keep the woman's from further clawing his face and laid it on her forehead. "The life within you was lent by the land of Faerie, and to the land I return it. *Codlata go deo.*"

The sidhe collapsed. Her body went limp in Dionnu's hands, the magic and madness and animation leaving her until she hung there like a doll, lifeless and empty. Danice watched with surprise as, instead of simply dropping her, the king strode the few steps to the stone altar and laid her across it. A beam of moonlight filtered through the trees and turned the now-smooth features into a porcelain mask of peace.

While facing the altar, Dionnu's back was to Danice, so she couldn't read his expression, or even guess at it, but when he turned back to the others, his habitual mask of arrogance had returned.

He fixed his gaze on Mac. "Well, Mac ni Tyra, will you now vow to avenge your mother's killing? If I am to wipe out an entire family, I would like to see the job done quickly."

Mac shook his head, but he watched the king warily. "She was never my mother. She gave birth to me, but she was a stranger to me my whole life. My family is in the mortal world. And from what I saw here tonight, there was little else you could have done. What she attempted wasn't sane. Tyra was sick, and as far as I'm concerned, her illness killed her, not you." His gaze flicked to Danice. "Of course, if you have any intention of harming either of these women, I won't hesitate to try to kill you myself."

"You wouldn't succeed."

"Maybe. Maybe not."

A small smile curved the king's lips. "Then it appears I am indebted to you, and that is a situation I cannot tolerate. You might not wish to call Tyra your mother, but she gave you life, and I took her from this existence before her natural end, so I must repay that act. Name something I can give you to balance the scales."

Danice shook her head. "Do you think there's any price that equals a life?" she asked, incredulous. "I mean, don't get me wrong, the bitch needed to die, but you can't put a price on her life. Twisted and effed up as it may have been."

Mac shushed her. "I already told you, you don't owe me for that. But we have gone to a great deal of trouble that you, however indirectly, caused us." He glanced meaningfully from Dionnu to Rosemary and back again. "So for that, I would accept a favor."

"Name it."

"The three of us want to go back to New York immediately," Mac said. The sound of a throat being cleared somewhere in the vicinity of his kneecap had him looking down at Quigley's frowning face.

"Four of us," the imp corrected.

Mac rolled his eyes. "Fine, the four of us. We would

like safe passage back to New York through the nearest gate. Right away."

Dionnu looked mildly surprised at the request, but he waved his hand. "You could have had much more, half-breed, but you shall have what you ask. Consider it done."

And before Danice had the chance to blink, it was.

Twenty-six

Large hands reached down and pulled Danice to her feet. A hard, masculine body pressed itself against her for a moment, then those same familiar hands gripped her by the elbows, carefully avoiding her injury, and shook her like a rag doll. The dark, oscillating cityscape she glimpsed out of the corner of her eye reassured her that Dionnu hadn't been messing around. They were right back on the corner of C and 6th, almost as if they'd never left. It didn't even look like an hour had passed.

"What the hell were you thinking, you little idiot?" Mac shouted, pressing her against him again, then repeating the shaking. "Don't you ever, ever pull a stunt like that again, do you hear me? You could have been killed! Twice! Goddess, I wanted to strangle you myself."

"For what?" Danice asked weakly, the back and forth of the shaking and hugging making her a little dizzy. "For purposely knocking Rosemary out of the way of Tyra's blast o' magic, or for accidentally knocking her out of the way when Tyra tried to stab me in the back?"

"Yes! For both of it. For all of it. For ever putting yourself in danger. You can't do that kind of thing to me," he growled, smoothing the hair back from her face and cupping her cheeks in his hands. "You can't scare me like that, Danice. I can't take it. The thought of losing you makes me crazy. When I saw that knife, I think my damned heart stopped."

"Isn't the important thing that mine didn't?" she asked, wrapping her fingers around his wrists and smiling up at him. "And that's because you warned me. I heard you yell, Mac. You're the reason I got out of the way and ended up with a slice on the arm instead of a knife in my heart."

Mac frowned and peered at her sleeve. He didn't look all that reassured. "How is your arm? Do we need to get you to the hospital? It looked like you'd probably need some stitches, but I never got a chance for a close look."

With a start, Danice realized she could no longer feel the wound. In Faerie, the thing had burned and ached as if her entire arm were on fire, but now she couldn't feel a thing.

"I don't know," she muttered, pulling away and shrugging out of her leather jacket.

She smoothed her hand over her shirtsleeve but couldn't find the tear in the fabric. Impatient now, she pushed up her sleeve and stared at the caramel skin of her upper arm. She saw not a drop of blood. The only thing that marred the smooth muscle was a thin, pale line, so faint it was nearly undetectable until the moonlight hit it. Then it shone with a faint silvery sheen.

Amazed, she lifted her gaze to Mac's.

He shrugged, but he was smiling. "I guess Dionnu really didn't think the favor I asked for was enough."

"Well, I think you should have asked him for a whole

lot more," Rosemary whined, reminding Danice for the first time that she and Mac were not alone on the quiet street corner. "After all the shit he put me through, I would have asked for some big, fat magic ring, or something."

Danice shot the girl a quelling look. "Oh, really? Maybe you'd like to go back and ask for your own favor?"

Rosemary went pale, but quickly recovered, schooling her expression into one of disdain. "As if! I never want to see that jerk's face again as long as I live. I can't believe I even slept with him. I mean, if he and that crazy lady had a thing, and she's Mac's mother, he must be at least fifty. Gross!"

"Yeah, gross."

Mac and Danice exchanged grins. From what Mac had told her about the Fae, Danice was guessing that Rosemary would have to multiply that figure by about a hundred to get closer to the truth. After all, the Fae were immortal.

"Anyway, I'm just glad to be home," the girl continued. "I want to put this whole mess behind me and forget I ever followed the creep into the country. It is so good to be back in Manhattan. Will you guys walk me up to First so I can get a cab?"

Danice was already nodding before Rosemary's words actually sank in. She gaped at the girl.

"Into the country?" she repeated, her voice sounding almost as strangled as Tyra's had near the end. "Rosemary, where exactly do you think you've been for the past couple of days?"

The girl shrugged. "I don't know, but I'm guessing it was somewhere out in Westchester. Where else would there have been a forest that big so close to the city? I mean, the trip back didn't even take an hour, did it?"

Danice opened to mouth to ask what the heck Rosemary had been smoking that she didn't remember being teleported to another dimension and back, but Mac stopped her with a hand on her shoulder.

"Don't," he murmured, leaning close so Rosemary wouldn't overhear. "It's a coping mechanism of the human mind. It's what makes people who've seen Lupines in the city convince themselves they were only big Siberian huskies, or homeless guys with really bushy beards. Since she probably wasn't aware of the existence of The Others before Dionnu, her mind is working to fit everything that happened into a frame that makes sense. The Fae and other dimensions don't exist, therefore that can't be what she saw or where she went."

He helped Danice into her jacket and wrapped his arm around her shoulder, holding her against him as they began to trail Rosemary up 6th toward First Avenue.

"But that's insane," Danice protested in a low whisper. "I mean, what does she think that is?" She pointed toward the small red figure of Quigley strolling along the curb, parallel to them but partially concealed by the shadows of parked cars.

"She probably hasn't even noticed him, and if she does, she'll think it's someone's weird pet. A monkey or something. The human mind is a pretty amazing thing."

Danice snorted. "It would have to be. But since we are speaking of the monkey at the moment . . ." She looked back at Quigley. "I owe you a thank-you for helping Mac tackle the lunatic, you little turd, but I don't want you to think it means I'm forgiving you for your part in this enormous mess. You were Tyra's spy the whole time. She had you keeping an eye on Rosemary until the girl decided to head to her parents' summer house, and she had you hire Mac when you couldn't find Rosemary in the city. You knew all along what was going on and why Tyra cared about the girl, and you never said a word."

"You never asked," Quigley whined. "I never lied to anyone. I was just doing my job. Tyra always had me watching Dionnu when he came to New York so I could tell her who he'd been with and whether he ever saw the same woman twice, not that he ever did."

"Because he's a great big man-whore," Danice muttered.

"I didn't know there was anything special about this particular girl, even when Tyra asked me to get a mortal investigator to pick up her trail."

"That is one big, fat coincidence I'm having a little trouble swallowing," she said. "How is it that out of all the private investigators in Manhattan, you managed to pick the only one who was actually Tyra's blood relative?"

Mac laughed. "You're having trouble swallowing it because it's not a coincidence. I'm sure that as soon as Quigley got the order to hire some help, I was the first one he thought of, and not because we've worked together in the past. His imp's sense of humor would have found the idea irresistible."

"And you don't want to smack him for it?"

"Why would I? If he hadn't hired me for this particular case, I might never have met you."

Something inside Danice melted, leaving her slightly more gently disposed to the interfering imp.

"Right," she said, wrapping her arm around Mac's waist and snuggling against his side. "I suppose in that case I can forgive the little jerk."

"Aw, admit it, Danice," Quigley prodded, "you know you secretly like me."

"No way. If I liked you, I wouldn't mention that I have a very strong hunch you'd sell me your right arm if I introduced you to the concept of a root beer float."

The imp's pointed ears visibly perked up. "Float? Root beer float? What's a root beer float?"

"And then I certainly wouldn't refuse to tell you anything else."

"Why haven't I ever heard of this before? Are you trying to trick me?" The imp scowled up at Mac. "Is she trying to trick me? Have you ever heard of a root beer float?"

Mac laughed his way through a groan. "Great. You just had to go there. I hope you realize that you've just created a monster."

Danice grinned. "He deserved it."

"Guys, come on! What's a root beer float? Man, you've got to tell me now. I can't stand this."

Mac and Danice just laughed and ignored him. They were too busy savoring the feeling of being safe and alive and together all at once. And thankfully, once they reached the much better-lit expanse of First Avenue, the imp had to drop back and find a darker way home.

They walked a couple of blocks along the avenue until Rosemary managed to flag a taxi and slip into the backseat. She barely spared Mac and Danice a backward glance.

As the cab pulled away from the curb, Danice glanced up at Mac. "Do you think we can trust her to actually get home safely at this point?"

He sighed. "I think she'll be safe enough for tonight. And as of first thing tomorrow when you let her grandfather know the real story about her supposed pregnancy, she will no longer be any concern of ours."

"Thank God."

Mac spotted another cab coming down the quiet street and held out a hand. When the vehicle stopped, he bundled Danice into the back and gave the cabbie the address of her apartment building.

She arched a brow. "How did you know where I live? I don't remember giving you that information. As I recall, all I gave you was my business card."

"I'm a private investigator." He grinned. "I investigated."

Danice let her head fall back against the leather upholstery. She couldn't remember ever being this tired in her life. Now that they were back safe in Manhattan, the enemy vanquished, the mystery solved, and the inviting comfort of her apartment mere minutes away, she wondered how she'd made it this far. Between the full day in Faerie, the battle, the sex, the running, the sex, and the stress, she was amazed that only now had she begun to shake with the tremors of extreme fatigue.

Mac said nothing, but he pulled her closer against his side to lend her his body heat. He had one strong arm wrapped around her back. The other clasped her hand in his, their joined fingers resting in her lap.

Neither spoke during the remainder of the ride. When the cab stopped in front of Danice's building, Mac got out with her and paid the cabbie, then turned to follow her upstairs. She didn't protest. She didn't want to walk into her empty apartment while he rode off toward his. She wasn't sure she ever wanted to be separate from him again, but for tonight, at least, she couldn't imagine having him anywhere but by her side.

Her cold, stiff fingers fumbled with her key until Mac gently took it and unlocked her door himself. Danice stumbled over the threshold and mumbled an apology, but her own voice sounded slurred and foreign in her ears. She could barely keep her eyes open. The lids felt as if they'd been weighted down with lead. In the end, she let Mac take care of her, let him lead her into the bedroom, strip off her clothes, and bundle her into bed between crisp cotton sheets.

She remembered murmuring with pleasure when she felt him crawl in beside her and press his warm bare skin to hers. He gathered her to his side, and she went gratefully, pillowing her head on his shoulder and resting her hand on the smooth, strong surface of his chest.

The brush of his lips against her forehead was the last thing she knew of for several, dreamless hours.

When Danice woke again, she realized she was lying in the exact same position she'd been in when she fell asleep. That in itself was unusual, since she tended to change position several times during the night. But even more unusual was the feel of a warm, solid male body beside her.

She ran an appreciative hand over his chest and felt his muscles tighten.

"You're awake," Mac murmured, his voice drowsy with sleep.

"Mmm. What time 'sit?"

"No idea."

She chuckled. "Some help you are." She lifted her head and squinted at the digital clock on the nightstand. Then she frowned. "Nine-thirty at night? That can't be right."

"Why not? I was certainly tired enough to sleep the whole damned day. In fact, I think it was my top priority."

"But that would make it . . ." She frowned. "What day would that make it? We met Quigley on Monday and went through the gate into Faerie on Tuesday. We were there all day Wednesday, and came back early in the morning on Thursday. So that means it's Thursday night?" She groaned and flopped back onto Mac's chest. "Shit. That is so not good. I can't have been gone for two days. Missing that much work with no explanation? They're gonna can my ass."

Mac rubbed his hand over her bare back as if he couldn't get enough of the feel of her skin. "There's no way to know if you have been. Time passes differently in Faerie than it does here, and there's no way to predict it. Sometimes a month there is an hour here and vice versa."

Her head shot up, and Danice glared down at him.

"Are you telling me that I might have been gone an entire month?" She felt the surge of horror at the idea, but tamped it down with the use of cool logic. "No, that's impossible. If I'd gone that long without calling my mother, she would have already had the National Guard out looking for me, and she and my dad would be camped out here in my apartment in case I came home. So it can't have been a month."

Mac slanted her a sleepy grin. "How long would your mom give you before she pulled out all the stops like that?"

"Ten days. At the outside. And then only if she had something else to distract her." She shook her head. "You don't understand how close my family is. Or my friends. If Mom didn't call the police by day ten, Ava or Corinne or one of the other girls would. They're a little protective. Actually, we're a little protective of each other."

"I think that's nice. It's that way with me and my dad, but then, it's always just been the two of us."

Danice heard what he didn't say and propped her chin up on her hand to gaze down at him. "I'm sorry I didn't say it before, but I'm sorry you had to lose your mother. And I'm sorry you had to see her like that. You shouldn't have had to."

He smiled up at her. "Don't be. I meant what I told Dionnu. I know Tyra gave birth to me, but I never considered her my mother. I never had a mother, or maybe I lost her before I even got the chance to know her. Either way, Tyra didn't mean anything to me, other than someone who tried to use me. I know who she was because my father told me about her, and when I was a teenager, he sent me to Faerie for a couple of weeks so I could learn about that side of my heritage.

"That's where I learned about the culture and everything. But I didn't spend the time with her. I stayed with the family of another changeling I had met at an after-school program. My dad sent word to Tyra that I'd be visiting, and she never even bothered to come and meet me. And the weird thing was, it didn't even hurt me then.

"I had a great childhood. My dad is the best father I could have asked for, so good that I never really missed having a mom."

She eyed him skeptically. "If you're sure . . ."

Mac laughed. "Why wouldn't I be?"

Danice shrugged. "Maybe it's because my family is so close, but I have a hard time believing that not having a mother, or having Tyra for a mother, didn't mess you up even the tiniest bit."

He sighed and sank back into the pillows, curling a strand of her dark hair around one of his fingers. "Well, I don't think it messed me up, and I think that's all my dad's doing. I give him a lot of credit, not just for doing such an awesome job raising me, but for not trying to turn me against her when I was growing up. I'm sure it would have been easy to do. After all, she offers the kind of ammunition money can't buy."

Danice snorted at that.

"But I mean it when I say I grew up just fine." He shifted a bit, his eyes sliding away from hers to gaze over her shoulder. "Honestly, the worst moment I ever had over having Tyra for a mother came tonight, and it wasn't because of what she was or what she did. It was because of you."

Danice felt a jolt of surprise and frowned at him, waiting for his gaze to slide back to hers before she shook her head. "Because of me? Why?"

Mac shrugged, but the tension in his long frame belied the casual nature of the gesture. "Because part of me was—still is—afraid that you'd look at her and think that since I came from her, I might have that kind of hate inside me. Or that kind of crazy. I mean, you have to admit, by the end of the night she wasn't in her right mind."

She shook her head, feeling the creases her frown was etching in her brow. "What on earth are you talking about? Why would I think you have anything at all in common with Tyra? Have I said or done anything that makes you think I view you as a potential psycho bitch in the making?"

His mouth quirked, but the expression in his clouded-blue eyes remained serious. "No, but I can't deny that part of her lives on in me. We share the same genes. What's to say that I won't go off the deep end, too, one day?"

"You're to say it," Danice insisted, understanding dawning. Not that she understood how he could feel that way, but at least now she understood that he did. "You are nothing like Tyra and you could never become like that. You couldn't end up in the same place as her because you don't have the capacity for that kind of selfishness. Even if you tried to be entirely self-centered, you wouldn't be able to stop yourself from helping other people. That's just who you are. Who you're always going to be." She let her smile tease him as she leaned down to brush her lips against his. "Besides which, I'd smack you down way before you got to that point. So stop thinking like an idiot."

Mac chuckled and cupped her head in his hand, pulling her down for a longer, deeper kiss. When she drew back, he smiled and she could see the traces of his worries fading. How could anything like worry or sadness survive when the two of them lay together like this?

"I appreciate your willingness to hit me," he said, still grinning, "as well as the fact that you just implied you plan to stick around long enough to notice if I develop any bad habits. Does that mean you care about me?"

Danice snorted and shook her head. "How could I not care? In case you've been too thick and male to notice it, I'm kind of in love with you, you idiot."

"Good, because I'm absolutely in love with you," he grinned. "You little she-devil."

Danice laughed, feeling joy welling inside her. If Mac loved her, everything must be right with her world. Then a thought occurred to her. Instead of making her frown, it only brought on a fresh wave of excitement.

"No, you know what, Parish Hampton is not going to can my ass," she said, her mouth curving into a grin of pure delight. "They won't be able to, because first thing on Monday morning, I am going to march into that office and turn in my letter of resignation."

She felt Mac stiffen beneath her and knew he would be remembering the argument they had had in Faerie, after the first time they made love.

"Are you sure?" he asked softly.

"Positive," she grinned.

During that fight, he had tried to make her see how ill suited her job at Parish Hampton was to who she really was inside. She had been struggling for so long to be Danice Carter, young urban lawyer on the rise, that she'd forgotten to be herself. And Danice was beginning to suspect that who she was would end up being more along the lines of Danice Carter, kick-ass lawyer to the underdog.

Just the thought made her dizzy with glee.

"You were right," she told him, her grin so wide she feared it would split her face in two. "Working at Parish Hampton is not where I belong, and I don't want to do it anymore. I am going to resign, and then I am going to find a job that I'm not just good at, but that I love. Who knows? Maybe I'll even start my own practice."

Mac's mouth curved, and Danice could see the love and approval glowing in his gorgeous stormy-sea eyes. He tugged her down and kissed her soundly.

"I think that is a fabulous idea," he murmured against her lips a few delicious seconds later. "In fact, I think it's such a good idea that it's going to be very difficult for me to resist taking all of the credit for it."

"Oh, you can have the credit," she told him, squirming around above him until he hissed through his teeth and she could feel the proof of his arousal pressing against her stomach. "I'm happy to give you all the credit you want."

She pushed herself into a sitting position astride his hips and wriggled enticingly.

Mac reached up to cup her breasts in his hands, cuddling the soft mounds with tender care. "Is that a new euphemism you're adopting? *Giving credit?*"

She laughed and leaned into his palms, loving the feel of him touching her.

Loving him.

"Not at all," she grinned. "It just means that if I give you all the credit, I can also saddle you with all the blame if something goes wrong."

Mac shifted his grip to the back of her neck and pulled her down for a kiss. "Nothing is going to go wrong."

And in her heart, Danice knew that he was absolutely right.

Look for the next heart-pounding Others novel from
New York Times bestselling author

CHRISTINE WARREN

BLACK MAGIC WOMAN
ISBN: 978-0-312-35720-7

Coming in summer 2011

...and don't miss this never-before-released FREE
Others short story

"HEART OF THE SEA"

Visit www.christinewarren.net to find out more.

Vampires, Werewolves, and Demons,

Oh, My...

Step into the Thrilling World of
CHRISTINE WARREN
and The Others

Wolf at the Door

Sullivan Quinn didn't travel 3,000 miles from his native Ireland and his wolf pack just to chase rabidly after the most delectable quarry he's ever seen. Quinn is in America on a mission—to warn his Other brethren of a shadowy group willing to use murder and mayhem to bring them down. But one whiff of this Foxwoman's delicious honeysuckle fragrance and he knows that she is more than a colleague or a conquest . . . she is his mate.

Anthropologist Cassidy Poe is a world-renowned authority on social interaction, but the overpowering desire she feels around Quinn defies every ounce of her expertise. Working by his side to uncover The Others' enemies poses risks she never expected—to her own safety, to those she loves, and to her heart, as every encounter with Quinn proves more blissfully erotic than the last . . .

Now, with no one to trust but each other, Quinn and Cassidy face a foe that's edging closer every day, threatening to destroy the lives they've always known, and the passion they've just discovered . . .

Cassidy crouched beneath the potting bench and trembled. Not with fear, but with the hot rush of adrenaline pumping through her.

She didn't know who the wolf was. She couldn't remember ever seeing him before—in either form—and he wasn't the sort she would have forgotten. She sure as hell couldn't picture forgetting him now. A girl never forgot a werewolf who attacked her in a deserted greenhouse. Or so she assumed.

To be honest, "attacked" was a pretty strong word. While the Lupine *had* reached for her, she hadn't detected any sort of threat from him, and she usually had pretty reliable instincts about those types of things.

She usually had pretty reliable instincts, period.

Peeking out from among the foliage, Cassidy sniffed the air and tried to pinpoint the wolf's location. He'd been right on her heels from the moment she shifted, not missing a beat even when she changed from woman to fox right in front of him. Of course, when one attended a party at the oldest and most exclusive private club for Others in Manhattan, one had to expect to see some things beyond the ordinary.

Like this Lupine.

She sensed something extraordinary about him, something beyond the average and not-so-average pack members she had met through the years. Oh, he smelled like wolf, that dark, earthy, evergreen smell they all had in common. And he certainly looked like one. She'd caught a glimpse of him over her shoulder when she took a corner at top speed, so she'd seen the huge white teeth, the rich charcoal-colored fur, and the deep black pigment of his skin. The eyes she'd noticed the moment she'd turned after hearing his growl. You couldn't miss those eyes—a dark, rich color something like ancient gold that seemed to glow in the dim moonlight.

They had fixed on her with an intensity that set her pulse racing. Along with her feet.

She'd read his intent to touch her in those eyes and instinct had kicked in, sending her darting out of the way a split second before skin made contact with skin.

Skin against skin, flesh against flesh, mouth against mouth—

Down, girl.

She shook her head again. Where had that come from? Clearly, the adrenaline was messing with her head. She pricked her ears forward, listening for the sounds of his movement. He was still out there somewhere; she just couldn't pinpoint where.

"Arrrooooooooooooooooooo!"

She bolted, sprung like a pheasant by a spaniel, at the sound of the howl so close behind her. He'd managed to sneak up on her somehow, but she sure as hell didn't intend to stand around and ask about his technique. She ran as if the hounds of hell were on her heels. Some might argue they were.

She felt her sides heaving as she ran, air billowing in and out of her lungs, her paws searching for purchase on the slick slate tiling the floor. When she hit a corner, her hind legs skittered out from under her, and she lost a valuable nanosecond righting herself. The slip let him get so close she could feel his breath ruffling her fur. Desperately, she poured on another burst of speed and dove frantically for the greenhouse door.

She never made it.

She managed to get herself airborne only to collide mid-flight with a much larger and more vigorously propelled body. He knocked her off course and sent her hurtling back to the floor before she could so much as wriggle away.

Cassidy lay there, dazed, the wind temporarily hammered out of her, while he stood above her, tongue hanging out, one massive forepaw planted against her chest, pinning her in place. She had about as much chance to get away as she did to become the next Mr. Universe. Faced with that harsh wall of reality, she gave one disgruntled yip and shifted.

If she had counted on the element of surprise to give her an opportunity to escape, she needed a recount. She stretched and shivered, fur replaced with smooth skin, newly broadened palms planting themselves on the slate to help her slither away.

They didn't.

She blinked, and he shifted with her. Though she had spent her entire life moving between forms, between worlds, and watching other shifters do it, too, she'd never been this close to anyone during the transformation. She'd never gotten to watch skin expand to envelop fur, bones shifting from animal to human, features shifting from muzzle to nose, jowls to lips. She'd never felt some- one shift against her skin, tickling in ways she would have tickled him. It fascinated her, and put her just far enough off balance that her movements slowed to give him an advantage. Before she could scoot away, he dropped, his weight pinning her to the cold slate, legs between hers, hands darting to capture her wrists and pin them to the floor above her head.

He smiled down at her then, and somehow the ex- pression looked as feral on the human face as it had on the wolf. Her eyes widened, and she became acutely conscious of her nakedness as this man pressed inti- mately against her. She kept her gaze fastened on him as the grin widened and he dipped his head toward her throat. She braced herself for the pain of teeth in her flesh or the intimate lash of an exploring tongue, but in- stead he pressed his face to her skin and inhaled deeply.

"God," he growled, in a low, smoke-and-whiskey voice, "you smell so damned good. It's been driving me crazy all night. I have to know if you taste half as deli- cious."

She felt his mouth open against her skin . . .

She's No Faerie Princess

Queen Mab's niece, Fiona, has long been bored to tears by the intrigues of Court life. She'd prefer to cut loose at a punk club, knock back a few Thai beers, and hook up with a likely lad of similar interests. But when Fiona goes AWOL, she only gets as far as Manhattan's Inwood Park before a nasty demon nearly puts a permanent crimp in her plans—and a dark stranger sparks her desire . . .

All work and no play make Tobias Walker one cranky werewolf. After six months of doing his part to keep the peace during the delicate negotiations between The Others and humankind, he'd like nothing more than a good night's sleep—preceded by an enthusiastic mating session. The alluring woman he rescues in the park might be the answer to his most lustful prayers, but only if they can both stay alive long enough to find out who wants her dead and why.

Now, Fiona and Tobias must unravel a tangled web of treachery that spans branches of the Fae, Other, and mortal worlds, all the while falling into a dangerous attraction that could be the beginning of a beautiful friendship—or the end for them both . . .

Walker wanted to grab the woman and shake her for being so stupid as to rush up to the demon like that. Then he wanted to thank her for distracting the demon with that spell of hers. And finally, he wanted to get a better look at what he remembered as being a truly fine backside, this time without the distraction of a rampaging demon to dull his pleasure. But at the moment, he had other things to do. Like getting them both the hell out of Dodge before the demon learned how to run with severed Achilles tendons.

Walker scooped her unconscious figure up in his arms and sprinted for home. The demon reacted about as positively to that as Walker had expected, but thankfully, the injuries slowed it to a point where the combination of werewolf speed and the thick tree cover foiled its pursuit. That didn't mean Walker slowed down any. He ran a good two miles before he felt safe in slowing to a brisk, ground-eating trot.

Through it all, the woman in his arms remained limp and still. His long strides ate up the ground between the park and his neighborhood. At a dead run, a werewolf could move faster than a sprinting racehorse and might even give a cheetah a thing or two to think about. Luckily, Walker could maintain his speed for distances closer to those of the equine than the feline, because it was a good couple of miles to his apartment.

He made it without incident, ducking into the alley behind his street and breaking his speed, slowing to a walk for the last hundred yards to his building. It took him a second to catch his breath, but both he and the woman had made it in one piece. And, he hoped, without being seen.

Hitching the unconscious woman higher against his chest, Walker let them inside and kicked the door shut behind them. Though the entrance to his apartment looked like it led to a basement, he actually occupied two floors of the narrow old building, and he used the bottom floor as a workroom and Spartan home gym. His living space was upstairs. He carried his guest up and directly to the sofa, depositing her on the soft cushions before he straightened and shifted back to his human form.

The woman never moved, and he frowned down at her, crouching beside the sofa to examine her limp form. He'd felt the steady beat of her heart and the rhythmic rise and fall of her breathing as he'd carried her home, so he knew perfectly well she wasn't dead. And that was what had him frowning. No human woman or witch should have survived the demon attack, which meant she must not be human. He knew from her scent that she wasn't Lupine or any other sort of shifter, for that matter. There was nothing earthy about her, nothing animal. She smelled too pure for that, and the fact that he could smell her at all meant she wasn't a vampire. Her skin felt too warm and smooth and elastic to belong to any other nonliving life-form, and she looked too much like a human for him to identify her origins by sight.

He didn't like that his sense of smell had failed him here. One good sniff ought to give him all the information he needed to place her species, but instead it only gave him a raging erection. He didn't know what the hell was the matter with him. Sure, just like any other male in existence, a good brush with death tended to bring out the horny in him, but this felt like more than that. He didn't just want sex; he wanted sex with her, with this woman—or whatever she was—and he wanted it now. In fact, he seemed to want it more with every breath full of her scent that he inadvertently inhaled. He struggled to block the tantalizing aroma from his mind and pushed to his feet. If he didn't get control of himself, she would end up getting a hell of an awakening. Maybe from the inside out.

Gritting his teeth and taking slow, shallow breaths through his mouth, Walker braced himself against his uncontrollable arousal and forced himself to take stock of her wounds. Starting at her feet seemed safest, and the ragged puncture marks in the leather of her high boots looked pretty nasty. He dealt efficiently with her laces and tugged the boots off, setting them aside under the coffee table. Without the heavy covering, her feet looked tiny and fragile beneath their veil of sheer black stockings, which were dotted with blood around her left ankle. The demon's claws hadn't bitten deeply, thanks to the leather, but the punctures would need a thorough cleaning.

His gaze moved up the length of her slim, graceful legs, which did totally inappropriate things to his libido, but they appeared to be free of further injury. The only other wound he could see was a slash across her stomach, and that was the injury that worried him. Carefully, he reached out to lift aside the hems of her skimpy tank tops, one eye on her face to be sure she hadn't woken up. Her eyelashes didn't even flutter, and her expression remained tranquil. Walker wished he could say the same for himself, but one good look at the ragged gash in her pale, freckled skin had him cursing a blue streak and gritting his teeth against the urge to howl in anger.

The cut bled sluggishly, much less than he would have expected, but it looked nasty all the same, with jagged edges darkened to black by the poison on the demon's claws. Jaw clenching, he dropped her hem and headed straight for the first-aid supplies in his bathroom. On the way back, he paused in the bedroom to grab a pair of jeans and ease himself into them. No reason to scare her to death by having her wake up eye to eye with the part of him most anxious to make her acquaintance.

He stepped back into the living room with his hands full of disinfectant and bandages, and he froze. The blue-haired punk he'd left on his sofa had been replaced by a dark-haired goddess with skin like whipped cream and a torn and tattered gown of a fabric so light, if it hadn't been for the pale lilac color, he couldn't have sworn it even existed. The clothes she had been wearing had disappeared, and she slept on as if nothing had happened. Now he had proof she wasn't quite human. A witch, maybe? That would explain her human appearance, since technically witches were humans who just happened to have evolved the ability to use magic, and a spell fading would explain the change in her appearance. At least, he thought it would. He wasn't all that up on the rules of magic.

And none of the rules he had heard before explained why the very scent of her made him want to strip her naked and introduce himself to her womb, up close and personal.

Forcing his mind off his crotch, he returned to the sofa and knelt on the floor at her side. Her wounds took precedence over his curiosity at the moment. Until he did find out who and what she was, he'd be better off treating her injuries than speculating about the effect she had on him. When she woke up, he'd get his answers.

Still, he was frowning as he poured disinfectant liberally onto a sterile pad. He parted the cut in her dress, ripping it slightly wider to get at the injury. When he pressed the cotton to her skin, the muscles in her stomach clenched reflexively, and he heard a soft gasp whisper between her lips. His gaze shot immediately to her face, but her expression remained relaxed and tempting in sleep. Reluctantly, he looked back at his task, only to see that the wound in her abdomen appeared to be a lot less serious than he'd thought, now that he'd cleared the dried blood and dirt away. In fact, it almost looked as if it had begun healing even before he'd washed it.

Oh, this wasn't good.

Swallowing a curse, Walker leaned back from his unconscious guest and took a really good look at her. One that had his stomach sinking into his toenails. He took in the moonlight-pale, velvet-smooth skin, the miraculously healing wounds, the magically transformed appearance, and saw that his bad day had just gotten a hell of a lot worse.

"Aw, shit."

Muttering to himself and whatever god currently watched and laughed at his predicament, Walker took a deep, bracing breath, eased his hands into the tumbled mass of the unconscious woman's raven black hair, and lifted it gently away from the delicate shell of her ear. An ear that swept gracefully up from small, unadorned lobes to a distinct and elegant point.

Fae.

The woman currently passed out on his sofa, bleeding from an unexpected and determined demon attack, was Fae. As in full-blooded, non-changeling, born-and-bred-beyond-the-gates-in-Faerie Fae. And high sidhe from the look of her. This wasn't a sprite but one of the aristocratic race. So what the hell was she doing in his living room?

Pushing to his feet, Walker shoved a hand through his already-rumpled hair and began to pace across the quiet room. He didn't need a Lupine sense of smell to know this whole thing reeked of trouble, and he wasn't just talking about the demon stench. He already had enough on his plate trying to keep The Others in the area from inadvertently starting a war with the humans. The last thing he needed was the Fae and demons putting in an appearance and throwing everything into chaos.

Walker bit back a curse and looked over at the sofa, directly into a pair of sleepy, darkly lashed eyes the color of African violets. It felt like taking a stone giant's fist straight to his gut. Even the demon hadn't packed this kind of punch. Asleep, the Fae woman had been beautiful. Awake, she stole the breath from his lungs and the brains from his head. All he had left was the blood in his veins, and that was sure as hell easy enough to prove, considering it had all rushed right to his groin the minute she opened her eyes.

While he stood there, blinking like an idiot and probably drooling like one, his guest raised her arms over her head and arched her body in a lazy, feline stretch that left him cross-eyed and half-delirious. Then she collapsed back into the cushions and her full lips curved in a sensual smile.

"Hi." Her sleep-husky voice had the same effect on his dick as the average Lupine female in heat waving her tail in his face, only magnified exponentially. He probably had zipper marks running up and down his shaft. "My name is Fiona. Who are you?"

Walker groaned and rubbed his hand over his eyes, quickly discovering that the image of Fiona stretching had been burned indelibly into his retinas.

"Shit. I'm screwed."

The Demon You Know

"Explodes with sexy, devilish fun."
—Romantic Times BOOKreviews

As a research grunt at a local television station, Abby Baker tends to blend into the background, which is where she's most comfortable. But when she ends up being the last resort to cover a hot story, Abby discovers a whole new side to her personality when she is possessed by a fiend—a type of rogue demon. Suddenly everyone wants a piece of her. And now the demon Rule—also a hunter of his own kind who have gone astray—is Abby's only hope . . .

Meanwhile, The Others—vampires, werewolves, and witches, oh my!—have come out of the supernatural closet and the rest of the humans are all aflutter. Mischief is afoot in the demon realm, and Rule knows that Abby is the key to figuring it all out before the fiends tip the fragile balance between the newly discovered Others and the humans into an epic battle. Now it's up to two lost souls to make love, not war. . . .

Tess had been right. Poker was definitely not Abby Baker's game.

Rule saw the intent to move in her eyes before her muscles got the signal. When she shot out of her chair, he leaped in front of her, and when she bolted for the door, he got ahold of her arm before she could so much as twitch in that direction. Judging by the frantic strength she put into fighting his grip—obviously augmented by Lou's presence inside her, because, Rule figured, her left hook didn't usually threaten to crack ribs—it was a good thing he'd been paying attention or she'd have been hell on wheels to catch.

No pun intended.

"Let go of me!"

Cursing under his breath, Rule grabbed her by both arms and spun her around to press her back against his chest until his arms crossed in front of her like a strait-jacket. The hold immobilized her upper body, but that didn't stop her from using her heels to try to dislocate his kneecaps. It was a good thing she was so bloody tiny or she'd probably have broken his nose with a vicious head butt.

Face set, he caught Rafe's gaze over the top of her tangled hair and jerked his chin toward the door. "I've got her. Take everybody else out. She may be feeling a little outnumbered just now."

"Outnumbered?! I'll show you outnumbered, you slime-sucking son of a syphilitic goat!"

Rafe nodded. "If you need backup, you know where to find us."

If this had been a movie set, Abby's eyes would have been glowing with red-orange flames. As it was, smoke was nearly pouring out of her ears.

Tess winced and ducked as Abby's increasingly loud tirade became increasingly moist as well. "Um, I think that's our cue to exit, baby. Come on. Getting Gabriel into his bath and pajamas will seem like a cakewalk tonight."

A moment later, the library door clicked shut, leaving Rule alone with the Tasmanian devil-woman in his arms.

His biggest problem, he realized as a particularly violent motion sent her undulating against him like a belly dancer, wasn't that the human female seemed in no hurry to calm down; it was that his attention had fixed more firmly on the warm, soft weight of her in his arms than on the fact of her determination to do him great bodily harm.

She felt amazing. Her soft curves and silky skin had obviously been designed for loving, not fighting, and the incongruous strength she currently possessed only drew more attention to the plush welcome lying in wait beneath her snarling attack. The exertion had begun to speed her heart rate, dampen her skin, and make her breathing fast and ragged just like it would be if he had her beneath him, bare and begging. . . .

Shit.

Gritting his teeth and banishing the image from his mind, Rule moved quickly to separate their bodies. He had more important things to think about right now than his sudden and obsessive interest in a human woman who never should have made him look twice. From a distance, she looked like a mouse. Maybe if she'd stayed that way when he got closer, his libido would have been easier to control.

"Calm down," he hissed into her ear, thinking about what good advice that was. For both of them. He saw his breath stir the baby-fine ash-brown hair at her ear and tried not to picture what the pale, plump lobe might taste like.

What the hell was wrong with him?

"I said, calm down," he repeated in a growl. "No one is going to hurt you. I swear it."

"No one is going to hurt me? What the hell is wrong with you? This is kidnapping! You think this is my idea of a good time?"

"I think nothing of the sort, but unfortunately, none of us have a choice in the matter just now."

"Oh, that's rich! No choice. Because, you know, you're under some kind of divine compulsion to grab me off the street, take me to your secret hideout, and keep me prisoner against my will."

The only compulsion Rule felt at the moment couldn't have been further from divine in origin, but he had no intention of discussing that with her.

He grunted when she landed another solid kick to his left knee. "You know exactly where you are; therefore, the 'hideout' is hardly secret. And I believe it would be better for all of us if you took Tess's suggestion and began to look at this as a form of protective custody. No one here means you any harm. In fact, it is quite the opposite."

She turned her head until her blue eye pinned him with a look of icy rage. "If you want to help me out, you'll let me go. I have friends and family to keep me safe."

"You're being ridiculous." Rule shifted his grip on her. "If we let you leave here, you would be dead within the hour, along with your friends and family. I guarantee it."

He saw her blink. It wasn't much as far as weakening went, but he would take what he could get just then. If she didn't calm down enough for him to let go of her soon, he was afraid he'd do something stupid. Like lick her. All over.

"And it is not only your life at stake," he reminded her. "If you die, Louamides becomes an open target, and if Uzkiel finds him, any chance we have of defeating Uzkiel dies as well."

Her compelling eyes narrowed. "Let me just tell you that reminding me of the thing that's currently *possessing me* is not going to put me in a very cooperative mood right now!"

Rule met her gaze squarely. "What if I remind you that if Uzkiel finds you and retrieves the *solus* spell from Louamides, your vision of Armageddon will look like a summer picnic in contrast to the hell those fiends will loose on the earth."

She heard that. He felt it in the way her struggles suddenly eased even as her muscles stiffened. He resisted the temptation to press the advantage and let the silence fill the space between them.

Rule slid his hands down to her wrists, ignoring the smooth glide of her skin beneath his hands. Gripping her wrists not tightly but securely, he turned her to face him.

Stars, but she was tiny. The top of her head didn't quite reach his shoulder, and the body that had fought so hard against him a few minutes ago looked delicate enough to break with a harsh word. She wasn't small or waiflike by any means, but she was so soft and so obviously human she may as well have been a baby bird.

"If you can remain calm for the next few moments, I will do my best to explain it all to you."

He didn't release his hold on her wrists. He used it to steer her the few steps to the sofa and urge her to take a seat. Settling beside her, he kept a wary eye on her. She might look like a baby bird, but she clearly had the temper of a rabid raptor.

Abby braced her elbows on her legs, burying her face in her hands. "This can't be happening."

He caught the mumble and wished for a way to reassure her. Hell, he wished for a way to reassure *himself*. "Unfortunately, I'm afraid that it is. It's happening right now. And the only way I know to keep the situation from getting even worse is to keep Louamides safely out of Uzkiel's sight until the rest of the Watch can locate him and bring him under control."

Rule braced himself for more screaming, but it didn't materialize. Instead, Abby turned her brown and blue eyes on him and studied him in silence for several minutes.

Her expressions might be easy to read, but her eyes were fathomless. He could see the doubt, the fear, the frustration, even the anger on her face, but in her eyes all he saw was a warm, deep calmness that made him want to crawl inside her. It was a separate instinct from the one that wanted to *get* inside her through an entirely different route. That one he understood, not so much its cause but at least its intent. This one confused him. This wasn't lust but something . . . sweeter.

It made his scowl deepen.

Abby sighed. "Look, I'm trying—I'm *really* trying—to see your point. I promise. But maybe if you tried looking at this from my perspective instead of just trying to intimidate me into cooperating—"

"I am not trying to intimidate you." Forcing the tension from his expression, Rule leaned back to try to give her as much space as possible while still staying close enough to grab her if she tried to bolt. "I'm just trying to explain to you why I can't let you wander around the city alone. Not while Louamides is still with you."

She laughed, but he heard no amusement in the sound. "So, what? I'm supposed to just nod and smile and take up knitting until you solve a problem you've clearly been fighting for a lot longer than I've been caught up in it?" She shook her head. "I don't know what world you come from, but I'm from this one, and around here we have to do things like pay rent. And buy groceries. That requires that I 'wander around the city,' as you like to put it."

He leaped on the opportunity to reassure her.

"We all realize that this is inconvenient for you. We would never put your livelihood in jeopardy," he reassured her. "The Council will be more than happy to pay your rent and see to any other bills for as long as you are required to stay in hiding."

She cast him a sour look. "Unless 'the Council' plans to keep paying my bills for the rest of my life, I have to go to work. If I don't show up tomorrow, I'll lose my job."

"You cannot tell them you are ill? Do you not have vacation time?"

"Vacation is what you call a week spent lounging on the beach, or touring Napa Valley. Being locked in a nightclub with a bunch of inhuman strangers is not a vacation. Besides, if I want to take a vacation, I have to request the time in advance. I can't just stop showing up and call it a vacation."

"Who do you work for? I will speak to her."

"It's a he, and trust me, that scowl will work even less on him than it does on me."

Rule cursed and rose, shoving a hand through his hair and prowling toward the fireplace on the other side of the room. "I am trying to make this easy on you, but there is only so much I can do. I cannot let Uzkiel find you, and I cannot protect you if you are not kept somewhere safe."

He knew while his mouth was moving that he was asking for trouble. He glanced back at the sofa and saw Abby's eyes narrow and knew she was about to give it to him.

"Well, forgive me for making your life difficult," she said, pushing to her feet. "Here I am with my entire life turned upside down, my body invaded by something I didn't believe in two months ago, and my freedom snatched away from me by a walking mountain with an attitude problem. What do I think gives me the right to get upset about any of it? I'm just behaving like an absolute crybaby!"

She stalked toward him with each step, her eyes blazing and the fear in her expression transmuted clearly into rage. She poked a finger at him in time with the cadence of her speech until she issued her last command with the tip digging into his chest and her gaze spitting fire at him.

Rule broke.

He couldn't help it. He'd been fine while he sat next to her; he'd even been in control while he'd been touching her, trying to keep her from hurting someone, herself included. But the minute she touched *him*, the minute her fingertip came to rest on his chest and the warm, sweet scent of her breath rushed over his skin, the grip he had on his control shattered like cheap glass.

As he muttered a prayer and a curse in the same breath, his hands came up to sweep her arms away and drag her hard against him. He saw the look of shock and the quick shiver of fear before his last rein broke and his mouth slammed down over hers like an invading army.

And he knew his troops had hers hopelessly outnumbered.

Howl at the Moon

"Christine Warren knows how to write a winner!"
—Romance Junkies

Noah Baker never wanted to betray The Others. But if his military commanders want him to covertly investigate a Lupine scientist—whose extraordinary research on sensory perception in werewolves could be used to develop werewolf-sharp senses in human soldiers— Noah must oblige. Even if it means deceiving the woman he desires the most.

Samantha Carstairs is the personal assistant to the Alpha of the Silverback Clan, and as best friend to the Lupine community's most brilliant scientist, she is privy to its most dangerous secret. Noah knows that Sam will never leak the scientific research . . . so he must find another way to get it, while keeping Sam close. But someone else is after Sam's secret. Who is the other *spy infiltrating The Others? If their genetic secrets get into the wrong hands, all hell could break loose. Now Noah's true loyalty is put to the test as he fights to protect The Others—and his beloved Sam—and find the imposter . . . before it's too late.*

Sam eyed Graham with growing suspicion. He wore his most charming smile, the one that said he was about to convince you to invest your last dollar in a housing development in the middle of the Okefenokee Swamp.

Sam could already feel her feet getting wet. "Whenever you get that look—the one you're wearing right now—it bodes ill for me. So stop stalling and lay it on me. I'm a big girl. I can take it."

"We need to clear off some desk space in here," he said. "We're going to be having a visitor for a little while."

"Oh, my goddess! We're being *audited*?"

Graham shuddered. "Bite your tongue. No, nothing like that. I've agreed to let a select branch of the U.S. military have the opportunity to recruit pack members. Strictly as volunteers, of course. An army officer is going to be setting up a minioffice space with us for a few weeks."

Sam's glimmer of suspicion exploded in a siren-blaring and red flag–waving supernova of alarm. "Who?"

"Noah Baker."

Yeah, that's what she'd been afraid he would say.

On the surface, there was nothing wrong with Noah

Baker. For a human, in fact, he'd made quite a few friends in the Other community since his sister had gotten mixed up with, and subsequently married to, a sun demon. Everybody seemed to like the man, from his demonic new brother-in-law, Rule, to Graham, to Rafe De Santos himself. Even Rafe's wife, Tess, liked Noah, and she wasn't one to suffer fools lightly, or even at all. But then, Noah Baker had proved to be no one's fool. A major in the army's highly selective and newly developed supernatural squadron, he had grit, training, and a cool head under pressure. Not to mention a talent for making large objects make even larger booms.

The only person Sam knew who *didn't* see the human as an all-around swell guy was Sam herself.

Something about Noah just made Sam's hackles rise every time he got within twenty feet of her, and it didn't seem to matter what form she was in at the time. Human, wolf, or were, Sam's teeth went on edge when Noah walked into a room and her hormones went haywire. She'd gotten to be friends with his sister, Abby, but with Noah, the best Sam could manage felt more like a tense cease-fire. And now Graham expected her to share office space with Noah?

Too much a Lupine to directly challenge her Alpha's word, Sam took a more subtle approach. "So he's going to be recruiting for his own unit? This 'spook squad' he's on?"

Graham nodded. "His own unit and a couple of new ones. Apparently, the Pentagon has been pretty happy with the way the squad has handled a couple of recent incidents leading up to and resulting from the Unveiling." The revelation of The Others' existence had set a few backs up around the world. Riots, demonstrations, and protests had been the least of the trouble. "I think their successes have inspired the army to expand, put together a few new teams."

"Do you really think many members of the pack will be interested? Playing well with humans is a new skill for a lot of us."

"To tell you the truth, I think it's a great opportunity. As loyal as our members are to the pack, it's got to chafe a lot of them to know they're not going to get ahead without challenging someone in a dominant position for a better place in line. That's why we get into trouble from time to time with things like the Curtis incident." Graham made euphemistic reference to the time his cousin Curtis had tried to rip his throat out and steal his mate, but Sam got his point. "This should give some of our Gammas a good chance to get out from under my paw, so to speak."

"I'm sure no one has a problem with your paw, boss." But even as Sam said it, she uttered a mental curse. Graham made sense. Spending a lifetime in the middle of the pack didn't suit everyone. Graham's former Beta made a good example. Logan Hunter had chafed under the traditional pack system of hierarchy, and the only solution for him had been to leave Manhattan and take over as Alpha of the White Paw Clan in Connecticut.

Graham making sense, though, failed to make Sam feel any better. All she could think of was the impossibility of getting any work done while a pair of very human and disturbingly intense hazel eyes looked on.

The Alpha flashed her a grin. "You may be nearly as biased as Missy."

Sam forced a smile of her own. "Not quite." She drew in a deep breath. "Well, you're the boss. When can we expect the troops to land?"

"How about now?"

Noah caught the flash of surprise and annoyance on Samantha's face and stifled a grin. He knew he made the Lupine tense just by walking into the room, but then, she did the same to him. Unlike him, though, he suspected Sam had no idea why they disturbed each other so badly. She probably wrote it off as lousy chemistry.

Oh, it was chemistry, all right, but Noah couldn't describe it as lousy. Not by a long shot.

Samantha Carstairs made Noah Baker feel about as predatory as her closest friends and relatives actually were. He might not get furry on full moons, but looking at the luscious female Lupine made him want to howl at one. It had been that way from the first time he'd set eyes on her, while he still thought she was a kidnapper holding his little sister captive. He'd taken one look at Samantha and felt his entire body go on alert. A few parts had even gone on *high* alert.

She had the body of an athlete, not as sinewy as a runner or as fine as a gymnast but covered in sleek, firm muscle and decorated with curves just generous enough to make a sane man look twice. Noah had looked more than that, taking stock from the top of her mane of wavy, richly brown hair to the tips of her feminine feet. Of course, by the end of their first meeting those feet had turned into paws and tried to pin him to the ground in the middle of the small park down the block, but even that hadn't put him off. He'd dated women with bigger vices than occasionally shifting into timber wolves.

After a second of silence, Samantha started to squirm and Noah deliberately shifted his gaze to the other werewolf in the room. Stepping inside, Noah set a cardboard file box down on the chair beside the office door. "Thanks for agreeing to put me up, Graham. I appreciate it."

The Silverback Alpha shook his hand, relieving the last of Noah's worries that the Lupine might still hold a grudge over the way his sister had briefly set the pack's Luna in harm's way a few months back when she'd been pursued by demons. Apparently, Graham didn't like having demons surrounding his wife.

"It's no problem," Graham said. "In fact, I was just telling Sam I think it might be good for some of our young males. Give them a place to channel their aggression other than in a dominance challenge."

Noah smiled. "I'll do my best."

He looked around the spacious room, taking note of the territory Sam had already marked. The huge cherry desk stationed in front of the door to Graham's private inner office had the look of a sentry's gatehouse, and Noah had no trouble picturing her fending off intruders and interlopers. Her area only took up one end of the grand old sitting room, though. There would be plenty of space for him. And he'd be near enough to give the electricity between them time to spar.

This grin he didn't bother to suppress. "Where would you like me to set up?"

Graham shrugged. "That's up to Sam. She's the one who keeps everything in its place around here."

It didn't take a mind reader to see that Sam wanted to put Noah outside with the trash. Or maybe to banish him to another continent. But that wasn't her decision.

Sam forced a pleasant expression onto her face. "I'll have one of the staff bring in a desk and some chairs. If we set them up near the fireplace on the far side of the room, it should give you some privacy for your sales pitch."

And get Noah as far from her as possible without banishing him from the room. Still. He'd save his fighting for other battles. "That works for me. Why don't you just tell me who on the staff I need to talk to, and I'll take care of my own supplies? I'm sure you have plenty of work to do without worrying about me."

"Great." Graham clapped Noah on the back. "I'll leave you to it, then. If you think of anything you need, just let Sam know. I'm putting her entirely at your disposal."

Noah saw Sam's eyes widen and her lips part to protest, but Graham had already retreated to his inner sanctum and closed the door behind him.

Walk on the Wild Side

"Amazing characters & intriguing plots."
—Fallen Angel Reviews

Kitty Sugarman is a lot tougher than her name implies. Still, she's content with how her small-town life keeps her removed from all the changes happening in the world—like the Unveiling of The Others. That is, until a near-tragedy strikes and Kitty discovers she has abilities . . . thanks to a father she never knew was alive. He also happens to be a were-lion and leader of one of the most powerful prides out West.

When Kitty heads to Vegas to find out more about her father, it's his sexy, seductive second-in-command, or baas, of the Pride, Max Stewart, who commands her attention. Now that she has tempted Max's hunger for a mate, Kitty finds herself stuck in a vicious struggle for her father's fortune, while deadly unrest stirs within the pride. Kitty's rivals won't rest until she's gone for good, but Max will fight until his last breath to save her . . . even if it means going against the pride.

Max sat in the big leather chair at the desk in his office above the casino floor with his back to his paperwork. Instead of diligently completing forms and poring over spreadsheets, he faced the bank of windows overlooking the sea of gamblers and stared through the one-way glass, seeing very little of what was right in front of him. Every bit of his attention had focused on his memories of smooth, freckled skin, wide, green eyes, and the softest, sweetest, lushest lips he'd ever tasted.

The sleep he'd gotten last night—the little of it he'd managed—had done nothing to erase the building obsession he'd developed in the twelve or so hours that he'd known Kitty Sugarman. A humbling realization for a man who'd never before applied the word "obsession" to any member of the fairer sex. But when a man spent six hours doing nothing but reliving a kiss that your average college kid would have viewed as routine, he had to face a few brutal truths. Admitting to the obsession had only gotten the ball rolling.

From there, he'd had to think about the fact that the object of his obsession bore about as much resemblance to the women he'd become used to as she did to the calculating, money-grubbing tramp he'd originally envisioned her to be. Leo females as a rule were so-phisticated, elegant, and completely aware of their own seductive powers. They usually exuded the sort of confidence that bordered on arrogance and saw no ben-efit in underestimating their own worth. They believed the word "bashful" referred to nothing more than a character in *Snow White and the Seven Dwarfs*. They didn't have dinner with eligible men while wearing their hair in ponytails and their faces scrubbed clean of makeup, and they certainly didn't stare at him with wide eyes full of suspicion and innocence and tantaliz-ing vulnerability.

No, Kitty Sugarman was like no other woman he'd ever met. He certainly reacted to her in a way he'd never experienced.

That intrigued him, almost as much as the woman herself did. He'd never had any trouble responding to a woman; he was a healthy Leo male in his prime, after all, a future Felix of his pride. But his response to Kitty went beyond the ordinary. He'd known her for half a day, and he'd already decided to have her. She didn't know it yet, but the sweet, stubborn girl with the slow southern accent was going to be his. Soon.

Martin, he knew, would be delighted, but that meant little more to him than the knowledge that the rest of the pride would be horrified. Max's intentions had nothing to do with any of them, especially since he wasn't com-pletely sure how far beyond the initial possession those intentions went.

Oh, he knew one fuck wasn't going to satisfy him, not this time, but he couldn't decide how long it would take, or if this could end up being more than sex. There was no way of knowing this soon if the attraction between them could turn into a mating, not unless the Fates had a truly remarkable sense of timing, but wherever this took him, he intended to take Kitty along.

His mouth curved as he considered whether or not she deserved a warning. He had a feeling this might turn out to be a bumpy ride, but he also had a feeling that Ms. Sugarman was more than up to the challenge.

He was still grinning a few minutes later when he reached for his phone. He still had some work he needed to finish before he could take Kitty out to meet her father as he'd promised, and he couldn't be sure she wouldn't get restless waiting for him. Just in case she took it into her head to explore the city a little while she waited, he should arrange for someone to tag along with her. He felt pretty confident that the incident at the airport last night had been a random mugging, but with the recent tension in the pride over idiots like Billy Shepard and Peter Lowe grumbling over the line of succession, it couldn't hurt to be cautious.

Mentally, he sorted through the pride until he hit on a particular name. Ronnie Peters was about Kitty's age, had a warm, fun-loving personality, and could kick the crap out of most men twice her size. She and Kitty would probably get along like gangbusters.

Glancing at the clock, he paused. It was still early, but better to make the arrangements ahead of time. If his visitor ended up sleeping late, so be it, but if her night had been anything like his, lingering in bed alone would be the last thing in Kitty Sugarman's tempting little mind.

One Bite with a Stranger

"A hot, hot novel."   —A Romance Review

When Regina's friends insist on setting her up a "Fantasy Fix" to help her get over her cheating ex, she dreams up some kinky out-of-this-world encounters that they could never possibly bring to life. But the next thing Regina knows, her friends have got her laced into a shiny black corset, tight leather pants, and a sexy pair of stilettos. It's time for some downtown vampire-fantasy fun. . . .

The Vampire Ball in Manhattan's East Village isn't really Dmitri Vidâme's idea of a good time, but as a member of the Council that governs The Others, he has to keep an eye on all the young vamps who prey on the pretenders. After he feasts his dark eyes on fiery Regina at the bar, he knows that he must have her. But for the first time Dmitri meets a woman who is more than a match for his indomitable will. And he may be the fantasy Regina hoped for . . . until she—and her feisty friends—discover her sexy new lover's bloodsucking secret . . .

Dmitri Vidâme nursed his single glass of scotch and wondered if there might be enough liquid in the glass to drown himself.

Literally.

Because he was about four minutes away from burying his face in it and breathing deep. Perhaps the fumes would counteract the odor of sweaty, chemically enhanced humans with sex on their minds and cobwebs in their heads.

If it hadn't been for Graham's insistence that this "Vampire Ball" made a perfect place for a young rogue to hide in plain sight, Dmitri would never have let himself be caught within ten city blocks of the place. Such a gothic circus as this event hardly fit his normal thinking as to what constituted a good time, and frankly, the attendees who filled the Mausoleum's vast basement dance floor had begun to annoy him.

He wanted to go home. A quiet evening in front of his fireplace sounded infinitely more appealing to him than another five minutes surrounded by pretentious children in "gothic" garb. Even one of the endless, politically charged meetings of the Council of Others, which he currently headed, sounded more appealing.

Dmitri swore under his breath and tossed back half of his drink in one swallow. He had let Graham, his good friend and fellow Council member, talk him into coming to this torture session. Rumors had recently reached the Council about a few young vampires who had taken to frequenting these goth events and feeding off the eager attendees. The fledglings risked exposure with their behavior, and the Council had decided they needed a stern warning.

It hardly counted as a crisis of epic proportions, and Dmitri would have been happy to let a few of Graham's Lupine packmates do the Council's dirty work, but the werewolf leader had volunteered Dmitri and himself for the job instead. Dmitri was tempted to "volunteer" Graham for the French Foreign Legion in exchange.

Restless, Dmitri tapped fingers on the scarred wooden surface of the bar, sorely tempted to just forget his good-byes and leave Graham to his fate and his bimbo. He reached for his glass to drain the last drops of fiery whisky, and that's when he saw her.

Temptation.

She stepped up to the bar, swept along in the wake of four other women, but Dmitri could not have described a single one of them. He saw only her, with her face like a vision and her body like a gift from the gods.

The woman looked impatient and a little nervous and sadly out of place among the ridiculous throngs that surrounded her. For one thing, she had the look of a woman, rather than a child. He could see she was young, probably in her late twenties, but she wore her age comfortably, as a mature woman should. Her skin, milk white and dusted with freckles the color of honey, looked smooth and unlined.

Dmitri saw a great deal of skin, from her hairline to the generous swell of her breasts where they were cuddled and lifted by the black satin of her corset; from the graceful curve of her shoulder to the tips of her slender fingers. Her snug black leather pants and tall black boots covered everything else, hugging her curves with loving care and making his body tighten.

Lord, she is stunning.

He certainly felt stunned. He hadn't reacted to the mere sight of a woman in longer than he could remember, but he reacted to this one. Already he could feel his cock hardening beneath his trousers, filling with blood and heat, while his sense of boredom died a sharp and final death.

She stood out in stark contrast against the sea of sameness that surrounded her. She, too, had dressed all in black, but she shared nothing else with the other women in the room. Her skin had the pearlescent glow of natural fairness, and her hair had not been dyed a flat and light-absorbing black. It rippled over her shoulders and down her back in waves of burnished mahogany. When she turned her head, the light caught it and sparked dancing flames across the shiny surface. Dmitri imagined burying his hands in it, using his grip to hold her still while he drove into her body.

He wanted that body, he acknowledged, wanted to feel those pale, white curves against him, under him.

He sat there at the bar, staring and fantasizing and wanting her, and while he did so, he gave in to his instincts and slipped lightly inside her mind.

She didn't notice him, as wrapped up in her thoughts as she was, but he'd have been astounded if she had. Most people didn't notice his mental presence even when he didn't keep quiet, like he did now. Very few people out there had any sort of psychic talent, and even fewer knew how to use it. He didn't probe deeply enough into the woman's mind to see if she did; he just wanted to get a sense of her, to decide if more than her beautiful body intrigued him.

More than intrigued, he found himself entranced and unexpectedly entertained. This woman possessed a lively mind and a sharp-edged humor.

Look at that. He heard her voice in his head, husky and feminine and arousing. *Lord Velveteen thinks he's just the shit sitting there with those silly little stick figures fawning all over his poet shirt. Does he have any idea how ridiculous it is for a grown man to have a visible rib cage and lacy shirt cuffs?*

Oh, wait. That's right. He's a long way from a grown man.

He watched her raise a glass to her slick, painted mouth, and his eyes narrowed. He wanted those lips to part around his cock, and the violence of his lust surprised him. This woman had an unsettling effect on him.

Where is this guy Ava invited? If I have to wait around this circus much longer, he can kiss his chances for some nookie goodbye. I don't care how badly they think I need this. I refuse to consider sleeping with someone who can't even manage to show up on time for it.

Rage turned his vision black for a split second, and Dmitri actually felt his fangs lengthen in anticipation of the wounds he would inflict on any man who dared to touch her. He would show these pretenders a real vampire's fury if a single one of them thought to lay a hand on what Dmitri intended to claim for his own. His woman would not be touched by any man but him.

His woman.

Dmitri registered the possessive term with surprise and tested the phrase in his mind. In all his considerable lifetime, he'd never felt such an instant proprietary interest in any woman. He'd never been tempted to conquer and claim so quickly. But in this case, he wanted to mark the woman so the entire world would know to keep its distance.

When he saw the woman turn her gaze to him, he ruthlessly tamped down his emotions and moved his touch to the edge of her mind. He didn't think she had noticed his presence within her, but he felt it prudent to be cautious. Already, he detected a stubborn and independent streak in her. He didn't want her to struggle against him. Not yet.

He felt her gaze on him, and he met her stare with a bold one of his own. Heat arced between them, slicing through the crowd as if to remove all barriers separating them. He wanted no barriers, wanted her bared to him, body and mind, so he could sate himself with her flesh, her thoughts, and her blood.

She was perfect, and she would be his.

You're So Vein

"Filled with supernatural danger, excitement, and sarcastic humor."
—Darque Reviews

Ava Markham is beautiful, savvy, chic, and more at home with Kate Spade than with the idea of fangs and fur. She can't get quite used to the fact that some of her closest friends have crossed over to the Other side. Then one night she is attacked by a rogue vampire, and her deepest fears are realized when her body begins a dangerous transformation from human to immortal—a change she cannot survive without the help of an alluring stranger who comes to her rescue . . .

Vladimir Rurikovich, an elite member of the European Council of Vampires, is on the prowl for a murderous vampire fugitive on the night he saves Ava from the clutches of death. It takes just one look for Dima to know he cannot live another eight centuries without the stunning and seductive Ava—until he discovers a secret about her bloodline that could change everything . . .

Ava woke from the nightmare, her heart pounding, her brow covered in cold sweat. She hadn't dreamed that vividly in years, not since she'd taught herself to step back from her nightmares and will them away. This one had been a doozy, all dark shadows and sharp pain and something cold and powerful staring down at her with eyes the color of an arctic sky. It was almost enough to make her reconsider her true need for beauty sleep. Blowing out a deplorably unsteady breath, she reached out to preemptively silence her alarm clock.

Or she tried to.

She couldn't move her hands.

Her eyes snapped open and presented her with the unwelcome view of an unfamiliar ceiling, high, pale, and crisscrossed with the exposed steel beam work of an urban loft. She had never seen this place before in her life. And she couldn't move.

Panic began to well. She tugged sharply on her hands and attempted to sit up, only to find her feet similarly secured. Aghast, disbelieving, she craned her head around to confirm what her instincts had been trying to tell her even while she'd been asleep: She was a prisoner, bound hand and foot to a strange bed in a strange apartment in what she hoped to God and all his angels was not a strange city.

She'd been kidnapped.

Every synapse in her brain seemed to fire at once, attacking her with an explosion of pain and confusion more intense than anything she had ever experienced. Memory flooded back, dearly drowning her. She felt like she was watching a movie montage—seeing herself at the girls' night party at Reggie's house, staring into the powder room mirror, walking home with her anger keeping her company, passing by an alley she'd walked in front of a million times before. . . .

Then the film went cockeyed, a handheld camera tumbling to its side. She saw the flash of movement on her right, felt the stirring of air and the overwhelming, inhuman strength of the thing that had grabbed her, grabbed her and dragged her deeper into the alley. She saw the slick, dark brick, smelled blood and rot and sick coming from the body that lay in a lifeless pile against the alley wall, smelled it on the breath and the skin and the empty soulless void of the monster holding her. She felt its arm around her neck, corded with muscle and hatred, cutting off her air, leaving her choking and gasping for breath. She felt its hot, fetid breath against her skin, felt the sharp tear of fangs against flesh, and her welling panic took the freeway exit straight to the blind, instinctual, animal imperative to escape.

Gathering her breath, Ava opened her mouth to scream and threw every ounce of strength in her body into breaking the bonds that held her. She got out no more than a short, sharp whistle before a large male hand clamped over her mouth and cut off her cry.

Her gaze shot to an unfamiliar face, one that hardly looked like it could belong to the stink in her memory. This man looked like death, but not the kind of death that snuck up behind a woman in a dark alley and bled her dry—more like the kind of death that knights had once faced on the battlefield, strong and quiet and rigidly calm. He had features as sharp-edged as stone, intensely masculine and far too heavy to admire. Ava worked every day with models who epitomized the modern sensibility of male beauty, and if this man had walked into her office, she'd have turned him around and sent him right back out again.

Or rather, she'd have called security—and maybe a SWAT team—and had him *escorted* out again.

Beautiful he wasn't, not even with the slightly too-long hair that framed his face in a dozen shades of blond, from warm toffee to cold platinum (Ava had clients—both male and female—who would pay thousands for that hair and never quite be satisfied), but something about him compelled. Maybe it was the eyes—sharp, intent, and the pale blue-gray of an arctic landscape. Or the way those eyes watched her with the quiet, frozen patience of a hawk just waiting for the moment to strike.

Big Bad Wolf

"Another hot and spicy novel from a master of para-normal romance." —Night Owl Romance

Missy Roper's fantasies have revolved around Graham Winters since the moment they met. But the imposing leader of the Silverback werewolf clan always seemed oblivious to Missy's existence. At least he was, until Missy collides with him at a party and then abruptly runs away—arousing Graham's interest . . . and wild desires.

Lupine law decrees that every Alpha must have a mate, and all Graham's instincts tell him that the sensual, beguiling Missy is his. Trouble is, Missy is human—every delectable inch of her. Convincing his clan that she's his destined mate, and keeping her safe from his enemies, will be the biggest challenges Graham has ever faced. And now that he is determined to have her—as his lover and as his mate—Missy's world is changing in ways she never imagined . . .

Abstinence wouldn't be quite so bad, Graham decided, if not for the lack of sex.

Nursing his fifth scotch and wishing it were a fifth of scotch, the alpha of the Silverback Clan of New York City spent his Saturday night in a manner no self-respecting werewolf should ever have to endure—single and celibate.

At least he didn't have to spend it alone, he reflected, although the type of companionship he could expect to find at his friends' post-wedding engagement party left a lot to be desired. A bit long in the tooth for his taste. Graham preferred women who hadn't been painting the town red back when his ancestors still thought of the cotton gin as a newfangled contraption. Plus, seeing that he'd just broken off his on-again-off-again relationship with one particular vampire, he didn't feel any great compulsion to go start a new one. Immortal women all seemed to be just a little too demanding.

Why he bothered to sulk here in the corner, rather than excusing himself and getting out there to meet the Lupine woman of his dreams, remained a mystery. He couldn't blame a fear of commitment like so many hu-

man men seemed to do. Werewolves relished the idea
of a mate-bond and lived to beget lots of new genera-
tions of baby Lupines, and even Graham looked forward to the day when he would rear his own cubs in the
traditions of his clan and his ancestors. Commitment
sounded just fine to him. It wasn't fear that had him in
this mood; it was boredom.

Graham suffered from a huge, honking case of the
same old–same olds. Everywhere he looked, he saw the
same faces, the same habits, heard the same gossip, and
seduced the same women. Oh, their names and hair
color might change, but deep down, they were all the
same to him. The realization depressed him. What had
happened to the carefree, rakish wolf he used to be?
These days he acted more like a priest than a playboy.

He'd gotten sick of all the women, and all modesty
aside, Graham Winters had had a lot of women. Some
were little more than one-night stands, some recurrent
companions, and some had bordered on casual relationships, but none managed to hold his interest for more
than a few weeks.

Taking another sip of liquid fire, Graham glanced
around the room and wondered how much longer eti-
quette required him to stay. He viewed Dmitri as a
brother, and he genuinely liked Regina, so he was glad
to share in the celebration, especially since he'd had to
duck out on his best-man duties at their reception in
order to deal with a fire in the kitchen of the nightclub he owned. What he wasn't so glad of was the spec-
ulative glances currently being aimed in his direction
by a large number of the room's single—and some

not-so-single—women. He worked at ignoring their interest, but he knew it was only a matter of time before one of them decided to lay off the staring and make a move.

"I vote for the redhead. She looks like the type who's ready for anything. Plus I don't think she's wearing panties."

His friend and beta appeared at Graham's side, carrying a dark brown beer bottle and wearing a repressed smile. Logan Hunter knew all about Graham's predicament and seemed to find it amusing. Graham shot him a narrow look.

"She never does," he grumbled. "But I doubt Shelley is going to put the make on me, not after the last time we went out."

"Did you spill a drink on her dress or something?"

Graham shook his head. "I criticized her, um, technique."

Logan winced around a chuckle. "Ouch. Okay, maybe not the redhead then." He glanced back to where Shelley stood, whispering to a couple of other women. "Could be her friend, the one almost wearing the green dress. Do you think those are real?"

"On vampires, they're always real. They can't afford to bleed out during surgery just to get implants." He gave the other woman an assessing look. "Besides, not even silicone can make tits that firm. Hildie works out."

Raising his beer for a drink, Logan rolled his eyes. "And I'm sure you'd know. But you could at least make an effort. Lady knows you need to do something to lighten your mood. What the hell is up with you tonight anyway?"

"Three guesses," Graham muttered. "I'll even spot you the first two."

Logan grimaced. "Shit. Curtis."

"Right both times."

"What's he done now?"

"Same old, same old. This week he tried to get Bill Lakeland to take an interest in examining the validity of the challenge Dad and I fought when he decided to retire and leave the business of alpha to me."

Logan nearly choked on his beer. "You've got to be kidding me."

"I wish."

"I don't care how many packs consider Bill an expert of the traditional procedures for alpha challenges, you took that fight fair and square. Your father wouldn't even cut your *mother* any slack in a challenge ring, let alone the son he raised to continue his family dynasty!"

"You know that, and I know that . . ."

"And so does anyone who was there watching. You took that challenge fairly and by the skin of your teeth. For a few minutes, I wondered if both of you were going to leave the circle alive."

Graham's mouth twisted. "So did we."

"So how does he figure he can protest the outcome?"

"Beats me. I doubt he thought he'd really get anywhere with that kind of nonsense. Chances are he was just pulling my chain."

"And how long has that been his favorite hobby?"

"Let's see. I'm thirty-four and Curtis is seven years younger, so . . ." Graham pursed his lips and pretended to think. "About twenty-seven years, I think."

Logan nodded. "And you did what to set him off again?"

"Be born first, be my father's son, and be more of a Lupine than he'll ever be?"

"Right. So you're just going to go on ignoring him?"

"That's the plan." Graham saw the disgust in his friend's expression and smiled. "Trust me, it's easier to ignore him than it is to dignify his idiocy with a response. If I got worked up every time he pulled a stupid stunt just to piss me off, I'd be the first Lupine in recorded medical history to have to take blood pressure medication."

Logan sighed. "True enough." He took a long pull on his beer and gave the room another thorough glance. "Which means that you could definitely use a distraction tonight. So? Who's it going to be?"

"No one."

"Excuse me?"

"I'm not in the mood for a woman."

"You know, you've been saying that with distressing regularity lately, my friend," Logan pointed out. "I don't know about your blood pressure, but you might want to talk to a doctor about your libido if this keeps up."

Graham glared at him. "There's nothing wrong with my libido. It's not me; it's the women. Haven't you noticed they're all the same?"

"Well, where it counts, I suppose. . . ."

"That's not what I mean. Or maybe it is. I don't know. I just know I'm . . . bored." He gestured around the room with his whiskey glass. "Not a fresh face in sight."

"Since when do you go for a fresh face? I thought you were an ass man."

"Since I realized I'd seen all of these faces a hundred times before."

"Come on," Logan chided. "There has to be a woman here you haven't slept with."

"Regina."

"She doesn't count. Dmitri would break your legs, wait a couple of hours for them to heal, then break them again. And after that, he might get cranky. I'm talking about the rest of them. The ones who aren't married to your best friend, and aren't from our pack, since they're all practically family."

Graham took a quick look around, followed by a longer look. On his third sweep of the assembled crowd, he stopped and pointed toward a grouping of furniture occupied by three very attractive females. "There," he said. "Those three. I haven't slept with a single one of them."

Logan followed his gesture and sighed. "Yeah. Regina's closest friends, who are probably the only human women here tonight, and we both know you don't do humans."

Draining his glass, Graham scanned the room one last time, dismissing each of the women he passed. His eyes never seemed to pause more than half a second on any of them, no matter how attractive or how skimpily dressed, until they drifted over one curvaceous female bottom and skidded to a grinding halt.

He could almost smell rubber burning.

His eyes caressed the full, generous lines of her backside encased in a form-fitting skirt of some clingy black material. The fabric draped over that delectable tush, showing him each rounded curve in heart-stopping detail. To his surprise, he couldn't tell if she was wearing panties, but unlike Shelley's lack of lingerie, the idea of this woman bare beneath her dress aroused more than just his curiosity.

"And her," he growled, all his attention focused on the woman whose face he still hadn't seen. If it looked half as good as what he *had* seen, he'd be a very happy man. "I haven't had her. Yet."

Born to be Wild

"Warren takes readers for a wild ride, and when she is done, the reader begs for more."

—Night Owl Romance

Josie Barrett brings out the animal in men. Literally. As the local veterinarian in a town that's approximately seventy percent Others—mostly shapeshifters— Josie deals with beastly situations all the time. It's practically part of her job description. But when the werewolves of Stone Creek, Oregon, start turning down- right feral, Josie smells a rat—among other, more dan- gerous critters.

Teaming up with the ferociously sexy Eli Pace, a full-time sheriff and part-time were-lion, Josie tries to contain the shapeshifting problem before it spreads like a virus. But when more shifters get infected—and stuck in their animal forms—the fur really begins to fly. Josie and Eli have to find the cause, fast, before the whole town goes to the dogs. But first, they have to wrestle with a few animal urges of their own.

Eli watched the object of his fascination sway toward him and bit back the urge to reach out and haul her across the table. For most of the last twenty-four hours, he might have wondered whether Josie Barrett felt even a fraction of the attraction for him that he had developed for her; but if that slightly dazed look in her eyes and the smell of her sweet warm skin were any indication, his question had just been answered with a resounding yes.

He might actually have thrown caution to the wind and eaten her alive if her dog hadn't chosen just that moment to switch his allegiance from his clearly neglectful mistress and drape his huge, drooling muzzle on the thigh of Eli's jeans. Clamping his teeth together, Eli pulled back and sent the mutt an only half-joking glare. Somehow, the feel of canine saliva soaking through denim proved to be a real mood killer.

"What?" he growled at the dog, hoping Josie would assume he was teasing. "Are you trying to tell us it's time for dessert?"

The veterinarian blushed scarlet at that question and reached for the dog's collar. At least, he hoped it was from the question and the knowledge that each of them would like very much to have the other for dessert, instead of from the embarrassment of having a hungry hound assault her guest.

"Bruce!" she scolded sharply, grabbing her half-eaten dinner with her free hand and hauling both food and dog toward another room of the clinic. "You know better than to beg from company. Come on. You can finish my leftovers in the file room, if you can't be trusted to behave yourself."

Frankly, the only one whose behavior Eli distrusted at the moment was himself. He'd been about three seconds away from ravishing the pretty veterinarian on her own exam table, so what did that say about his company manners?

Josie returned a second later, already apologizing. "I'm so sorry about that. He doesn't normally do that to people he's just met, but I'm afraid that when it comes to Laura Beth's meat loaf, the idiot just has no self-control."

"Don't worry about it. I understand about the futility of resisting that kind of temptation."

Believe me, I know.

"I should thank you again for dinner," she said, beginning to fuss with the debris of their meal, balling up napkins and dropping them into the discarded take-out sack. "It was very nice of you to bring it over so late."

"Is that what it was?" Eli growled. He crushed his empty soda can in his fist and tossed it into the recycling bin under the counter. "I didn't buy you dinner to be nice."

Josie blinked up at him, her eyes wide and wary. "You didn't?"

"No."

"Then why did you?"

"Because I wanted to. I wanted to get to know you better. I still do."

She didn't say anything at first, just kept her eyes fixed on the shiny surface of the exam table as she sprayed it with disinfectant and wiped it with a wad of paper towels. Eli almost found himself wishing for the first time that he were a vampire, so he could get an idea of what was going on in that head of hers.

"There's really not that much to know," she said finally. "I've already told you most of it. I grew up here in Stone Creek. I became a vet. I took over my dad's practice when he and my mother decided to retire to Arizona. My older sister lives there, too, with her husband and two kids. And you already met Bruce. That's pretty much the full story."

They bumped shoulders when each of them reached to deposit their litter in the trash bin at the same time. Josie seemed to withdraw from the brief contact, and that pissed Eli off. He didn't want her trying to get away from him.

He didn't want her getting away.

Maybe he would have reacted differently if he hadn't seen that he intrigued her just as much as she did him. He could read it in her eyes, in the rhythm of her breath. And he could smell it on her skin. This was a mutual fascination they had going between them, and he refused to let her ignore it.

Grabbing her gently by the elbow, Eli turned Josie to

face him and softly tightened his grip. She lifted her chin, her gaze skittering away from his to settle somewhere in the vicinity of his left earlobe.

"That's not what I meant, Josie," he murmured quietly, but her shivers told him she heard. It wasn't that cold inside the clinic, no matter how chilly it had gotten outside. He reached up and tucked an escaped strand of shiny dark hair behind her ear, and the shivering intensified. "I think you know that."

She forced out half a chuckle. "Wow, wouldn't I sound like an arrogant so-and-so if I said yes to that."

"I don't think you'd sound arrogant. Just honest. You want to get to know me, too. Don't you?"

He could see that she wanted to deny it. He saw the impulse in her clear dark eyes, saw her wrestle with it, and saw when her conscience won out. She wouldn't lie to him, not about that.

"I . . . maybe," she admitted softly. "It's weird. I mean, we must have bumped into each other a hundred times over the last three years. Stone Creek just isn't that big. So how is it that this is happening now?"

"I don't know. I'm just glad it is."

A soft breath sighed from the softness of her mouth, and Eli could almost feel it part for him as he leaned down and brushed his lips against hers for the length of a stuttering heartbeat.

She tasted better than the scone he'd devoured that morning along with his coffee. Sweeter and richer and altogether more intoxicating. But what struck Eli wasn't the way she tasted, but the way she made him feel. Just that gentle touch of lip to lip, skin to skin, made his heart pound as if he'd sprinted up the side of a mountain. His head spun, and his fingers literally itched and flexed with the need to touch her. It didn't matter where. He just needed every bit of connection he could forge between them. He needed to convince himself that she was real.